The Eclipse

Mark Dahl

Copyright © 2023 Mark Dahl

All rights reserved.

Cover design by Martha Michelson.

Cover image adapted from "Columbia River Gorge view from near Hood River." Date: 18 June 2008. Uploaded to Flickr by user woodleywonderworks. https://flic.kr/p/58EsWm Accessed 30 January 2023. Creative Commons Attribution 2.0 Generic (CC BY 2.0)
https://creativecommons.org/licenses/by/2.0/

Text copyedited by Gant Wegner.

ISBN: 9798864893517

First Edition

This novel's story and characters are fictitious. Any similarity to real persons, living or dead, is coincidental and not intended by the author.

All errors are attributable to the author.

For my friends

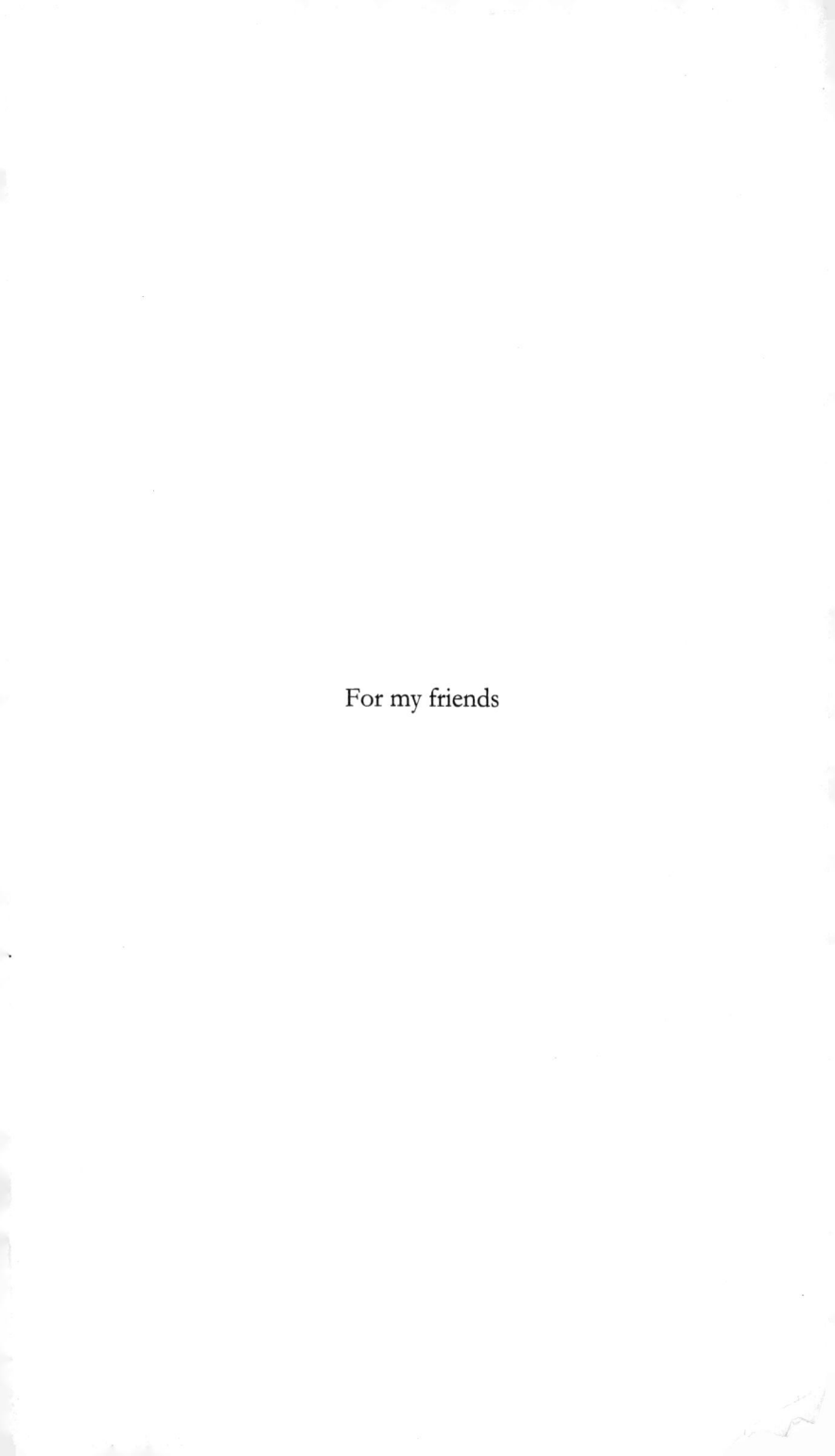

1

It was November in Portland, Oregon. Scott sat at his desk in the empty classroom in the somewhat worse-for-wear public high school where he was employed as a history teacher.

Even though the clock read 3:30, it looked like nighttime outside his classroom windows. A pineapple express weather system had ushered in gloomy, wet weather over the last few days.

He was grading AP European History blue book exams and was resolved to do them in batches of five before taking a break to check his phone or get a snack. His three-year-old Android device lay turned over on his desk to the right of the stack of finished exams.

He graded two exams and got into a third one, a total disaster, and then his hand found its way over to the phone. He unlocked it by swiping a pattern on the cracked display and found his way to the dating app.

> Tracy, 42, Hospitality, Camas, Washington

A busty figure in a halter top with a plastic cup of wine sat smiling next to a campfire. Right swipe.

> Angie, 46, Systems Analyst, Washington County Sheriff's Office, Portland

The quirky, anti-fashion type. She was sort of cute. Why not? Right swipe. He flicked through a handful of other profiles over the next couple minutes.

In a weak attempt to avoid the distraction, he stuffed his phone into his bike pannier, walked down the hallway to the teacher's lounge and made a cup of mint herbal tea.

He returned to the classroom and resumed grading. A couple minutes later, he heard his phone make a distinctive ding.

Digging the phone out he clicked on the Tinder notification: "You have a new match!" The screen filled with an image of an attractive woman who he'd right swiped on a few days before: Kim. He'd adjusted his settings in the app to include women that were up to a year older than his age of 46 and been surprised at how many attractive ones there were.

She was a striking brunette with dark brown eyes and a wide smile. He scanned the photos. They all had scenic backdrops: a beach, a foreign-looking cityscape, a resort pool, a ski slope. She was clad in fashionable, expensive-looking clothing that fit each setting perfectly. The app indicated that Kim and Scott shared a mutual friend, Sarah.

Next stop, Sarah's Facebook page and her list of friends. He clicked on Kim and scrolled down her feed: a few pictures with kids, good-looking kids, maybe tween-aged, a boy and a girl. There was a picture of Kim with Sarah and another woman, dressed up in cocktail attire at some kind of fundraising event. Kim was in the middle and totally outshined the other two.

Scott vaguely recalled seeing that picture on Facebook sometime earlier on Sarah's feed and taking note of the elegant woman in the middle. Sarah was an old friend of Scott's from college who also lived in Portland but they didn't really ever see each other.

He went back to the app and entered a message to Kim.

> Hey Kim, awesome photos! They all have such beautiful backdrops.

Scott returned to grading but not without a few breaks

to have a look over some of the photos he'd found of Kim on Facebook. The dating app tinged again. Kim had responded with a series of messages.

> Thanks!!! I know some pictures on this app are so bad.
>
> I'm sitting at the bar at Skamania Lodge right now.
>
> Such pretty Christmas decorations.

Scott responded and they texted back and forth.

> Oh sounds nice. I love Skamania. I'm out in the Gorge all the time in the summer to windsurf.
>
> Windsurfing? Old school.
>
> I've been doing it since the 90s.
>
> I miss the 90s.
>
> Me too.

The messages paused. Scott returned to his grading for about two minutes, then put on his bike commuting gear. It was still looking pretty damp outside for the five-mile bike ride to pick up Nate, but Scott didn't mind the rain or the physical exertion of cycling.

The transition in his half-time parenting schedule was always a bigger emotional ride than he expected. As soon as he walked into the afterschool program at Abernethy Elementary School on Portland's urban Eastside, his eyes met his son Nate's. Nate immediately stopped what he was doing and began to pack up to head home.

After some complaints about not being picked up in a car as happened with his mother, Nate climbed on the damp bench of the Xtracycle, a device that extended the length of a bike to take on passengers and additional cargo. Pretty standard stuff on Portland's crunchy Eastside.

Scott pedaled through the November gloom to their half of a midcentury modern duplex. Dinner was spaghetti and meatballs with a half-bottle cabernet blend from Trader Joe's for Scott, apple cider for 8-year-old Nate.

After being begged into reading two extra chapters of "Danny, Champion of the World," Scott managed to get Nate down to sleep but only after crawling into his twin bed next to him. Scott fell asleep too. When he awoke, he looked at his phone. 11:05. There was a message from Kim.

> I've tried windsurfing myself but I have to say I'm more of a runner.

Scott responded.

> Yeah, there's a learning curve. I'm sure you could get it. I'd love to give you a lesson sometime but meanwhile, would you like to meet up for a drink?

Kim returned the message in a minute.

> Sure. I just got back from Hawaii so I should go out on a lot of dates while I'm still tan.
>
> Right tan is hot!
>
> ;)
>
> How about the Rum Club at 8 next Wednesday?
>
> Great choice. I'll see you there.

Scott switched off the phone, got up and brushed and flossed his teeth. His 8-year-old dog Bob, a mix of Lab and shepherd and who knows what else, roused himself and followed Scott as he finished his nighttime routine.

THE ECLIPSE

Going on lots of dates while still tan? What the hell did that mean?

A few days later Scott had a date he had arranged with another woman he met online. He commuted home by running, showered, walked the dog and put on a pair of relatively new jeans, a T-shirt and a wool sweater with a turn-up collar.

The date arrived at his neighborhood bar after he ordered his beer. She was a social worker who was developing a line of organic hair products on the side. She was slender and pretty and 10 years his junior. He could see she was objectively attractive but there was a sort of oiliness to her skin and hair that turned him off. They had two rounds of drinks, then he walked her to her car. He wasn't sure how he felt about her, so he kissed her on the lips, just to see if there was something there.

It was common in online dating to connect with someone, admire their picture, fantasize about what life could be like with them and then be let down when meeting in person. When Scott went through his divorce five years earlier, he thought that meeting someone online sounded like a great innovation. It would save so much time and anguish for an introverted guy like him.

Scott got back home, put together a plate of snacks and sat down on the couch to watch some TV. Bob seemed happy that he was home.

Before starting up Netflix, he picked up his phone and thumbed through some pictures of the woman he had just met. Then he looked over the pictures of Kim on Tinder, then looked over a bunch of photos of her he had already found on Facebook.

After an episode and a half of "Fauda" he switched off the TV and looked at his phone. There was a message from last night's date.

> I enjoyed meeting you, Scott. Thanks for the drinks!

He wasn't inclined to respond.

Two days later, a blustery cold front moved into Portland and the days were filled with clear skies and bone-chilling east winds from the Columbia River Gorge.

Kim walked halfway down the stairway of her hillside home and called to her 13-year-old son Aiden, who was down in his room.

"Do you want pepperoni or cheese pizza?"

"I don't care Mom."

"I'm going out to meet a friend for an hour or so. Sierra is getting dropped off about 8:30. After dinner, I want you off screens and doing your homework and your 30 minutes of reading."

"Okay Mom."

Kim put the pizza in the oven and then went back down the hall to her room to the full-length mirror in her walk-in closet, where she tried on the fifth top.

Okay, she was really doing this. Since her divorce, Kim had never *needed* online dating. There was always a friend ready to set her up with someone or a connection that just happened. But with this separation, well, she wanted discretion. All their friends and connections were so intertwined.

And she had to admit to having a bit of curiosity about it. She'd helped her single friend Michelle flick through guys on Tinder. God some of the profiles were so hilarious. This one, Scott, looked cute. Scott's pics — in trail running gear atop a peak, skiing down a mountain slope and enjoying drinks with friends clad in an oxford shirt — made him an easy right swipe. She liked the athletic outdoorsy type but only if they were clean cut.

She finished touching up her makeup just as the clock ticked eight, the time they were supposed to meet. As usual, she was in a rush as she piloted her 2007 Range Rover down from Portland's West Hills into the center of the city.

Scott got to the Rum Club, a tropical-themed cocktail bar in Portland's inner Eastside industrial area, at 8 p.m. It was lively for a Thursday night and he was glad to nab a couple empty seats at the bar. He ordered a dry gin martini up.

Kim messaged him that she'd be there in 15 minutes.

He was already halfway through the martini when she walked in the door of the bar 20 minutes later. She smiled when she recognized Scott and he hopped off the bar stool to offer a greeting hug.

"I forgot about this place!" Kim said.

"It's one of my go-to's. Kind of reminds me of a bar in Madison, Wisconsin, where I went to college," Scott said, adding, "you certainly are prepared for the elements," as he helped Kim tuck her puffy coat, which looked large enough for an Antarctic expedition, under the bar where a hook was located.

As Kim climbed onto a barstool, Scott couldn't help but check her out. She was wearing a flowery Latin blouse, jeans, leather boots and half-moon silver earrings. Even in the dim bar light, Scott could see she cut a nice figure.

"I guess I'll notch that up to my Latin side. I like to be warm," Kim said with a laugh. She took the menu from the bar.

"Oh, they have such delicious-sounding cocktails here."

The bartender leaned in and asked Kim what she wanted.

"I'll have a margarita," Kim said. Turning to Scott, she added, "A classic."

"I just read in a novel that the margarita was invented in Baja California Sur in the fifties."

"Fascinating."

"What was that about a Latin side?" Scott asked.

"My mother's family is from Mexico City. My dad is Belgian, second generation. I've got relatives all over."

"As far as Latin America, I've only been to Mexico. Baja

specifically."

"Let me guess, La Ventana, Hood River South."

"You got it."

"I've had too many windsurfing lessons there," Kim said with a smile. "I never quite got the hang of it."

There was something about the sound of Kim's voice that Scott liked. At times it was soft, so soft that you had to strain a bit to hear it.

"Like I said, I'd be happy to give you a windsurfing lesson sometime."

"I wish we were there right now. Actually, anywhere tropical, with water. This is nice," she said, gesturing around the bar, "but there's no beach. I do like the snow, skiing and all, but just in small doses."

"What are you doing this weekend? It's supposed to snow on the mountain, I think."

"Oh, my daughter has a dance recital and I need to run a wine tasting. I work for a small winery."

"Very cool," Scott said.

"So how long have you been divorced?" Kim asked, changing the subject.

"Five years," Scott replied. "How about you?"

"Eight. I just got out of a 6-year relationship."

"Oh. I'm sorry to hear that. Well at least you get to experience the world of online dating," Scott said, regretting he'd said that as soon as he did. It was never a good idea to talk about the subject of dating on a date.

Scott, having practically polished off his first martini before Kim arrived, ordered a second drink while Kim was still working on her margarita.

"Look, your coat is expanding," Scott said with a teasing smile as he noticed her coat protruding outward between their legs at the bar. She playfully whacked his chest with a familiarity that seemed surprising. As he moved the coat away, he let his fingertips rest on Kim's thigh for just a second.

"How about another margarita," Scott asked.

"I need to get back to my kids," Kim said.

"Can I walk you to your car?"

"Sure," Kim said.

They walked about a block to her Range Rover and she gave him her cheek for a goodnight kiss.

When Scott got home, he flipped through some more profiles on Tinder before taking Bob for a walk. Then he hopped on Google and did some searches for "Kim Marseilles wine Portland." A website for Ross Wines came up first. The site featured vineyards with Pacific Northwest scenery interspersed with smiling middle-aged people drinking wine, mostly in outdoor settings. Under "About Us" Scott came across Kim's profile. "A veteran of the wine industry, Kim has been helping out with Ross Wines for almost six years now." Scott took in the picture of Kim in some form-fitting athleisure wear standing in front of a beautiful Hood River Valley backdrop.

At work the next day, he looked at the app a couple times, checking for messages. Details about Kim kept resurfacing in his head: that soft-spoken voice, those expressive brown eyes and that knockout smile she broke into when she laughed. He waited 'til noon to send her a message.

> Hi Kim, I had fun last night! Would you like to get together again sometime soon?

He checked the app continuously for the rest of the day at work and in the evening as he picked up Nate, fed him dinner and did the family dog walk. He left the phone sitting out in the living room when he went to bed, not wanting to think about it.

When he woke up at 2 a.m., like he often did, he walked out through the living room to get a glass of water. There was the phone on the table. He picked it up and entered the security pattern. There was a message from Kim.

> Great to meet you too. Yes, I'd be up for
> getting together again. Here's my number.

He crawled back into bed and laid awake for a while before falling back asleep.

Their second date was at La Moule, a French-themed restaurant in an old brick storefront in the trendy SE Clinton area not far from Scott's place. After getting dropped off by an Uber, Kim stood outside for just a minute before she saw Scott's lanky figure in the distance. It was another cold evening in Portland and he wore a retro western-style Patagonia down jacket, jeans and slip-on leather boots. His floppy brown hair blew in the slight breeze as he approached.

She felt a warm sense of anticipation as he walked toward her with a grin that she could see he was trying to suppress a bit. Soon, they were seated at a two-person table in one corner of the dimly lit restaurant.

"I love late dinners," Kim remarked in the candlelight.

"You look great," Scott said. She was wearing some tights, a loose-fitting sweater and hoop earrings.

She ordered a sparkling wine to start, while Scott went with an IPA.

"I like that Norwegian sweater," Kim said. "Can I feel it?"

She ran her well-manicured fingers along Scott's arm and hand.

They both ordered different variations on the mussels and tucked into a conversation that revolved around kids, winter vacations and the 2016 election.

After dinner, they walked back to Scott's house so Scott could give Kim a ride home. There was ice on the sidewalk and Kim was wearing boots with heels, so he guided her by the arm as they walked. By the time they got to Scott's place, they were holding hands.

"Come inside and meet my dog?" Scott asked.

"Sure," Kim said.

THE ECLIPSE

When they opened the door and entered, Bob gave a couple stern barks at this new figure but then calmed down. Kim leaned over and gave him a few hesitant pets without dropping to his level. She wasn't really a "dog person."

She turned and looked at Scott and smiled, wondering what was next.

Somewhat to her surprise, he opened the front door and they headed for the driveway.

Scott had the sense that Kim was a bit hesitant about online dating, so he didn't invite her to hang out for long. Bob joined them for the drive to her home by hopping in the hatchback of Scott's rig, a 1992 Saab that he had picked up while he was going through his divorce. Scott had developed an affection for Saabs when he first learned to drive as a teenager in the 1980s and had briefly owned a 900. When he saw a well-preserved, low-mileage 900 Turbo on Craigslist, he made an impulse purchase, thinking he would probably just hang onto it for a year or two. Five years later, it was still his daily driver.

"Gosh, it's been a while since I've been in one of these," Kim said. "One of my high school boyfriends drove one. It's cozy."

Scott turned the key and the engine warbled to life. He clicked on the seat heaters and they were off, heading west on Division Street, then north on Grand and then west on Burnside across the river.

On the way she asked him if he knew her last name. Scott laughed and said "of course," and explained that he'd Googled her.

Following her directions, he turned off West Burnside onto Macleay Boulevard, a winding road high in Portland's West Hills. He drove along curvy residential streets for what seemed like several minutes, passing by multimillion dollar homes perched above downtown Portland with stellar views of Mount Hood. Kim's house was a low-slung contemporary-style place.

"It's nothing special, built in the eighties. I got it after my divorce. I wanted something I could do a midcentury modern theme with," Kim said.

"Nice location," Scott said.

"The schools are good. And I do love nice views."

With the Saab in her driveway, Scott looked over at her with a hint of a smile on his face.

"So what did you used to *do* with your high school boyfriend in this car?" Scott asked playfully.

Kim rolled her eyes and Scott moved in for the kiss. She was receptive, though she didn't let it go all the way into make out territory.

The next week was Christmas and Scott took his son to visit his family in Madison, Wisconsin. This was the first family get-together since his mom had passed away in the fall.

The freeze and the snow had come early that winter. Scott, Scott's dad and Nate went out for cross-country skiing on Lake Mendota on a perfectly sunny, calm day. Scott couldn't resist sending Kim a lake panorama. Her West Coast sensibilities might be surprised at how pretty it was in flyover country.

She responded quickly.

> Beautiful! Did I tell you that I've been to Wisconsin?
>
> I'm running around doing Christmas shopping today and I have a holiday tasting this afternoon at New Seasons. Your day looks much more fun.

Scott wondered about the Wisconsin reference, but something told him not to ask about it.

Later Kim texted Scott a shot of her daughter in a holiday dance recital.

After Scott got Nate off to sleep that night and his dad

turned in, he sent Kim a message.

> How did your hectic day go?
>
> It's over. I've got a bottle of prosecco open and I'm watching that show you told me about, "The Affair."
>
> It's addicting, isn't it?
>
> I'm blaming you if I spend the next four hours binging it!

They continued the back and forth for a good 45 minutes, setting up a date for a couple days after Scott got back.

Scott was starting to feel like this thing with Kim had potential. Sure, they'd only kissed but they were texting a ton. He went all out preparing for their date at Helium Comedy Club. A haircut, a trip to J. Crew to get a new shirt plus he even washed and vacuumed the Saab.

When he spotted her in the bar area after he arrived, his stomach tightened up. Was she too good looking for him? Out of his league? They had drinks in the waiting area and then got ushered into the club and were seated on stools at a tall table. As the lights went down and the act came on, Scott moved his hand over to Kim's and she reciprocated his touch.

The act was a PG-rated comic and had a funny bit about Donald Trump's unexpected election to the presidency.

Afterward, they walked out to Scott's car. When he opened her door, she exclaimed, "Oh my God, it's so clean!"

"I cleaned it up for you!" Scott said.

Kim laughed and said, "I'm not going to show you my car."

Scott drove her to his house, a bit nervous about what might await.

Soon, they found themselves in Scott's kitchen.

"You know you come highly recommended by Sarah," Kim said as Scott opened a bottle of wine.

"Really?"

"So what are you looking for?" she asked.

"My soulmate," Scott said.

Kim laughed.

"What about you?"

"I don't know. My situation is complicated. I can't be involved in anything serious right now."

The words hung there in the air.

Scott couldn't quite process their meaning. He moved closer to her, reached out and took one of her hands and moved in for a kiss.

Her lips didn't reciprocate, so he paused, then went back to filling their drinks.

They moved to the couch, where they drank wine and talked. The evening had been going well but now things felt a bit awkward.

Sooner than he expected, Kim finished her wine and said she needed to get back to her kids.

When they headed out to Scott's car, they were surprised to see big snowflakes falling, a real rarity in rainy and temperate Portland. Once they got seated in the car, Kim said that she had left her phone inside the house.

They got out of the vehicle together and went back into the house. The phone wasn't hard to locate so they headed back out. Just as Scott was locking the front door, Kim reached for his arm, moving him around to face her. Their lips came together and they had a long sensuous kiss as the snow fell around them.

"I find you so attractive," she said.

Scott smiled and guided her to the car, holding her arm.

They were silent for a while on the drive west down Division Street to her house. Then Kim said, "We'll see how long you put up with me."

2

Scott pulled the Saab into the snow-dusted driveway of his duplex. He shut off the vehicle and sat for a few seconds.

It seemed like he could still smell a hint of her from the empty passenger seat, a delicate but elusive scent that he figured must be her perfume or body lotion.

When he got inside, he put some water on the stove, opened his laptop and Googled "it's complicated." A few hits showed up in the results list. The Urban Dictionary said:

> *Refers to a couple in an ambiguous state between "friends" and "in a relationship." May also be used to indicate dissatisfaction with an existing relationship.*

Scott Googled Kim again and looked over the results that came up: her LinkedIn page, her Facebook, the winery where she worked. What was it about her that made her so stunning? She had a facial structure that he recognized as objectively attractive, almost familiar, like she was a model or an actress he'd seen before. Even so, it wasn't a look that recalled any female whom he'd fancied in the past.

The water was boiling, so he fixed himself a cup of orange tea then went back to his laptop.

He looked at the winery webpage a little more carefully than the last time he'd been there. Camden Ross, the winemaker, adorned the front page of the site. He was a rugged-looking guy with wavy brown hair and a perpetual salt-and-pepper stubble. In one photo, he was clad in a flannel shirt kneeling next to some grapes in a vineyard and in another he was leaning on a barrel in a wine cellar with an earnest expression on his face.

No, it couldn't be him. That would be too simple.

Scott Googled "Camden Ross Kim Marseilles" and clicked over to the image search results page.

Fuck. There they were at some wine awards event a few years ago. A couple, arms around each other. Kim looked stunning in a cocktail dress with Ross, clad in an untucked dress shirt and jeans, right by her side.

Scott pulled up the Instagram feed for Ross Wines on his phone. The latest post was a set of shots from a snow-covered winery taken just a few days earlier. They were individual shots of Kim and Camden stomping around in the snow, obviously taken by each other.

He threw the phone at the couch.

Fuck.

He couldn't get the phrase "my situation is complicated" in Kim's seductive, self-possessed voice out of his head.

The next day, Scott went out to one of his favorite bars, the Landmark Saloon, with a couple friends. The place was a small house on SE Division Street that had been converted to an urban refuge for honky-tonk music enthusiasts, complete with autographed photos of Merle Haggard, Loretta Lynn and John Prine on the walls. Scott was on winter break from school and didn't have Nate, so it was a night he could let go a bit.

"So how did the date go?" his buddy Doug asked.

Doug was another divorced single dad, one whose dating life was even a notch slower than Scott's relatively uneventful one.

"She gave me this line about her love life: 'my situation is complicated.' What the hell does that mean?"

"What do you know about her?" Doug asked.

"She just broke up with her long-time partner. They still work in the same small winery business together. I gather that the complicated thing must have to do with him."

"Ah yes. They're taking a break. Getting space. Seeing other people."

Scott raised his eyebrows.

"I guess I was kind of figuring it was something like that."

"Fuck that. It's bullshit. For you and the other dude."

"I found some pictures of her ex online. He's a good-looking guy, an artisan winemaker. How can I compete against that anyway?"

"Move on."

Scott finished off his India Red Ale. He made his way forward to check out the singer, Matt Buetow, who was mixing in some covers of George Jones and Dwight Yoakam with some originals.

Scott ordered a double Bulleit on the rocks. Just as he took a sip, Buetow started on one of Scott's old favorites, "A Good Year for the Roses."

> I can hardly bear the sight of lipstick
> On the cigarettes there in the ashtray
> Lying cold the way you left them
> At least your lips caressed them while you packed

In his somewhat buzzed state of mind, Scott thought of Kim and wondered about this relationship she had been in or maybe still was in. What had attracted her to him? Had they been in love? What had caused the relationship to founder?

Soon, he was back home. As he was lying in bed, his friend's advice to just move on from Kim lingered. But for some reason his drunken mind kept trying to work out why it would be a good idea to keep seeing Kim. He was having trouble getting to the answer he wanted but he was almost there when he fell asleep.

The next morning, Kim got a text from Scott.

> I'm so hungover.
>
> Was it worth it?
>
> Absolutely. When are we going out again?
>
> Hmmmm ... how about Thursday?
>
> It's a date. There's a Mexican place near me you might like.
>
> Sounds good, I'm game.

Another date with Scott? Where was this going? She certainly had expected something a little different from Tinder. What? Maybe meeting someone fun who could take her mind off the heavy relationship shit she was dealing with.

She flicked through the pictures of Scott on the app. What was it about him that was so intriguing? He was awkward actually and dressed in this outdated preppy style. A high school history teacher. Really? But that lanky, lean runner's body, his disheveled hair, and those sexy green eyes. He had this Midwestern seriousness about him that was so different than herself.

In two days, they met at the Mexican spot Scott picked out. The food was odd and their table was in a somewhat inadequately heated zone of an enclosed patio area.

"Brrrr," Scott said, "I bet you wish that you still had that trip to Hawaii ahead of you."

"Who said I'm not going back?" Kim replied in a playful tone.

"Are you?"

"I am," Kim replied, somewhat sheepishly.

"Oh really? Which island is it this time?"

Kim paused, trying to think of a way to redirect the conversation.

"I don't want to talk about it," she said.

Scott nodded his head and took a sip of his beer.

THE ECLIPSE

After dinner, they retreated to Scott's place and sat on the couch talking, laughing, holding hands and watching funny YouTube videos. There was one that made fun of gluten-free diets that they both thought was hilarious. The question about the trip to Hawaii hadn't left Kim's mind.

She felt weird about what she was about to do with Camden but she knew she shouldn't feel guilty. She and Scott were just dating.

She finished her glass of wine, announced that she had to leave and gave Scott a perfunctory parting kiss.

Scott had thought things were going well on their date, but the mention of the upcoming Hawaii trip and the abrupt ending left him a bit confused. Later that week, a forecast for another big snowstorm in Portland came through. Scott texted Kim.

> Want to get together this weekend (if we survive the oncoming storm and time at home with offspring)?
>
> I don't know if I'll survive! Remember how I said I was going to Hawaii again. Well. I'm going to Kauai over MLK weekend.

She sent a few tropical emojis.

She didn't mention *whom* she was going with but Scott wasn't going to ask. It had to be him. Scott felt a tension well up in his gut. She was really doing it. Going off for a romantic getaway with her ex or whatever he was. Fuck. He sucked it up and sent her a text.

> I have to admit I'm a bit envious. Do bring back a nice tan.
>
> Hahaha

It was uncomfortably quiet after Kim and Camden rolled in their carry-ons and closed the front door of their

Kauai condo. They were alone together again in an enclosed domestic space, the first time since he'd moved out in August.

"Ah this is nice," Camden said, coming over to her and giving her an embrace. Kim allowed a gentle kiss on the lips and then broke away, walking out on the balcony to take in the ocean view.

"I think I'll take a swim," she said, "and then book a massage before dinner."

"Okay, I'm going to try the surf. It's light but it'll be a good day to get my sea legs."

The swim in the tropical water followed by the massage was a combination that always worked for Kim. Three hours later, she sat on the balcony in the late afternoon tropical sun with a glass of the pinot gris they'd picked up at the little grocery store on the way to the condo.

She could already feel the anxiety about the trip melting away. The relaxed, sensual mood that she sought on a tropical vacation was coming over her.

She thought about Scott and picked her phone up to text him.

> Aloha! Just wanted to say hi from the island, Scott! I've been seeing all the pictures of the snow in Portland and they look so pretty.

Just as she sent the message, Camden came out on the balcony in a towel with a glass of the pinot gris. He leaned over, ran the back of his fingers slowly down the outside of her arm, then kissed her cheek, then her lips and it felt good.

Over MLK weekend, Scott tried to occupy himself by working on some neglected house projects but he had a hard time finding the motivation. He mustered up a positive reply to the text Kim sent him from Kauai but in his mind he tried to write her off.

THE ECLIPSE

The previous October, Scott had traveled to Bainbridge Island for the fourth time in so many months to visit Melinda. They'd had a sweet thing going all summer but it was long distance. One Friday night, Scott arrived on the ferry with all the specific organic products that Melinda had requested from the mainland Whole Foods.

When she greeted him on the porch, he was struck by Melinda's presence, her dark eyes and shapely feminine figure. He was lucky to have this good-looking woman waiting for him on a Friday night.

The next evening, they were hanging out on Melinda's loveseat, getting ready to watch a movie. Melinda had somehow managed to steer the conversation to the topic of their relationship.

"So, it's been so much fun, Scott. How are you feeling about things?"

"Things are great. I'm so glad to be here. Do you want a top-off on your wine before we turn on the movie?"

"So how about dating? I mean, seeing other people. Are you still interested in that?"

Scott paused for a while. He started to speak a couple times and then couldn't figure out what to say. Then out it came.

"I think I'd like to see other people."

"Oh really?"

She put a couple inches of distance between them on the loveseat.

"I am looking for something not long distance," Scott said.

The truth was Scott wasn't sure about Melinda.

The conversation cooled things off for the rest of the weekend. But they cooked, hiked and talked for another day. When it came time to go on Sunday afternoon, Scott had felt inexplicably emotional. They had a few long hugs and then he left for the ferry terminal.

Now Melinda was moving to Portland and she had asked Scott to help her move into a new apartment on Sunday afternoon. They hadn't seen each other much since that weekend in early October.

He spent the afternoon unloading furniture from a rental truck into her new residence in the Belmont neighborhood, an area a bit north of Scott's place that was a mix of older homes and apartment buildings, independent coffee shops and vintage clothing stores. Scott was in a funky mood the whole time. He was thinking of Kim.

After they were done unloading, Melinda bought takeout Thai and they cracked a bottle of wine and then another. Even the alcohol and flirty Melinda couldn't take Kim off his mind. Scott got drunk and laid down on her couch to sleep. In the morning, she came out to check to see if he was warm.

He took her hand and joined her in bed. In the January dawn twilight, they enjoyed a carnal reunion of sorts. Then they spent the next day together as a couple, cooking for each other and taking long walks. Scott could almost imagine forgetting about Kim and making the choice to start something up again with Melinda.

But in the days afterward, she didn't text him and he didn't take the initiative to text her.

The following week, Scott's friend Rick from Wisconsin visited for a long weekend. Rick Leyden was a professional photographer and perennial bachelor, aged 47 going on 25.

Like his previous visits, this one consisted of carousing at bars, late-morning brunches, and some casual sightseeing and photography during the day.

Just after Rick arrived, Scott got a text from Kim.

> Back to Portland from the Islands and finally caught up after this trip. How are you?

Scott and Rick were out at Stammtisch, a German-themed bar and restaurant on Portland's Northeast side.

"Damn, I can't believe she texted me. I thought she was

gone forever," Scott said.

"Who's that?" asked Rick.

"Kim."

"Let me see a picture."

Scott retrieved one from the Ross Wines Instagram feed.

"Not bad, Mr. Larson. She's smokin' hot."

"There's something out of reach about her. I don't know her full story but I think she's from money. In a strange way, she kind of reminds me of Lauren Hill."

"I remember your infatuation with her in high school. The popular girl who had a crush on you for two minutes. The doctor's daughter.

"So, what's the story with Kim?" Rick asked.

"Met on Tinder. We've gone out on a few dates. No sex, just making out a bit. And she's told me her situation is 'complicated.'"

"No sex and you met on Tinder? What's the problem, Mr. Larson?"

"Just recently, she said she was headed to Hawaii with her ex-boyfriend. I pretty much threw in the towel on her but here she is texting me. What do you think?"

"Hmmm," Rick said as he took another draw on his Kölsch. "She's in a messed-up situation. She's trying to work it out with this guy but she's not sure. If she really liked him, she wouldn't be messaging you. You're the new guy on the scene, the excitement. There's opportunity here."

"You really think so? But the situation is so fucked up."

"It *is* fucked up. But dude, you need to play the bad guy. She wants you man."

"I don't know. It seems demeaning."

"Just keep a couple things in mind. The situation is fucked up and will stay fucked up. You won't be able to change that.

"And don't put pressure on her to commit. If you put pressure on her, she will flee."

Rick ordered another round.

They ended up at the Landmark. The band Countryside

Ride was playing. They did an old Merle Haggard tune that made Scott think of Kim and Camden's Hawaii getaway.

> If we're not back in love by Monday
> We can't say we didn't try
> But before we bury our love
> Let's make sure we've let it die
> Sleep a few more nights together
> Say the things we used to say
> If we're not back in love by Monday
> We can go our sep'rate ways

The next day was a Sunday, and Scott and Rick had brunch at a Mexican spot. They enjoyed a couple Micheladas along with some huevos rancheros.

Scott brought up the situation with Kim and her ex. "There's no way that I can compete with him. He has his own winery. There are all these pictures all over his website of him in these manly poses holding grapes, leaning next to wine barrels, magisterially directing operations of this winery."

"Where is this fucking winery?" asked Rick.

"Well, it's out in Hood River, you know, the windsurfing town."

"He doesn't know you, right? Let's pay him a visit."

Scott frowned disapprovingly. "Bad idea, Leyden. That would be so embarrassing."

Two hours later, they were at the Hood River waterfront. Rick was into artsy photography of highly engineered structures and wanted to get some close-up shots of the Hood River Bridge. They walked out on the sand spit that extends into the Columbia River and Rick launched his drone. He piloted it up over the bridge roadway for some high overhead shots, then he dropped the drone alongside the bridge to get some close-ups of the metal work. After about five minutes of trying different angles, he lost his signal and the $3000 device crashed into the side of the bridge and plummeted into the water.

"Fuck! That's the second one of these that I've lost."

"Ouch," Scott said.

"I need a drink. Where did you say that winery was?"

"I thought you'd forgotten about that," Scott said.

In a few minutes, they were walking toward Ross Wines' tasting room, which was situated in a storefront just off Oak Street, the main drag of Hood River's compact downtown.

"Not sure this is such a good idea," Scott said as they approached the entryway.

"Steady as she goes, my man," Rick said.

The interior of the tasting room was clean, open and modern with floor-to-ceiling windows, a reclaimed fir bar top and minimalist Scandinavian-style stools. Scott's heart raced as he caught a glimpse of some pictures on the wall of Kim and Camden Ross.

A tall, white-haired man with a goatee stood behind the bar in lively conversation with a seated couple who were enjoying a tasting. Rick and Scott took two open spots, one seat removed from the couple.

It didn't take long for the tasting room attendant to address them.

"Hey guys, I'm Axel. Can I pour something for you?"

"Tell us a little bit about what you've got," Rick said.

They absorbed Axel's spiel and chose a pinot noir.

"So can I ask how Ross Wines got its start?" Rick inquired, making a conscious effort to turn the conversation toward Camden Ross. They got some of the same info that they already knew from the website: that Camden Ross had been a software developer in Silicon Valley and had nurtured a taste for Northern California wine. Enrolling in the wine program at UC Davis and a growing fascination with the Oregon wine scene had prompted a move north to Oregon.

"So how does a guy *start* a winery?" Rick asked.

"Do you mean the actual process of making the wine, or the business side of it?"

"More the business side of it," Rick replied.

"It takes some equipment and some know-how," said Axel. "Actually, quite a bit. Ross Wines uses a shared winemaking space currently, but soon we will have our own production space in the Hood River Valley."

"So how did Ross get started? Did he have an investor?"

"Well, I'm not exactly sure about that, he started pretty small."

"Well, that's impressive, to follow a passion like that and build something like this," Rick said, gesturing around the tasting room. "Is he around today, could we meet him?"

Scott cringed.

"Actually, he should be here any minute."

Rick and Scott drank a while longer, conversing amongst themselves. Soon, in walked a dude who came up to the bar and greeted Axel with a fist bump.

"Hey Cam, I haven't seen you since you got back from Kauai, how was it?" Axel asked the man across the bar.

Scott looked Camden Ross over. He was a bit shorter than Scott, more wide-set and muscular. He had blue eyes, thin lips and a sharp-edged smile, and wore scuffed leather boots, Carhartt pants, a heavy plaid flannel work shirt and a trucker cap. His outfit seemed just right for the part of the manly artisan. That it came together so perfectly suggested a fashion-conscious female partner might have put it together, Scott surmised.

"You were just in Kauai?" Rick jumped in. "Do you surf?"

"It was amazing. Had two epic days. I went with my girlfriend so I couldn't be in the water as much as I would have liked. You know, romantic getaway sort of thing," replied Camden.

Scott's face burned.

"Nice," Rick said. "How was the swell?"

Rick got Camden started, first on the Hawaii trip and then on his winery. As he talked about his surfing and winemaking adventures in an easy-going dude-to-dude sort of way, Scott could understand the guy's appeal.

"Get these guys another pour, Axel," Camden said after he discovered that they were all from Wisconsin.

"This wine is fantastic, Camden. I mean I've never experienced pinot with this ..." Rick paused, lifting the glass into the air and swirling its contents in an exaggerated manner.

"Depth and character?" Scott suggested.

"Exactly," Rick said, taking a large belt of the wine.

Rick and Scott, who'd both grown up in Madison, Wisconsin, learned that Camden's dad owned a large freight transportation business based out of Milwaukee. They recognized the names of the private schools that Camden had attended while growing up.

"And so she's the one you went with to Hawaii?" Rick asked, pointing to a picture on the wall of Kim and Camden.

"That's the girlfriend," Camden said.

"Damn, she's a looker. If I were in Hawaii with her, I don't know if I'd want to leave the hotel room," Rick said.

Camden seemed a bit taken aback by such a forward remark but then said with a sort of half smile, "She's pretty special," and then began walking away, as if to deliberately end the conversation.

"Sometimes the good ones are hard to hold onto," Rick said.

"She's an independent woman," Camden said, turning back around.

"The beautiful ones always smash the picture," Rick said.

"If Prince says so," Camden said.

"May he rest in peace," Rick said.

With that, Camden moved to some other guests.

Rick seemed to be walking a little funny as they left the tasting room. "What a conceited rich fuck," he said as they got into Scott's Saab.

"I actually thought he seemed like an alright guy," Scott said.

"He's a rich kid who gets to play instead of work. Fuck him. This was such a nice picture I couldn't resist," Rick said as he held up a framed photograph of Camden and Kim that was along the walkway to the restroom. He'd stuffed it into the giant winter coat he had brought from Wisconsin.

As soon as they got back on I-84, Rick unscrewed the top off the bottle of Ross Reserve Cabernet. He handed Scott the bottle so he could take a drink.

"Dude, what are you doing?" Scott asked as he reluctantly took a belt of the Cab.

"Where to next? How about another winery?" Rick asked as he put down the window and chucked the photograph into the ditch.

Rick flew back to Wisconsin the next day, a Monday. Scott had been playfully texting Kim over the weekend but had consciously not broached the topic of them getting together.

That morning, with the week beginning in earnest, he messaged her.

> Good morning! I'm back in school after my lost weekend. Wondered if you had plans on Thursday?
>
> Hmmm, let me check my social calendar;)
>
> Of course.
>
> Actually, I do have something planned Thursday night. Thanks for the invitation. I'd love to get together soon. Maybe next week?

Scott's students were filing into the classroom. Today's topic was Bismarck and the balance of power following the Crimean War, usually one of Scott's favorite subjects. His mind kept drifting as he lectured and conversed with the class.

He had time for a walk during his next break between classes, so he did his regular loop on some residential streets near the school. He kept thinking about what Leyden had said: Kim wanted him. This was an opportunity.

When he got back to his desk, he sent Kim a text.

> I don't think I can wait til next week.

Scott put the phone in his pocket and kept walking. No response. Then he texted her again.

> I want you.
>
> How about we try something different? Wednesday afternoon we could meet at my place when I have a break from teaching. We can have a little wine, talk and see where things go.

No reply for about a half-hour. Then she sent an open-mouthed emoji.

> Scott, I'm shocked. I'll have to think about this...indecent proposal.
>
> Okay.

It had been a week since Kim had returned from her long weekend with Camden in Kauai. They'd seen each other on Wednesday to interview a new tasting room attendant but hadn't managed to spend any real time together.

Things *had* clicked in Kauai but as soon as they got off the plane, something felt different.

It was close to 10 p.m. and the kids were in their rooms. Kim heard a gentle knock on the front door and knew it must be him. She hadn't returned any of the texts that he'd sent earlier in the day. Something in her felt irritated by his persistence, his assumption that something was different now.

She went down and opened the door. Camden was dressed in one of those cable knit sweaters she liked on him. She knew what he wanted.

"Hey there," she said. "I'm sorry I didn't respond to your texts. I was just not sure how I was feeling. I think I'm coming down with something."

"Happy to just hang out a bit," Camden said. "How about a massage?"

"I'll take a rain check on that."

"Okay," he said with a neutral expression on his face.

"I'll see you soon," she said and gave him a goodbye hug.

It was sad, she thought. This was *their* home just five months ago.

Then she flashed back to that morning last April.

After a poor night's sleep, Kim had risen with the sun while everyone else in the house slept.

She had made breakfast, pried all three kids out of bed, including Camden's daughter, and mobilized them all for school. Camden remained asleep, probably hungover from a night out with friends. Minutes before she had to get the kids loaded up, he came rushing into the kitchen to tell her that she'd forgotten to cover a shift at the tasting room.

In fact, that had been *his* responsibility, his fuck up. She was already overloaded with preparations for the wine tasting dinner that weekend.

It was the culmination of tension that had been building for months. She wasn't used to this supporting role that he just *expected* her to play in the business and at home. She wanted to be an equal partner and she couldn't do that while taking care of every goddamned thing with the kids and all the most mundane aspects of the business.

"Your breakfast is ready," she'd said to Camden. Then she'd taken the plate with his breakfast sandwich on it, raised it into the air, and smashed it on the floor. He muttered something about her Latin side.

Then she'd sent her breakfast plate airborne.

"I am fucking done with this," she'd screamed in front of him and the kids. She'd stormed out of the house, leaving him to figure out how to get all three kids off to school.

Two months later, he moved out.

Scott's Monday and Tuesday slipped by with a few inconsequential text messages with Kim. After Nate went to bed on Tuesday, Scott hurriedly cleaned up the duplex on the off chance that Kim actually took him up on the "indecent proposal." On Wednesday morning, Scott texted her at about nine when he knew she'd be done with her kid drop-offs.

> Meet me at my place at 2? I'll have a bottle of something chilled.

Scott didn't hear anything back for over an hour and then he did.

> Okay.

Holy shit. It was on.

When he was done with teaching at one, he changed into his biking clothes and made the bike commute home in record time. He put on a pair of jeans and a t-shirt, still warm and slightly sweaty from the ride.

Kim arrived fifteen minutes late. She was wearing some athleisure wear and no makeup. He greeted her with a soft kiss on the lips and he asked her if she'd like a glass of rosé as he motioned for her to sit on the couch.

She looked different in the daylight to Scott. Her skin appeared paler and he could see the subtle lines on her face revealing her age. This exposed state only made him want her more.

As they began making small talk, Scott could feel the chilled wine go right from his stomach to his head. He let the conversation drift on for what seemed like a long time, probably just five or 10 minutes. Then he leaned over to kiss Kim.

Her lips felt cool and they had a long, sensuous kiss. Scott took Kim's hand and led her into his bedroom where she began to undress him, looking at him with those large, wide-set eyes.

Despite the wine, Scott's heart raced as he could see fantasy becoming reality.

Free of their clothing, they rolled around and made out. Scott paused the action for a second and they just laid there, Scott caressing Kim's body.

Soon, Scott felt desire well up in him and their bodies came together.

Afterward they lay there in Scott's bed, letting 20 minutes or so pass until kid retrievals were imminent. Kim started to get up and get dressed but Scott couldn't keep his hands off her as she clothed.

As he cooked dinner that night for Nate, Scott thought about Kim in the space of his home. It was hard to believe she had been there just hours earlier. It was almost like she was an apparition.

They repeated the Wednesday afternoon rendezvous thing a couple more times. Kim liked to wrap them up at the door with long, sensuous kisses. "I see you're getting better at goodbyes," she'd say in a teasing tone.

The rendezvous were erotic, but somehow Scott wanted more of Kim. He had an AP history teacher's conference coming up in Seattle over a couple of in-service days on a Thursday and a Friday. What if he booked a little extra time up there and Kim met up with him?

The time window turned out to work for her and to Scott's surprise, she agreed to come.

The conference was a meeting of Advanced Placement European History instructors in the Pacific Northwest. It was hosted in what might be described as a boutique

European-style hotel near the University of Washington campus. The place was clean and modern but the rooms were pretty tiny.

During the meetings at the conference, Scott worried constantly about Kim's impending arrival. Before she got there, he upgraded to a room with a view. At a $75 premium, the room turned out to be just as small as the one he'd initially occupied but was a few floors higher up.

When he spotted the contours of her head inside her Range Rover as it passed by the hotel lobby on the way to the parking area, his heart leapt and he rushed outside to meet her. Suddenly Kim was there in the flesh.

It was a rare sunny March afternoon in the 50s in Seattle and they took the free bikes offered by the hotel for a ride along the waterfront. They stopped at Gas Works Park on Lake Union and wandered around a bit in the sunshine.

The waning daylight got them back to the hotel where they cracked a bottle of prosecco and let one thing lead to another. Afterward, they Ubered over to a downtown French restaurant and had a long, leisurely dinner before returning to the hotel.

Neither of them slept well. But just as the first signs of daylight came through the windows, Scott got up, made coffee, brought a cup to Kim in bed and then slipped back under the covers. After a couple sips of joe, Kim began kissing Scott's chest playfully. One of her kisses turned into a bite. The sharp pain aroused Scott unexpectedly and they made love intensely in the dull light of the misty Seattle morning.

After checking out of the hotel, they enjoyed a leisurely breakfast, visited an art museum and dawdled around some second-hand stores in the Ballard neighborhood. For some reason, Scott liked watching Kim examine the merchandise. There was just something about the way that she took in the world that fascinated him.

They tucked into a quirky Mexican restaurant for a late lunch — the last meal of the short trip. Over a margarita

Kim told him about her life in her late twenties and early thirties before she got divorced.

"It was such a different world. My husband was in finance during the dot-com thing and moved into commercial real estate in the early 2000s. I worked in PR before we had kids. We lived in San Francisco and had a beautiful place in the city and a winery in Napa plus a condo in Tahoe.

"I spent winters in Maui and much of the summer at the winery. I had a full-time nanny to take care of our kids. We took private planes.

"In 2008, it all went crashing down. He had several development ventures that totally fell through. Our 30 million in paper wealth evaporated overnight."

Scott drew from his Pacifico, listening intently.

"I also found out that he was fucking his executive assistant, not to mention a string of other girls at the office. A woman he worked with took me aside and told me. I was the last to know, of course. That's when I moved back to Portland to be with family."

"My divorce story isn't quite that exotic," Scott said.

Kim laughed.

Scott had hitched a ride with a colleague to the conference, so they drove back in Kim's Range Rover. Scott had never been inside Kim's car, but was surprised at how worn out the 10-year-old SUV was on the inside. It was a relic of flusher times in her life.

On the drive, they joked around and took a quiz on the NPR website that was supposed to assess whether you live in an elitist bubble. Somewhat unexpectedly, the results of the quiz deemed Scott more of an elitist than Kim.

Kim dropped off Scott at his home. As he sat in his Portland living room with his dog Bob, a wave of emotion came over him. He decided to send Kim a text expressing a little more genuine feeling than their usual banter.

THE ECLIPSE

> So glad we made this weekend happen. I had such a nice time with you.

Kim replied.

> I know YOU had a nice time;)

Then a pause.

> Thank you for such a pleasant getaway.

The reply stung a bit. Scott was hoping for something more.

3

Spring Break arrived the next week. Scott took Nate to central Oregon for a few days of skiing, snowboarding and mountain biking. The late March sunshine made the high desert an attractive escape from the ongoing gloom on the west side of the Oregon Cascades. They stayed at Seventh Mountain Resort, a cluster of condominiums nestled in ponderosa pines just outside of the booming town of Bend and on the way to Mount Bachelor, Oregon's top ski resort. The spot was a favorite with Nate because of the outdoor heated pools.

On the second day, they skied Mount Bachelor with Scott's friend Ted, a long-time Bend resident, and his daughter. Ted was married and about the same age as Scott. Afterward, they all hung out at the condo Scott had rented. Scott kept checking his phone and sending messages while he was sipping a beer and putting together a spread for tacos.

"So who's texting, dude? Got a lady back in p-town these days?"

"Sort of. It's complicated. That's how she puts it. I'll tell you about it more later."

Scott had messaged Kim a few times already, sending her some shots from the slopes. After dinner, while the kids played in the outdoor pools, Ted and Scott hung out in one of the hot tubs. They could hear eighties music including songs by Prince, Bon Jovi and Phil Collins coming from the adjacent outdoor skating rink.

"So it's complicated, but you're getting laid?"

"More or less."

"Sounds better than my marriage. I just have the complicated part," Ted said, taking a sip of beer.

"It feels more like an affair than a real relationship. She never invites me over to her place. Sometimes the only time we get together is on a Wednesday afternoon. She'll come over. We'll drink some wine and … you know."

"Dude! Details, please."

"She doesn't want to commit. She says she can't be involved in anything serious."

"This is sounding better all the time. I wish I could afford a divorce."

"I like her though. She won't let me into her world. Last weekend, she sent me a hot picture from some fundraising dinner she was at and I'm wondering 'why didn't you invite me along?'"

"Don't worry about that bullshit, just enjoy time with her."

"I know I should, but I think about her constantly. I'm always checking my phone. It's frustrating. I'm on a high when I'm with her or after we've had a good text exchange, but then it wears off and I'm anxious and miserable."

"Wait a second," Ted said, "I think this song playing has your punchline." The eighties tune, "A Total Eclipse of the Heart," could be heard from the skating rink.

Scott shook his head and Ted smiled.

"You've got it bad for her, dude. That's hard. But you'll get past it. It's not going to change the course of your life."

After Spring Break, a couple weeks ticked by. Scott and Kim managed to get together a couple times. One Thursday afternoon in mid-April, Scott was finishing up in his classroom and his phone buzzed with a text from Kim. She'd sent a picture of snow-capped Mount Adams and a cobalt blue sky.

Guess where?

The Gorge?

Wish you were here!

I can be there in about 90 minutes.

That would be so fun.

They went back and forth a bit, at first not taking the idea seriously. But soon enough, Scott was on I-84 bound for Hood River.

The transition from Portland to the Columbia Gorge was one that Scott knew well from his regular summer commute to windsurfing sites along the river. As the East Portland concrete jungle gave way to the thickly forested slopes of the western Gorge, Scott felt a sense of anticipation for one of his favorite Pacific Northwest destinations and a bit of anxiety about what awaited at Kim's place.

The clouds thickened as he approached the Bonneville Dam and then Cascade Locks. A few miles later, the clouds started to break as he passed the exits for Wyeth and Viento. An azure sky opened as he entered the Hood River corridor. Soon the small city of Hood River appeared, hugging the hills on the right.

He took Highway 35 up the Hood River Valley as Kim had instructed. The white blooms on the pear trees that lined the highway looked pretty in the early evening light. Soon after the mile marker Kim had given him, he made a left turn and drove up a quarter mile on a private gravel road through a vineyard and into a grove of fir trees in which her house was nestled.

The place was a simple midcentury farmhouse. He walked up the driveway to an orange front door that popped against the gray siding.

Kim answered the door in jeans, a sweatshirt and a baseball cap. He'd never seen her dressed in such a domestic way. Somehow, that made things feel more intimate.

They entered the living room, which had a picture window with a decent view of Mount Adams. Kim flicked on the gas fireplace to take the chill off the cool April evening. She poured wine and they talked for what seemed like a long time.

With the day's light fading, Scott slowly moved in to initiate a kiss. When their lips touched, Scott felt an electricity as they finally closed the gap of time and space that had separated them earlier in the day.

After they made out a bit, Kim got up and pulled a sheepskin throw off one of the sofas and laid it out in front of the fireplace. As she took his hand and guided him over, Scott couldn't help but surmise that this wasn't the first time that she'd pulled this move with a man.

They undressed each other and enjoyed the radiant heat as they made love.

Afterward, they lay there for a while in front of the fire with their long-stemmed glasses of wine.

"I don't understand what you see in me," Scott said.

"I could say the same thing about you."

"A real estate mogul, a winemaker. I just don't see where I fit in."

"I find you so attractive," Kim said, as she wrapped her arms around Scott and initiated one of those long kisses that she liked.

The house was booked on the Vacation Rentals By Owner website the next day, so they slept in a small anteroom in the daylight basement. The next morning over breakfast, Kim got to talking about the winery. She and Camden had purchased the 10-acre parcel a year earlier with the intention of creating an estate vineyard for Ross Wines, which at that time consisted of winemaking in a shared warehouse facility and the tasting room in Hood River.

They had done some basic renovations to the house to make it suitable as a vacation rental, converted 4 acres of pear orchards to vineyard, and had gotten the permits to open a tasting room and a wine production area.

"It's just been so overwhelming," Kim said. "The permitting has been hell. And there is so much still wrong with it. The layout of the house is terrible. The view from the living room cuts off the top of the mountain view. This is a nice parcel we have, but this whole area is a little trashy in my opinion, too many funky-looking places with old cars and trailers on the lots.

"The building that we're converting to a tasting room, well, it's an old barn. And Camden will be making wine in that ugly oversized garage that you drove by as you came in.

"I just don't know if buying this was ever such a good idea." She continued, "The vacation rental income doesn't come close to covering the mortgage. There's the hassle of leasing out the remaining orchard. I really don't know if the winery part will ever work out.

"When I was married, I thought I'd be running my own nonprofit by now. This is at least a shot at creating something I can call my own business. I know it's messy with him involved, but that's where I'm at right now."

A week later, Scott headed out to the Gorge again, this time with his board atop the Saab and the rest of his windsurfing gear loaded in the back. He drove past Hood River, continuing east on I-84 toward The Dalles. Shadows from the clouds slipped over the hillsides of the Eastern Gorge, which were green for these few weeks of spring every year.

It was beautiful, but he also felt a sense of isolation in this vast expanse. He wouldn't be making the long drive back to Portland solo after sailing as usual, though. He'd be going to Kim's place again and this gave him a warm sense of anticipation.

As he drove, he attempted to analyze his feelings toward Kim. The funny thing was that before he met her, he could never have imagined her. She tapped into a desire for something that he didn't even know was inside him. She was fascinating. But the ambiguous, uncommitted nature of their relationship was disturbing and, most likely, made it a bad idea. But it was undeniable that he wanted her.

Once he reached the Sam Hill Bridge, he crossed to the Washington side and drove along Maryhill State Park and through the small town of Maryhill. The gravel road that went along peach orchards took him to one of his favorite sailing spots: The Wall. The Wall's namesake is an imposing basalt cliff that abuts the Washington side of the river. The massive John Day Dam lays seven miles to the east.

When he arrived, there were two windsurfers already ripping back and forth across the river.

The sage smelled good as he rigged up in the grassy area between the gravel road and the river. The sky out here was clear as far as you could see and he could feel the strong late April sun on his skin.

Once his sail was rigged, he put on his wetsuit, picked up his board and sail and waded out into the little protected inlet area. He could feel the icy spring water seep into his wetsuit as he paddled to the rocky outcropping where the wind line was located. As he held the sail in the air to water start, it pulsed with the power of the wind gusts.

Soon, he was up and ripping across the river. His sailing skills were rusty, but he managed to get in the groove and have some fun jumps and swell rides.

After about two hours, he'd thoroughly worn himself out and it was time to derig.

He knocked on the door at Kim's place at around 6:15. She was excited to show him the new tasting room.

"They just stained the floors and painted it. Let me show you," Kim said, handing him a glass of sangiovese.

They walked out to the odd little building, which had originally served as an outbuilding for the farmstead and had more recently been employed as an artist studio. Scott listened as Kim went over the details of dealing with the renovation.

He ran his hands over the reclaimed wood bar top and looked around at the space. The walls were now painted and wires dangled from the open electrical fixtures.

Kim came up to him, put a hand on his shoulder and whispered in his ear, "Ever done it in a tasting room?"

The idea of getting it on with her in this space she was creating with her business partner and sometime lover seemed bizarre. They began to kiss, at first slowly and then more intensely.

Forty-five minutes later, Scott chopped onions and fresh cilantro for the tacos that they were making.

"What are you doing for the eclipse?" Kim asked. She was referring to the total solar eclipse that would happen that summer on August 21.

"Seems like that's what everyone is talking about these days," Scott replied. "I think it all sounds overhyped. I figured I would just stay in Portland to get ready for my classes, keep clear of the crowds."

"Oh, I'm so fascinated by it. I have to see it. A friend of mine has a beautiful ranch right in the zone of totality. It's out east of Redmond. We could camp there in the desert under the stars together. And then the next morning, we could watch it. He's having a big party."

Scott felt a warm feeling in his gut as Kim made reference to them doing something together months down the road. Maybe they did have a future after all.

4

It was 6:15 a.m. on the third Saturday in May. Despite a late evening with friends at the Lyle Hotel restaurant, Kim was up and at work on her laptop in the kitchen of her Hood River Valley home. Camden remained asleep in the master bedroom.

The arrangement she had with Camden, that they would take a "break" from their romantic relationship and see other people while continuing as business partners and friends, wasn't working the way she'd planned. Collaborating on the business, staying together out in the Gorge, the lines had become blurred.

And so what if they slept together now and then? Maybe that proved the relationship still had legs.

Today was the Grand Opening of Ross Wines Gorge Estate. The tasting room had been open three previous weekends, but the weather had been lousy. Today's forecast looked promising: sunny with a high of 81.

She retrieved her coffee and returned to her laptop screen. The unread messages on her overloaded Gmail account went far beyond the scrollable screen space. Had she remembered to follow up with the guy from the band that was supposed to play today? Did the caterers need another update on the number of guests?

The early morning light shone through the living room windows. Kim remembered coming out to the kitchen about this time a couple days ago. Scott was sitting on one of the stools with his tousled hair and the early morning sunlight in his face.

She had walked over to him and wrapped her arms around him. An unguarded moment, before they both returned to the reality of their lives. So many people in her life wanted things from her — her kids, her ex-husband, her business partner and sort-of ex-boyfriend. Her relationship with Scott was an escape from all those obligations.

"Fuck buddy" wasn't the right term for Scott. They had a connection, but she wanted to keep the relationship casual. He didn't demand anything and he listened to her. His adoration for her made her feel wanted. She knew she still could turn heads, but how much longer would that last? Maybe another 10, tops.

The morning went by quickly as Kim ran errands and organized the tasting room for the Grand Opening. One couple showed up right when they opened at 11 a.m. By 1 p.m. the pace of arrivals had picked up quite a bit. Kim's heart raced as car after car arrived and the space that she had spent so much time developing filled with visitors.

Kim, Camden and Robert, the tasting room manager, circulated about, chatting up the customers. The picnic area filled up with parties seated at the tables, on the Adirondack chairs and on blankets that they brought themselves. The band started up at three. What was their genre? Blues? Rock? Jam Band? It didn't matter. They had an easy, pleasant sound that the aging Gen Xers and Baby Boomers appreciated. Kim and her team moved quickly as they attended to the customers, alternating between relaxed conversation and harried efforts to serve what was becoming a daunting crowd.

Many of the winery's regulars stayed late. Kim was exhausted as the last group filtered out. The estate was bathed in early evening rays of light. A wave of elation came over her. There was nothing that made her feel better than throwing a party. Maybe this winery was it: a success she could call her own.

She saw Camden walking toward her in the distance. He had wandered out onto the vineyard as she was finishing up.

With a beaming smile, he lifted her in an embrace and swung her in a circle. After serving others all day, it was time to crack a bottle for themselves and celebrate.

When Thursday rolled around, Scott maintained the pattern of the last few weeks and took off early from work to head out to the Gorge, windsurfing gear loaded in the car. On the hour-long drive, he started thinking about Lauren Hill.

It had been his junior year of high school back in Wisconsin in the late eighties. He ran cross country and track. Being on those teams had been an opportunity for him to meet girls. At the end of the cross-country season, someone had told him that Jessie Lutz, the captain of the girls' team, liked him and around the holidays, they started dating. She was a slim, smart, cute achiever. She was Scott's first real girlfriend and he enjoyed spending time with her, though she wanted to take the getting physical thing kind of slow.

Track practice started up in early March and then Spring Break happened. Many of the wealthy kids in Scott's high school took off to Florida, including Lauren Hill, a member of the track team who Scott had always admired. She wasn't super athletic but she had this glow about her. She was shorter in stature with a voluptuous body, beautiful hair and eyes and radiant skin. She was popular, a sort of social nexus on the team and went out with a senior, Steve McCormick, who was the captain of the men's team.

When Lauren returned from Fort Myers Beach, the team was all abuzz that she had broken up with Steve down in Florida. Scott got word that Lauren liked him and he immediately cooled things off with Jessie and began making a play for Lauren in his own awkward way, writing notes to her that he put on the windshield of her Volkswagen Cabriolet in the school parking lot.

He convinced her to skip track practice one day and do their own "training run" instead. They ended up at her dad's house in a leafy, upscale part of Madison.

Scott could still recall that afternoon vividly. It was a sunny early spring day and the trees were still barren of leaves. They entered Lauren's house from the daylight basement. The contemporary home had expensive modern furnishings, wall-to-wall carpet and was obviously cleaned by outside help on a regular basis.

Lauren got Miller Lites for them from the mini fridge.

"My dad will never notice they are missing," she said.

They hung out and drank them on the wraparound couch situated around a fireplace. Then she led him to the guest room where they started making out and rather quickly took things to the next level.

It was Scott's first time and she guided him through the experience.

He couldn't think about much else in the days and weeks that followed. They were a couple, sort of. She would see him and then she wouldn't. When he asked her to the prom she said yes, but then a week later, she said no because she'd gotten back together with Steve McCormick.

Scott remembered a moment walking in the crowded halls of Madison West High School. He saw Lauren and Steve come together after she got out of class. As the two embraced like lost lovers, Scott felt like someone had stuck a knife in his back.

At Doug's Beach, the wind was gusty and the air temperature cold. Scott shared the launch with two other sailors and eventually found himself out on the water alone after they left.

On his last reach, he flubbed a jibe and to his surprise his mast slid back on his board, popped out and disconnected. As Scott fell into the water, he reached for the board but the wind and swell pushed it out of reach.

He was alone and a quarter mile offshore in the cold Columbia. He needed that board and swam frantically toward it, yet another wave caught it and propelled it further away.

THE ECLIPSE

He swam as hard as he could. He could see it bobbing there just out of reach, but then another swell would catch it, just before he could grab it.

After a few tries, he finally caught the back of the board just before another swell grabbed it.

Fuck, I'm distracted, he thought as he paddled back to the sail. He had probably neglected to tighten the universal joint onto the board.

Still out in the middle of the river, he went through the frustrating process of reattaching the sail to the board while both were being jostled about in the choppy water. After several tries, he got it.

Exhausted, he headed back in.

Kim welcomed him to her place as usual. Scott grilled salmon and asparagus and opened a bottle of Ross Wines Pinot. They were through with the first bottle before the food was ready.

For some reason, Kim was in a mood to ask questions.

"Tell me about your last relationship. I want to know about the kind of girls you usually like."

"I guess most of them are more introverted than you. Quiet achievers. I do tend to fall hard for the popular, glamorous ones, like you. The ones out of reach."

Kim smiled and just kept looking at him, waiting for him to continue.

"To tell you the truth," Scott went on, "I've just felt I've been on my own since my divorce five years ago. There was a night when my ex announced that she didn't want to be together anymore. I remember the day after that conversation thinking, 'Wow, I'm alone. I haven't felt like this in a decade.' It's been that way ever since."

Scott looked over at Kim and she was crying.

"Why are you crying?" he asked.

"It's sad," she said.

"What about you? Where do I fit in? Am I part of your perfect polyamorous mix?" asked Scott.

"No, that's not me," Kim said.

"What's the status of your relationship with your ex? Is it platonic?"

"I don't want to go there."

"It's a fair question."

"It's *largely* platonic."

Scott was silent.

After dinner, they smoked some pot that the last vacation rental tenants had left at the place before departing weed-legal Washington State. Instead of mellowing things out, the marijuana put them in a strange emotional state that caused them to vacillate between sex and a continuation of the fraught emotional conversation they started at dinner.

The next morning the early spring light had them both up early and sleep deprived. After breakfast, Scott had limited time to beat it back to East Portland for class. But neither of them could stop at a passionate goodbye kiss and one thing led to another. As Scott rushed out, now really late, Kim said something about "things needing to change."

Even though the weekend back in Portland was packed with kid activities — soccer games, dance recitals, etc. — Kim managed to schedule a "play date" with her girlfriends, Michelle and Sarah. Their SUVs converged for the meetup on the streets outside Besaw's, a popular restaurant located in the recently built-out section of Portland's upscale and urban Northwest District. As Michelle and Sarah pushed the pace on their walk through the network of stairways and sidewalks that thread through the residential streets of the Portland West Hills, Kim could sense that she wasn't as fit as the last time they did this.

Afterward, they settled into brunch at Besaw's, starting off with mimosas. It wasn't long before Michelle and Sarah turned to Kim for an update on her love life. She was the only single one among the threesome and they were keen to hear about all the details.

"Scott and I click in a way that I haven't felt in a long

time," Kim said.

"What's the attraction of this guy? He's a high school teacher, right?" Michelle asked.

"Well, he's athletic, a runner and a windsurfer. Two sports I've attempted various times in my life. They say you want someone who excels at things you find difficult."

"Is he fun?" Michelle asked.

"Oh, he's a serious guy, but he has fun with me. We text, we joke around, we rendezvous and drink wine. We've got such a good back and forth, I don't know why but I'm so intrigued by him."

"Rendezvous? Ooh là là," Michelle said.

"I haven't seen Scott in so long, but he's such a nice guy," Sarah said. "Do you see this getting serious?"

"I don't think it can be. Timing just isn't right. I really need to concentrate on the winery. Camden thinks that if we get that off the ground together, maybe we should give it, I mean our relationship, another shot. And he may be right."

Michelle asked, "So what's going on with Camden, are you seeing — "

"You mean fucking," Sarah interjected.

"Him too?" Michelle finished.

Kim rolled her eyes. "It's complicated. We've been together a long time. I'm not sure it's the right thing to leave this behind. We had a plan to be business partners and be friends while we took a break, a pause, from our relationship. But now, he's talking like if we don't get back together, he's going to cut me out of the business that we created together. It's all of his family's equity in the winery, so he could just leave me high and dry and I'd need to start over."

Kim thought about ordering a third mimosa, but she decided a latte would put her in better shape for her daughter's upcoming dance recital.

"What are you going to do?" asked Michelle.

"I don't know," Kim said.

"You'll figure it out," Sarah said.

They gave each other hugs outside Besaw's before returning to their respective SUVs.

On Monday, Kim broke the pattern of Thursday Gorge rendezvous and asked to meet Scott for lunch in Portland. It wasn't a lunch meeting at his house with a bottle of rosé, but lunch at a spot close to Scott's school, a Thai restaurant. Scott thought about what she had said about things needing to change. He figured that maybe she was coming around. That this conversation would lay the groundwork for them getting serious with the relationship.

When she picked him up from the front of his school, they joked around a bit in the car like things were normal.

At the restaurant, as they were waiting for their order, Kim switched to a more serious tone. She explained to Scott that she couldn't see him anymore because her life was "too chaotic" now.

Scott felt a sense of shock and resentment.

"It's him, isn't it?"

"I'm so sorry, Scott."

"This can't be right. I haven't asked you for anything, any kind of commitment."

"The situation. It's not fair to you," Kim said.

Scott pleaded, "There must be a way. Find a way forward, for us, Kim."

She told him that her life was so intertwined with her ex-boyfriend and business partner that she had to give her relationship with him another chance.

"But you just broke it off with him last summer," Scott argued. "You went to all the trouble of kicking him out of your house. What about giving your life without him a chance?"

"I know, I know," Kim said.

The conversation continued in circles like this with Kim revealing more and more details about her on again off again relationship with Camden, whom she never identified by name.

After leaving most of their lunch unfinished, they continued talking in the car on the way to Scott's house.

As they parted, Kim's last words were, "I'm sorry."

5

Scott first started windsurfing in the late eighties when he was in high school in Madison, Wisconsin. This was back when the sport was exploding.

Scott was part of a growing tribe of windsurfers in Wisconsin who'd drop everything to get out on the water whenever whitecaps appeared on the local lakes. Though windsurfing's most high-profile activity happened in coastal locales like Maui, the sport also developed a freshwater tradition, practiced in places that included the lakes of southern Germany and the American Midwest.

Like many Midwestern windsurf fanatics at that time, every summer he would load his car to the gills with windsurfing gear and drive 30 hours west to the Columbia River Gorge. While the Midwest was stuck in the summer doldrums, the Gorge offered strong wind almost every day on a freshwater river with conditions akin to a large inland lake on an exceptionally windy day.

After college, Scott joined many others like him and made Oregon his home to be in close proximity to the famous Gorge winds.

In the early 2000s, kiteboarding became the hot new wind sport and windsurfing stopped growing in America. By the 2010s, most windsurfers in the Gorge were middle-aged or older with the exception of a few young up-and-comers, often imported from Canada or Europe.

The wind in the Gorge had been a bit fickle in May 2017. But when Scott pulled up the online windsurfing forecast blog, "The Gorge is My Gym," on the first Wednesday of

June, he saw that the wind was forecast to go "nuclear" that day.

Part of the challenge of windsurfing is that the practice of the sport is dictated by the capricious nature of the weather. For this reason, specialized windsurfing weather forecasts are a longstanding tradition in the Gorge, at first on the radio and now on the internet.

Scott considered the condition-dependent nature of windsurfing a feature, not a bug, one that rewarded patience, preparedness and the readiness to set aside other life obligations. A great day on the water wasn't something one could plan. It was a gift to be savored. Sometimes, rarely, there could actually be too much wind for windsurfing to be enjoyable and Scott worried that this could be one of those days.

Portland was socked in with clouds and a light drizzle when Scott pulled onto I-84 East. It stayed that way for 30 miles, but as soon as he hit Cascade Locks the clouds began to break up and his car was buffeted by huge gusts of wind. Where the highway provided a view, he could see the river covered in whitecaps and large swells. He felt that combined sensation of anxiety and excitement in his gut.

The clouds cleared completely from the sky once he hit Hood River. He continued on to the last highway exit, the one for the Hood River Bridge. As he crossed the Columbia to the Washington side, he had to hold the steering wheel of the Saab tight to stay in a straight line as it was jerked sideways by wind gusts.

At the end of the bridge, he took a left on Highway 14 and headed back west. The steep rocky cliffs of the Gorge were to his right and the river, a field of whitecaps, was to his left.

In the distance, he could see the cloud line and translucent sails skidding back and forth on the surface of the river. In a couple miles he came to the turnoff to the Spring Creek Fish Hatchery and saw giant river swells crashing into the rocky outcropping at the entrance to the park. The parking lot was already filling up.

"The Hatch," as it is commonly known, is ground zero for windsurfing in the Pacific Northwest. Situated in the central corridor of the Gorge, it is known for strong wind, giant swells, and its natural rock amphitheater. When windsurfing was at its peak in the late eighties and early nineties, the volcanic rocks at the Hatch seated hundreds of spectators for competitive windsurfing events.

Scott had been windsurfing the Gorge for decades, and he knew that this was an exceptional day. With gusts up to 50 mph and swells the size of motorhomes, it was survival sailing conditions. As he was rigging up, he peered out anxiously at the roiling river. "Liquid smoke" rose off the tops of the swells.

He rigged his smallest sail, a 2.9 meter, and entered the river from the rocky outcropping at the west end of the Hatchery. Usually this was a matter of walking to the end of the rocks, dropping his board in and then hopping on. But today swells broke like ocean waves over the platform of volcanic rock at the launch, creating a potentially treacherous board- and bone-breaking scenario.

Scott made his way down to the rock platform and then made a quick move to toss his board into the water and jump in after it when the launch spot was free of crashing river swells. Then he was off.

He and a handful of other sailors hung on for dear life as they made reaches back and forth and rode the giant swells downwind.

On his second session out, Scott was sailing on a starboard tack next to a guy with a long gray mane of hair and beard. This man's windsurfing skills were superb. Just as Scott was banking off a steep swell into a jibe, he caught the dude in the corner of his eye pulling off a hard and fast port tack forward loop, the classic Gorge windsurfing move where one jumps the board off a wave and performs an airborne rotation using their speed and the power of wind in the sail.

The man's board smacked the water at high velocity, making a cracking sound. After Scott jibed, he sailed past the man and saw that his board was broken in half. Scott sailed a bit further away and then did another quick jibe and returned to the man and dropped his sail. He yelled over to the guy to ask if he'd like a tow in. He got an affirmative thumbs up.

The guy hooked his uphaul line to Scott's back foot strap, which was then attached to the broken board's mast base. Scott water started up, then he slowly and jerkily pulled the guy and his broken rig back toward the protected area where sailors exited the river.

After they'd hoisted their rigs back up on shore, the man gave Scott a hearty handshake. "I'm Dimitri," he said with a disarming smile and some sort of Eastern European accent. "You rescued me! Come on and have a beer with me!"

Scott was pretty beat already from the extreme conditions so he assented and soon they were sitting together on the rocks of the Hatchery's amphitheater area, sipping cans of Everybody's Brewing Country Boy IPA and commenting on the handful of sailors daring enough to take on the extreme conditions. Dimitri enthused about the small cadre of younger windsurfers who were out and taking it to the next level.

Dimitri was from the Republic of Georgia, spent his winters in Maui and had been coming to the Gorge for the past few summers. He talked as if he knew half of the population in the Gorge, or at least anyone who windsurfed.

The next morning, Scott woke up in the tent to dog breath. Bob was eager to get out and sniff around Tucker Park, a Hood River County campground nestled among ponderosa pines and scrub oak along the rushing Hood River. At 6 a.m. the park was cold and quiet.

Scott relished the morning dog walk. This was the time of day when he didn't think about Kim as much. It felt good to move the sore muscles from yesterday's windsurfing session. He made a couple of hard-boiled eggs and checked his phone to get a read on the wind conditions that day. Things were forecasted to pick up midmorning. He headed into town for coffee and a pastry.

When he walked into The Coffee Spot, his favorite Hood River cafe located across the street from Sailboard Warehouse, he spotted Dimitri's shoulder-length gray hair immediately. Sporting cutoffs and an old school Patagonia pullover fleece top, he was holding forth with a couple of other middle-aged windsurfing types. They all appeared to be regulars at the place.

Dimitri greeted Scott with a warm smile and an animated spark in his eyes.

"Hey! You're the guy who saved me at the Hatchery yesterday! Have a coffee with us!"

Scott got an Americano and took a seat with Dimitri and his buddies. The conversation initially focused on the windsurfing conditions in the Gorge that year but drifted into all sorts of other topics that ranged from the food and wine scene in the Gorge to global equity markets.

"Well, it looks like a good one at the Hatchery today. It's already 27 gusting into the 30s. I'm going to get down there," Scott said.

"I can't make it out there today," Dimitri said. "But come on by to my house tonight. I'm having a party."

Scott had to be back in Portland to pick up his son the next morning, but this opportunity sounded interesting. He entered Dimitri's address into his phone.

The windsurfing conditions were mellower that day, but in a way more enjoyable. Classic 3.7 at the Hatchery. Scott was beat when he got off the water, but he didn't feel like heading home. He had been thinking about Kim all day long on the water. He wanted to go out and talk to others, have new adventures and forget her.

He had a burrito from a food cart, took Bob for a long

walk along the waterfront and at dusk, headed up to the address Dimitri had given him. It was a large contemporary sort of place built into the hills above downtown Hood River. The street level was relatively unassuming, mostly dominated by a garage door.

Scott could hear a Wilco tune, "Impossible Germany," playing when he approached the door. He pressed the doorbell and about 30 seconds later a dark-complexioned, slim 20-something girl with a trucker hat and a tight halter top opened the door,

"Welcome to the party!" she said.

"Thank you! Margarita, right? I'm Scott."

Scott recognized her from the beach. He'd admired her well-toned figure and graceful windsurfing skills many times. Her numbered sail made it clear that she was a pro in the Gorge to train for the summer.

The second floor of the house had a vast open floor plan that spilled out onto a balcony overlooking the town and the central Gorge. A crowd of tanned, flip-flop clad impossibly athletic-looking types were hanging out on the balcony next to a pony keg of Double Mountain beer. Scott headed over. They were good for 15 minutes of conversation about the big wind the previous day.

Then he wandered into another group situated around the kitchen bar that had some open bottles of wine on it. Catching sight of a label from Syncline Winery, one of Kim's favorites, Scott struck up a conversation with a bearded and tattooed vintner about twenty years his junior named Azan. Soon they were deep into details about natural wine and viticultural trends in the Pacific Northwest.

Scott knew almost zero about winemaking, but his time with Kim had elicited at least a mild curiosity about the process. Sometimes, Scott liked to get other people going in conversation about something they were passionate about and just sit back and fuel the fire. Listening to people talk about wine could be hilarious in a way — all the adjectives they used to describe it could get ridiculous quickly. The

Millennial Azan was more than happy to oblige as he detailed the awesomeness of natural wine and his own philosophy of connecting with the universe through winemaking.

Eventually Scott got drawn into a group conversation led by a tall, boisterous and bejeweled woman named Jamie. Supposedly Jamie was an influential Pacific Northwest wine critic followed by thousands on her blog and Instagram account. She had the group in stitches as she described various debacles she'd encountered in her ventures at wineries across the West Coast.

"The tasting room was literally a trailer someone had pulled out onto the farm. But oh my, the depth and electricity of that cabernet franc was phenomenal."

Scott began talking one-on-one with Jamie about Gorge wineries. He was curious if she'd heard of Kim's place. She had. She said she'd just done a blog post on it and commented, "A nice atmosphere, and from what I've heard, good wine, but terrible service."

When Kim awoke, the early morning light revealed the familiar sight of Camden's wavy brown hair and freckled back. They had slept together last night for the first time in a while. She slipped out of bed and headed into the kitchen, cringing as she always did at its datedness. After the coffee was on, she reflexively opened her laptop. A Google alert for Ross Wines was at the top of the inbox. She eagerly followed the link to a blog post on their winery.

The post was a commentary by "Wine Jamie," the blog's author, on her visits to some of the newer wineries in the Gorge, including Ross Wines. Kim skimmed ahead to the part about Ross Wines, reading the paragraph that started out by describing the setting of the winery, the inviting picnic area, and the festive atmosphere of their Grand Opening a couple weeks back. Kim's sense of excitement turned to panic as she read on.

Wine Jamie had approached the bar and found no one

to help her. She'd positioned herself at a table in the tasting room and amidst the chaos hadn't been able to get a glass of wine. She left after 20 minutes.

Kim was horrified. How could they have missed this customer? It had all gone so well, she had thought.

She rushed into the bedroom to tell Camden about it. He was just waking up.

"What a load of shit," he said, rubbing his eyes. "I need coffee."

Kim returned to the kitchen.

When Camden emerged in his bathrobe, Kim handed him the cup silently. Neither of them particularly liked cooking nor, generally speaking, serving one another. But Kim toasted a couple bagels and boiled some eggs. Kim was hoping to talk over the bad review with Camden at a sit-down breakfast, but instead he stood and munched a bagel and slurped his coffee, finding a travel mug and emptying the rest of the coffee pot into it.

"I need to run out to Dundee to figure out a harvest buy this fall."

"I thought we could talk about this review," Kim said somewhat sheepishly. "About what we could do to prevent this. Should we hire more staff?"

"That's not going to work. You need to train Robert better and stop talking to each set of customers for so long."

He came over to Kim and embraced her, even though she looked irritated. "Don't worry about this, it means nothing," he said, his mouth still full of bagel.

Camden was soon gone and Kim was alone again. She would help open and run the tasting room again today and then head back to Portland to pick up her daughter and son.

She couldn't get the bad review off her mind. It was not like her to get a bad rating on anything. She'd always been a straight-A student and had carried an expectation of perfectionism into all arenas of her life. She spent most of what remained of the morning frantically Googling and reading other reviews by Wine Jamie, trying to think about how to right the wrong.

She also made up her mind about that vacation getaway Camden was planning. It wasn't going to happen. It just wasn't the right time. She needed a pause.

6

Home with Nate in Portland, Scott invited his friend Catherine and her daughter over for a backyard grill-out. They had been friends since Scott's early days in Oregon and a few years ago, they realized they were both single and divorced. When they discovered that their kids got along pretty well, they began hanging out as friends, bonding over the challenges they shared raising kids on their own and navigating the dating scene in their mid-forties.

As Scott got Cat her second cider and himself a second beer, he started talking about what was really on his mind: Kim.

"I can't stop thinking about her. We had this *connection*. If I could just break through, somehow it could work with her."

"But think of all the shit you've put up with, Scott. Think of the stress. It's good she's gone. How about her?" Cat was flicking through women on Scott's Bumble account for him.

"She's okay. Outdoorsy, but kinda manly looking." He sighed. "Kim just does it for me. She's so bright and magnetic. She seems to attract others. I know she's snobby and, well, indecisive and unavailable. But somehow when she turns her attention to me, it excites me so much. It just does it for me."

"You can do so much better than her drama and fake tits. I just don't see you guys together. You need someone real, Scott," Cat said.

Scott noticed that she was tapping on his phone.

"There, I deleted her from your phone."

After he got Nate to sleep, Scott lay in bed, still a bit buzzed. He couldn't fall asleep right away, so he read some of "My Struggle: Book 2." He could often relate to the Norwegian author Karl Ove Knausgaard. At this point in the book, Knausgaard was describing the tedium of being a caregiver for small children in the 21st-century world of equalized parenting roles, lamenting that he was a 19th-century man at heart.

Scott dozed off for a bit. At about 11:30 he heard his phone vibrate out in the kitchen. He knew he shouldn't get up and get it. Better to let the devices rest for the night. But he was thirsty. Couldn't hurt to just get a drink of water.

He got up and went into the kitchen. He entered the security pattern on the phone and saw the alert from a number not associated with a name on his phone. He recognized it as Kim's number.

Hey. Are you up? Want to talk?

Scott could feel his blood pressure skyrocket. He threw the phone on the sofa and started pacing the room.

It had been a couple weeks now. He stared out the window for a while wondering why she was texting.

He figured he should just leave it be and not call her back. After she'd let him down like that, well, she didn't deserve to talk to him. At least not promptly.

He thought about his conversation at Dimitri's with those wine people. He had to admit that he wanted to share that with her.

Was it really the strong thing to do not to call her back, or would that just show that he was upset? He brooded a bit on this point.

Fuck it, maybe he should just call her, he figured.

It was late. If he was going to call, he should just do it.

He picked up the phone, went to her call record and pressed the phone icon.

Kim answered after the third ring.

They avoided talking about what happened a couple weeks back. Kim slipped into a monologue about the domestic dramas of her week. Scott listened.

Hearing Kim's voice was a balm. The anger and hurt vanished and hope returned. It just felt so right to talk with her.

Soon, Scott told her about the wine crowd at Dimitri's party. "The ringleader was this hilarious lady. I can't remember her name, a wine blogger."

"Wine Jamie?" Kim asked.

"Yes, that was her."

"You're kidding me! All I have been thinking about the last few days is her bad review of my winery."

"Yeah, she mentioned that she'd paid you all a visit."

"Yes, she did," Kim said in an irritated tone.

"Do you want me to see if I could set up a meeting with her?" Scott asked, without really thinking the idea through.

"You know, that might be smart. I'd appreciate that, Scott."

"I will do that," Scott said.

Soon they wrapped up their conversation and Scott went to bed.

The next morning, Scott texted Dimitri and got Wine Jamie's number. Then he texted her.

> Hi Jamie, Scott Larson here. We met the other night at Dimitri's. My friend Kim is a co-owner of Ross Wines and she'd love to meet you. I wondered if you might be up for a glass of wine with her?

Jamie returned his text in less than 10 minutes:

> Good morning Scott! Would love to meet her. How about tonight at Bar Norman, you guys could both come?

Kim was a bit annoyed at the format of the meeting. She would have preferred to meet this wine critic in a more formal, controlled environment and put on a show. But she guessed that this would be a good first step.

She'd been to Bar Norman before. Founded by one of Portland's most well-known sommeliers, it had such a fresh, European feel to it. And the emphasis was on natural wine. She loved the ambience of the place but had to admit that the tattooed Millennials and the DJ'ed electronica left her a little out of her element.

Shuttling her son to his soccer practice and her daughter to dance class made for a hectic afternoon. But she got them situated with a halfway decent pesto pasta dinner without feeling too much "mom guilt." Aiden would probably spend the rest of the evening playing Fortnite while Sierra tried out makeup techniques that she found on YouTube.

With the youthful Bar Norman crowd in mind, she put on skinny jeans, heels and a form-fitting silk cami and spent some time in the mirror getting her look just right.

Camden popped by as he was prone to do. Kim explained how she now had a big chance to fix things with Wine Jamie.

"You look great, babe," he said, squeezing both of her shoulders.

She frowned. The kids were supposed to think that they were just platonic at the moment.

"Can I come along? Don't you think she might like to meet the winemaker?" he asked with a hopeful look.

"Next time."

She crossed the river in an Uber running her usual 20 to 25 minutes late. Upon entering Bar Norman, she quickly spotted Scott seated at the long wooden table with the mismatched chairs. Lots of beards and ink as expected. Wine Jamie was easy to identify with her highlighted hair, hoop earrings and colorful dress. A fun-looking group, Kim

THE ECLIPSE

thought, as she approached the table.

Kim sat down next to Scott and Wine Jamie was right across from her, but Jamie was already engaged in another conversation. Kim turned to her right and met David and Mel. They also had a small winery that they were starting up in the Gorge. They shared their experiences of long hours at harvest time, the chaos of the wine festivals, the Instagram publicity game, wine club subscriptions and more. Kim loved connecting with the energy of younger people.

Scott seemed a bit quiet, as usual, but he eventually got to talking with one of Jamie's friends.

After 15 minutes or so, Jamie finally got a chance to chat with Kim. She went on and on about the trollinger that she was drinking. It was one of those orange wines that were so huge in the natural wine scene. Kim decided that she should have a glass.

She and Jamie found some common ground chatting about some of the Oregon vintners that they knew. Eventually, Jamie brought up the visit to Kim's winery. She made a sorry, not sorry apology for the harsh review and agreed to pay Ross Wines another visit soon.

After a third glass, Kim was feeling like things were going in the right direction. Scott put his hand on hers. It was unexpected and she reciprocated the touch. Somehow it felt natural. They fell into a conversation with Wine Jamie about the burgeoning Gorge wine scene and all the amazing new winemakers and vineyards that had been found footing the Gorge in recent years. Kim couldn't help but comment on how small scale many of them were compared to the vineyard that she had owned in California way back when.

Scott talked about warming up to the Gorge lifestyle after spending time at the Ross Wines estate. Jamie said that there were some interesting investing opportunities in winery properties. Scott pursued the topic more, explaining that he was a bit of a real estate investor himself, owning a duplex and all, and that he aspired to add to his real estate investment portfolio. This was news to Kim.

"Visiting Kim at her place has made me realize how awesome it is to own property in the Gorge."

Jamie said that she knew of some cool opportunities for "co-investment" in vineyard land with a foreign investor who sought a U.S.-based partner.

"They get the vineyard property to use as a winery and you get to use the residential part of the property."

When the group broke up, Scott asked Kim if they should have another drink. She suggested they just go for a walk, so they strolled in the Clinton/Division neighborhood a bit. This was the first time that they'd seen each other since the "breakup."

Before her Uber came, they made out for a delicious minute on the corner of SE 26th and Clinton.

Scott walked home. He was on a high. It was rare that he facilitated anything social, but somewhat surprisingly, this appeared to have worked. He couldn't help but have hopeful thoughts about Kim run through his head.

Maybe he'd been thinking about Kim all wrong. He shouldn't have taken her intention to break things off so seriously. She was an emotional, impetuous creature and could be indecisive. When Kim said no, it didn't really mean no, it just meant no *at that time*. He was buzzed and he knew he wasn't thinking logically, but there was something to this.

He switched to thinking about Gorge real estate. The old agriculture of the Gorge was shifting to the new. Wineries were replacing orchards and it was an opportune time for investment.

For a while now Scott had thought of himself as a clever, if amateur, investor. He had become a high school AP history teacher because he loved learning and ideas and got the summers off. But as he had entered serious adult life and faced the prospect of buying a house and providing for a family, his analytical mind had been drawn to finance and investment.

When it came to searching for a house and making arrangements to have a kid when he was married, he'd felt real financial pressure, something he hadn't quite foreseen when deciding on a career back in his twenties. He and his ex-wife had managed to do alright for themselves, finding a house in a hot Portland neighborhood. But there was always pressure to have more than a teacher's salary could deliver.

He watched the stock market continuously and often fiddled with his retirement investments. After getting divorced, he'd purchased the duplex to dip his toe into real estate investing.

Even though he was a public-school teacher pushing 50 whose finances were anything but exciting, there was a part of him that thought he had the potential to make an investment move that would get him set up right. And he did have a modest stash of cash sitting in some CDs that he had inherited from a great uncle who passed away a few years ago. Ostensibly, that was for Nate's college but he had been contemplating using it for the purchase of a vacation rental in Bend or Hood River.

Still quite buzzed from the wine, Scott laid out a plate of cheese and crackers on the kitchen table and opened his laptop to scan the Zillow listings for rural properties in the Gorge. Panning and zooming the aerial view map, five or six multiacre properties came up. The prices were mostly a million plus but there were some in the high six figures. There were some interesting rural properties in the hills above the central Gorge, farmsteads that had mostly been used as orchards.

He emailed Jamie and asked her about the co-investment opportunity that she had mentioned. Her instantaneous response didn't surprise him. They agreed to meet for coffee soon.

7

Scott's next kid-free day was on Wednesday. The wind was nil, but he went out to the Gorge for a run on the Eagle Creek trail and then headed to Hood River to meet Wine Jamie for coffee at Stoked, a cafe along the Columbia River waterfront.

He got an Americano and a scone while she opted for a triple-shot oat milk latte. They sat on the stools looking out the front windows of the cafe at Waterfront Park and watched parents chase after their kids on the grassy playground. Scott remembered many weekends there when Nate was little.

Jamie was on her way back from visiting the Walla Walla, Washington area and couldn't help but regale Scott with descriptions of the fabulous wine she had experienced on her two-day visit. Soon she turned to the matter at hand. "Mr. Chen and his firm, Darden Wine Holdings, are very interested in Gorge wine right now. The artisan wine scene is just exploding here and they'd love to establish a vineyard with an up-and-coming winemaker. Part of their formula involves a local co-investor who can purchase the vineyard property."

"Tell me more about how it works," Scott said.

"Well, they review your credit history, your stability. They're interested in small investors. People like you who are well-established in the community. They connect you with special financing and you buy the property with a five-percent equity interest in the deal. They like vineyard properties with a residence on them. You'd get the right to use the residence yourself or even to rent it on Airbnb. The firm then leases the vineyard land and constructs a winemaking facility on the property."

"What's the motivation for the company to involve me?" Scott asked.

"The firm prefers to have a local individual acquire the property and hold the title. Makes things easier when it comes to permitting and developing, especially in the Gorge National Scenic Area, where any kind of development faces so many obstacles. There are also some tax advantages to individuals holding property versus corporations."

"Okay, I'm intrigued," Scott said. "Where do I start?"

"Mr. Chen has a real estate agent here. Her name is Denise. Here, give me your phone and I'll put her number in. The firm has their eye on about three properties right now. She'd be glad to show you them all."

Scott connected up with Denise that evening. With school out for the summer, he stayed in the Gorge and caught an early windsurfing session at Doug's Beach the next morning. At 2 p.m., he met Denise at the park-and-ride where Highway 35 comes into Hood River.

Denise was a well-coiffed brunette who was dressed in form-fitting slacks and blouse, a little more businesslike than the typical Gorge resident. Scott hopped into her Lexus SUV and they crossed back over the Hood River Bridge.

They first headed for the winding back roads of Underwood, Washington, a rural area that hugs the hillsides high above the Columbia a little bit west of the central Gorge population centers. As Denise piloted her Lexus up Cook Underwood Road, Scott occasionally looked off to his left to catch the spectacular view of Mount Hood. Eventually she turned onto a side road and drove a half a mile to the first property.

The driveway led past a recently planted vineyard to a somewhat dilapidated homestead. As they surveyed the yard and the home, Denise said, "This 30-acre property needs work but has fabulous potential. The current owner has been leasing out the farmland as a vineyard."

The tired ranch-style home did not impress. It had an eighties-era kitchen inside and a funky DIY hot tub platform appended to the back. There was a partial view of the mountain from the rear, but the overall package seemed somewhat underwhelming.

Scott had never considered owning semi-rural property before. As they wandered through the vineyard, Scott examined the tiny tubes protecting the baby vines. It all seemed a bit overwhelming, but somehow the idea boosted his spirits. He could become part of the "landed gentry," a history term he used every year when introducing the concept of feudal life to his students.

Next, they went over to the Hood River Valley where Kim's place was. The property for sale was off Country Club Road and consisted of pear and apple orchards which could be converted to vineyards. It had a double-wide manufactured home on it and a so-so view of Mount Hood as well as a desirable south-facing slope.

"Of course, the home would need to go," Denise said, "but this place could evolve into an incredible vineyard."

"I agree," Scott said, without a lot of conviction. "Is there anything else out here?"

"There is another place that is supposed to be coming on the market soon," Denise said. "It belongs to Chuck Bodenheimer. Mr. Chen is very interested in that one."

"Oh, I know Chuck," Scott said. "He was in 'Hard Winds A Blowin',' a famous windsurfing video in the 1980s. It was that video that got me to move out to Oregon from Wisconsin."

Chuck was practically a Gorge institution, one of the early pioneers of windsurfing there who had done quite well for himself in the area as the sport really took off.

"How well do you know him?" Denise asked.

"Only casually, from saying hi here and there when we're

windsurfing at the same beach."

"Well if you see him around town, or could get in touch with him, you might ask him about it. I know he's going to list it with another agent. I think it could be exactly the type of property that would work well for you and Mr. Chen."

The Ross Wines Summer Solstice Dinner was an annual tradition, but this was the first time hosting it on the Ross Wines property. Kim had been rushing all week to get the lawn and landscaping prepared. She also had to work with new farm-to-table caterers in the Gorge that Camden had selected.

As the day unfolded and the 6 p.m. start of the event neared, Kim became increasingly frustrated with Camden. He seemed to have no understanding of all that she was juggling and remained fixated on some details about his winemaking that really could have been dealt with at another time.

In addition to all of the pressure involved with putting the event on for the first time in the Gorge, Kim also had to contend with Wine Jamie and her entourage attending.

The beginning of the event did not go smoothly. Some of the staff were late for the setup and the caterers did not supply enough waitstaff. While Camden jovially greeted the visitors with a glass of wine in hand, Kim was rushing around in the background putting out fires.

Despite some frantic moments, Kim managed to pull it off. So many guests gushed about the food and wine as they bid farewell to Kim at the end of the event. Even Wine Jamie and her entourage seemed happy enough, especially with six comped bottles of wine.

By the time the last guest left, Kim was exhausted and still irritated with Camden. Some of his old buddies had come to the dinner and he had headed into town with them for drinks. She was left on the estate to tidy things up with her tasting room manager and a girl that they had hired for the event. After the two of them left, she popped a bottle of rosé and sat out on the deck.

With a buzz from the wine coming on, she reached for her iPhone and texted Scott.

> I'm so exhausted. The event was insane.
>
> Oh really, can't wait to hear about it.
>
> Where are you?
>
> In my sleeping bag at Tucker Park.
>
> Get up now and get over here. I need to go out for a drink.

Scott popped out of his sleeping bag in a matter of seconds, any feeling of drowsiness gone, throwing on some jeans and a halfway decent-looking shirt. He hopped in the Saab and headed out of the campground and up the road to Odell and then south on Highway 35 to Ross Wines.

The signs for the big wine dinner were still in place as Scott pulled into Kim's driveway. Kim walked into Scott's headlights before he even had a chance to get out of the car. She was wearing a skirt and looked ready to hit the town.

"Hey there!" Kim said.

"I wouldn't mind just hanging out a bit here," Scott said as he began to get out of the car.

"No, we're going out, Scott," Kim said, getting into the passenger seat.

They sat at the loft bar at Sixth Street Bistro & Pub, a long-time downtown Hood River establishment that had recently had a contemporary facelift. It was a quieter, adult-oriented kind of place among the town's drinking establishments.

Kim told Scott about the chaotic but ultimately successful dinner. She was already a bit tipsy and touch between them came easily. Scott shared details about the potential real estate deal that he learned about from Wine

Jamie and that he'd been out looking for properties.

Into her second margarita, Kim began to wax nostalgic for the Napa winery property that she and her husband had to sell as part of the divorce. She had a certain way of saying "property" that sounded snobby and elitist, but Scott kind of liked it.

Scott tried to temper his excitement, but he could feel Kim's assessment of him subtly rise with the prospect of him buying a vineyard. As he was talking about the possibility, her bare foot found its way up his leg.

With Camden in the Gorge, Kim's place wasn't an option. And they weren't going back to Tucker Park so they checked into Prater's Motel at the edge of downtown. It was a small, rough-around-the-edges motel still in business despite Hood River's seemingly relentless rise toward unaffordable good taste. It had been weeks since their split and their bodies came together with an urgency that took Scott by surprise.

Afterward, they both drifted off to sleep. Scott awoke to hear Kim gathering her things. The clock read 2:37. He pulled her back into bed.

She left after 3.

Scott had Nate for a few days and they headed out for an annual campout among several families they knew at Timothy Lake, a scenic spot for lakeside camping south of Mount Hood. The kids had a blast out on the beach all day, making forts out of the driftwood and splashing around on inner tubes. The parents hiked, boated, SUPed or just took it easy on the beach.

Scott had a hard time getting his mind off that recent night in the motel with Kim and the potential real estate deal. He took the 13-mile trail run around the lake to clear his mind. When he got back to the campsite, he took off his shirt and jumped into the lake for a swim. Afterward, he popped a beer and hung out by the campfire.

His friend Ray and his daughter always came over from

their place in Silverton for the annual trip and Scott hadn't yet had a chance to catch up. Ray's camouflage camping gear stood out a bit from the standard issue REI stuff that the other families had.

Ray was a fisherman, hunter and all-around sportsman. Scott had struck up a friendship with him as Ray was upgrading the fire alarm system in Scott's school. A random conversation in the hallway had led to the discovery that they were both knee-deep in divorce proceedings, which led to beers at the local watering hole near the school and a long-term friendship.

"So are you still spending lots of time in the Gorge, Scott? We should meet up again at Tucker Park one of these weekends. That was such a blast last year. Molly loved windsurfing."

"Definitely. Maybe one of these years I'll have my own place out in the Gorge."

"Really? They must be paying high school teachers in Portland pretty well these days."

"I've got an interesting investment opportunity that I'm considering."

"Do tell."

"There's a Chinese investor and he's interested in purchasing a winery. A vineyard property. He'd like an American as the owner of the property. I'd get a sizable stake in the deal."

"Would you really want to get involved with something like that, with some Chinese oligarch? How did this guy get his money anyway? And why can't he just buy it himself? They own half of Manhattan."

"It's a complicated thing. I think they want me involved because as a local I could help shepherd the permitting process. And I'd have the use of a home on a beautiful Gorge vineyard. I could cover my stake in the deal easily with vacation rental income."

"Scott, you need to be cautious about this. The Chinese are working their way into our economy in all sorts of nefarious ways. You know what's happening in Africa and South Asia, right? They do these major infrastructure projects and then leave the locals in debt up to their eyeballs. Then they seize the assets: the mines, the mineral wealth."

Here he goes, Scott thought. Once Ray got a couple beers in him, he could go off on conspiracy theories like an AM radio talk show host.

"If they are interested in you at all, they've probably hacked your phone and are watching everything that you do. They can probably hear this conversation."

"Are you serious? I think it's just a rich foreign dude who likes wine," said Scott.

"It doesn't sound that simple to me."

Scott suggested that they build up the fire and get the kids back to the camp to start putting together their camper's stew dinners: hamburger, potatoes, carrots, butter, and salt and pepper wrapped in foil and cooked in the coals of the campfire. It was a combination that the kids and adults both appreciated.

After dinner, Scott took some time away from the fire to check his phone. There was just enough signal to catch text messages. He'd contacted his old Wisconsin windsurfing buddy Sam to see if he could get an introduction to Chuck Bodenheimer and possibly a private viewing of this property that was about to come on the market. Sam had lived full time in the Gorge since the early 1990s and knew all the old-school Gorge windsurfers.

It worked easier than he thought and after some texting back and forth, Scott had an invite to come out to the property in a few days for an informal evening viewing.

Ahead of the viewing, Scott arranged to meet Kim at Henne's, a favorite restaurant of hers in White Salmon, a town on the Washington side of the river not far from the Bodenheimer estate. Over cocktails and appetizers, Scott told her about the opportunity to see Chuck's place.

Kim didn't know Chuck Bodenheimer as a windsurfer

like Scott did, but she was very intrigued by the prospect of this property. She loved browsing real estate, especially if it was a vineyard and it didn't take much for Scott to convince her to head over with him.

They made their way back down to Highway 14 and up the Cook Underwood Road. After a few twists and turns they pulled into a wooded private drive that wound around a bit and then revealed a farmstead. When they got out of the car and walked to the house, they turned to the right and beheld an absolutely spectacular view of an open field with Mount Hood in the distance. They were so high up, it looked like there was nothing but wild land between them and the mountain.

The property had a main home and a number of outbuildings, including a big garage outside of which Chuck's familiar seventies-era Ford F-100 sat, Dakine pads on the tailgate for his windsurfing boards. Chuck's big silly golden Lab met them with tail wagging hard as they approached. Chuck wasn't far behind and greeted them with a generous smile.

"Hey I'm Scott. I think we've chatted a few random times at the windsurfing sites."

"Right on, I remember you, Scott. Chuck Bodenheimer."

Chuck was wearing some Patagonia hiking shorts, trail running shoes and a baseball cap. His weathered face and white hair suggested that he was in his sixties, but his body was extremely fit and muscular. Not an uncommon configuration in Hood River with its large population of aging extreme sports nuts.

"Kim, I knew of Chuck way before I moved to Oregon. Back in Wisconsin in the eighties we used to watch him in the video 'Hard Winds A Blowin'.'"

Chuck laughed heartily. "I remember those days well. This is my daughter Emma," he said, introducing a young woman clad comfortably in athleisure attire.

"So you guys think you might want to buy this place?

I'm done with the rural lifestyle, moving into a newer home in town and committing to Maui for the better half of the year. I'm tired of clearing brush, even though I've got the perfect rig for it." He laughed, gesturing at the old Ford.

He suggested they take a tour but got them set up with beer and wine first. Chuck and his wife had renovated the old farmhouse, bumping out its footprint a bit and installing a modern kitchen and a great room with a view of Mount Hood. It wasn't ostentatious but the quality of construction was evident. Scott eyed the hot tub, built into the ground and rimmed with basalt.

Much of the estate land was now leased as a vineyard as the property had a perfect south-facing view. They wandered along a cedar chip path down to an old barn and open field with another stunning view of vineyard land, forest and Mount Hood. Spectacular.

"This would be an awesome picnic area," Kim said.

After they looked around, they hung out on Chuck's patio a bit, just off the farmhouse.

"Man, you've got it made here, Chuck," said Scott.

"I know, I know, it's pretty sweet. This property has been a way to stay connected to my Missouri roots. Grew up on a farm out there. With this location, I am able to be in the bustle of Hood River and the freeway and then in 10 minutes be up here. It feels remote, like the end of the world.

"The Gorge has changed so much since I got here in '81. It was so much more rural at that time. It was we kooky windsurfers that started all the change. I hardly recognize Hood River anymore. But this place hasn't changed much. Since we leased the land for grapes about 15 years ago, it's been a nice source of income and makes me feel like I'm in Tuscany. Though I'm not a big wine guy myself.

Chuck continued, "I'm glad the Gorge is doing well, but I have to admit, I miss the way it was just 10 or 15 years ago. A lot of the people who come here now don't even care about getting outside and experiencing the natural beauty.

They're not windsurfers or into fishing or mountain biking. They just want to pull into town in their Tesla and go shopping, maybe snap a picture or two with their phone at a winery."

After they finished their drinks, Chuck suggested that Kim and Scott wander around a bit on their own. They strolled back down the path to the barn. As soon as they were a good distance from the house, Kim started gushing about the property.

"Oh, the way these buildings overlook the vineyard land and the mountain view. It's all amazing. The little farmhouse would have to go, of course."

"I like the farmhouse," Scott said, "It's cozy and look what they've done to it."

"But for this property with this breathtaking view?" Kim replied. "It is cute, but there is so much potential to develop this place into a destination winery."

They reached the barn again. "*This* is the spot," Kim said. "The tasting room and winery could go right there. I'm imagining dinners, parties and picnics."

They were bathed in the evening summer light and Mount Hood stood in all its glory. Kim reached out to hold Scott's hand.

"I just wonder if the truck comes with the place," Scott said. "That just seems like the ultimate setup. Throw the board in the truck and down to windsurfing at the Hatchery in five minutes. Hot tub afterward."

They drove back to Kim and Camden's place, which suddenly felt mediocre after their tour. Kim kept talking about the Bodenheimer place, though she didn't press Scott on his plans for making an offer on it or not. Truthfully, seeing the place and how amazing it was had made it seem that much more out of reach to Scott, but he relished the fantasy of checking out the property with her as if they were a real couple who could contemplate serious plans for the future.

The next morning, Kim brought up the idea again of spending the eclipse together at her friend's ranch.

"It would be amazing to experience that with you," Kim said.

"Let's plan on it," Scott said.

It was the Fourth of July the next day. Scott called Denise and gave her a rundown on the private tour of the Bodenheimer property and shared some photos as well. She said she would get them to Mr. Chen.

Scott met Dimitri and Wine Jamie at The Coffee Spot that morning. Dimitri greeted Scott with a huge bear hug.

"We heard that you got a private showing from Chuck," Dimitri said. "That place is so beautiful, isn't it? I was over there to grill out last summer."

"It's amazing," Scott said. "And so close to windsurfing at the Hatchery."

"Right on, man."

"I know Jamie told you a little bit about my son, Sasha. He's been making wine since he was 16 and he's been apprenticing with one of the best winemakers in Georgia. His wines have already won awards in Georgia and I think he's ready to break out on his own. Mr. Chen wants to get behind him and bring Georgian wine to the Gorge."

"The whole wine scene is definitely taking off here," Scott said.

"The Georgian method of winemaking is so cool, man. We use these vats buried in the ground to age the wine. And the flavor is amazing. If we bring this to the Gorge, I'm telling you, Oregon will go crazy for it."

As they finished their coffees, Wine Jamie wrapped up the conversation. "This sounds like a great possibility, this partnership. I'm going to tell Mr. Chen about this. And I hope we can move forward from there."

Kim thought about inviting Scott to the Fourth of July party that her neighbors in the Portland West Hills always threw. But she decided against it. Scott had his son and it would be a little awkward introducing this new partner of sorts to the neighbors.

Instead, she invited her friend Michelle who lived in the neighborhood. Michelle arrived at Kim's at about 8. Kim got her started with a little prosecco as she finished her makeup and they chatted about their respective weeks. Soon they were strolling along Kim's winding street in festive summer dresses. Chris and Tamara's place was just a couple of blocks away.

"So give me an update on the men in your life," said Michelle.

"I'm single. Unattached. A state that I have been in rather infrequently in my adult life. It's something my therapist recommended."

"Really?" Michelle said, twisting her head and giving Kim a skeptical look.

"Really," Kim said.

"Well, I suppose that's probably healthy. It was a year ago that Camden moved out, right?"

"A year ago in the fall."

"How are things with Camden?"

"We've been working well enough together at the winery. But when I cancelled on the summer trip he'd planned to Lake Chelan, he was furious. Those trips are part of his long-term vision for us to return to couplehood. He disinvited me and my kids to the camping weekend we always do with three other families. I've made it clear that for the summer, I want us to stay separated, just business partners. He seems okay now, like he's mellowed out. But that's probably because I had just had sex with him."

Michelle's mouth dropped open.

"Did your therapist give the okay to occasional sex with exes?"

Kim laughed.

They arrived at the chateau-style home and made their way around the side to the large yard, which was filled with fairly uptight-looking doctor and CFO types and their wives plus two or three gay couples. There was a bartender doing custom cocktails off to the side. The Portland skyline and Mount Hood, illuminated by the late-day sun, stood as the backdrop. Kim said hi to a few neighbors as she and Michelle procured whiskey sours.

The chit-chat with various acquaintances didn't last too long and Michelle and Kim found themselves on their own meandering across the lawn.

"Whatever happened to the guy you were seeing this spring?" Michelle asked.

"Scott. Well, I'm seeing him again. Just a bit. Being single means I can date, right? With Scott, it's different than with Camden. There's something about the way we are together that just clicks."

"Maybe this experience is telling you something was missing with Camden," Michelle said.

"Or maybe it's just that one wants what one can't have. I just don't know if I have it in me to cut it off with Camden and start all over again for love. In a few years, that stuff wears off."

"Oh, come on Kim, don't be so cynical."

"I own a business with Camden. We've lived together as a blended family. I picked his daughter up just last week. We've got a shared social circle. Should I really give this up and start something with some guy I met on Tinder?"

"Right, it's something to think about."

"The money situation isn't great right now, either. The alimony still comes on time but it never covers my expenses. I'm eating into my nest egg every month. Sure, I could cut back on the travel. And I suppose I could find a stylist that charges less than $400 to do my hair. Then there's the spa and, you know, the other sorts of doctor's visits."

"Let's face it, being Kim Marseilles is not inexpensive," Michelle said. Kim gave her a mock frown.

"Seriously, I'm almost 50. I'm not giving up my stylist and my winter getaways. I need to finally get serious about a real income and career and I keep thinking this business with Camden could be it."

Kim continued, "Scott and I saw this amazing property together yesterday. Oh my god, this was what I really wanted when Camden and I were looking for a winery. It hovers above the Gorge. Scott is connected up with some funky scheme to buy the place in conjunction with a foreign investor. It's not going to happen, but we were on such a high imagining ourselves there. I'd have my winery and he'd have his windsurfing."

"Sounds like this time with Scott is a big fantasy, an escape. Enjoy it while you can."

They both sipped their drinks as the fireworks show from the Portland waterfront began.

8

Back in Portland, Scott retrieved Nate from his mom at 5 p.m. for the 4th of July holiday. They met up with his buddy Doug and his daughter and biked up to Mt. Tabor Park on Portland's SE side to see fireworks. Mt. Tabor was one of Scott's favorite Portland parks, a small extinct volcano with giant Douglas firs, a network of hiking trails and three large 1930s-era water reservoirs.

They found a patch of grass in a field above the main reservoir, spread out a couple of picnic blankets and cracked open beverages and snacks while their kids explored and played.

Just then, Scott got a text from Kim.

> Happy 4th of July! Just a low key get together in the neighborhood.

She sent a picture of the fancy West Hills backyard party with a view of the downtown Portland skyline.

Scott replied with a shot from Mt. Tabor.

> Down here in the lowlands. Still not a bad view;)

As dusk descended on Mt. Tabor, the scene got a bit too wild with lots of drunken kids dancing around and some insanely large fireworks. Scott and Doug made their way home before the fireworks show was over.

Scott tried to put the Bodenheimer property out of his mind. However, the next day he spotted his neighbor Mark, who had built a large new home across the street a few years back. Scott knew he was a real estate lawyer.

"Hey Mark, I'm wondering if you could help me with a real estate deal I'm considering? I'd pay you, of course."

"Well sure, Scott."

"I've got an opportunity to do a co-investment on a Gorge property, a vineyard. I would be able to use the house on the property and the other entity would use the vineyard land and create a winery."

"Sounds intriguing, can I get in?" Mark said, chuckling.

"Maybe I can send you some paperwork to look over?"

"Okay, I'll take a gander at it."

Scott emailed Mark some documents that he had received from Wine Jamie and they agreed to meet out for a beer in a few days.

Scott had Nate for several days and he found it hard to keep his mind off the potential deal. Kim was unavailable to rendezvous, but they did text some back and forth. He was tense with anticipation when he approached the Imperial Bottle Shop & Taproom for the meeting with attorney Mark.

The Taproom was a relatively new drinking establishment in Scott's neighborhood that combined a bottle shop with a curated selection of microbrewed beer on tap. They ordered beers off the extensive selection listed on the flat-screen display.

"So what do you make of this deal, Mark?"

"Scott, this is somewhat of an unusual arrangement, but not totally out of the ordinary. Usually the foreign real estate buyers want to hold title themselves. In this case, this company, Darden Wine Holdings, has a somewhat indirect strategy for purchasing and controlling the property through you. The term of art is a 'straw man buyer.'"

"These papers have been drawn up by one of the most

reputable firms in the Portland area. It appears they have a couple of these holding arrangements already going in California wine country.

"The company is funny, though. It's hard to find out much about them. It's owned through a trust and I can't find out the names of the people who are part of the trust.

"On the other hand, it could be a very lucrative deal for you. For putting up $100K, you'd be able to do an all-cash offer on the property. Your stake in the property will start out at $100K, about 5 percent, but it'll increase to 20 percent after five years and that's currently worth ... oh, something over $400K."

"Damn, that's not a bad return," Scott said.

"After the deal is closed the bank will issue you a loan. Darden agrees to make the loan payments. You get use of the house. They just want the agricultural land and a build-out of an on-site winery. As the owner of the property, you are committed to pursue the permits and such to get the winemaking facility off the ground. They also have a provision here to transfer the property to a new owner or a real estate partnership agreement, so you or they could eventually disengage."

"Why would they want me to own the property instead of them?" Scott asked.

"A number of possible reasons. For one, it lets them control the property without actually having their name on the title. It might be easier for you as a local to get the necessary permits for development. Also, there can be high taxes when corporations own real estate, so there's that angle. It's also possible they are trying to obscure ownership from scrutiny by the authorities."

"Interesting. That last reason makes me a bit uneasy," Scott said.

"Would you like me to look into the deal any further?" Mark asked.

"That's okay," Scott said. "This sounds like it would be way over my head. But man, you should see this place, it's amazing." Scott pulled out some photos on his phone to show Mark.

"Hey man, now I'm intrigued," said Mark. "Unfortunately, I don't have $2.2 million lying around." They ordered another round and talked about skiing and summer backpacking adventures before they headed out.

Two weeks later, Kim invited Scott to accompany her to a birthday party in Portland for one of her friends who'd just turned 50. It was on the roof deck of Revolution Hall, a renovated high school turned hip entertainment complex in southeast Portland.

Kim informed Scott that cocktail attire was required. Portland was experiencing a heat wave, so he struggled a bit regarding what to wear and eventually landed on a blazer and khakis.

He was stressed about the party. What would her friends be like, he wondered? Would he be able to hold his own in conversation with them?

Kim was there when he arrived, looking stunning in a black cocktail dress and well into a glass of chardonnay. It turned out the cocktail attire really seemed to only apply to the women — most of the dudes were dressed casually, even in shorts. Oh well.

The people at the party were all connected to the private school Kim's kids attended. Scott sipped a Maker's Mark and let Kim take the lead as they mingled with various acquaintances of hers.

"This is my friend Scott," Kim said, introducing him to Danielle, a friend that Kim had mentioned before.

"Looks like a very special friend," Danielle said with a wink.

"We're dating," Kim said, as if to emphasize their status went no further than that.

The crowd wasn't all that intimidating to Scott. He chatted casually with a few folks as Kim drifted in and out of conversations with various people, though he did have a few moments on his own. At least there was the bourbon and the beautiful skyline to contemplate.

By the end of the night, Kim was tipsy and pulled him aside to make out in an out-of-the-way corner of the roof deck. Scott went with it but it seemed a bit bizarre, almost like an attempt to compensate for her noncommittal attitude toward the relationship.

On their way out, they snuck into a Psychedelic Furs concert happening in the auditorium below. He, Kim and all the aging Gen Xers at the concert shook their bodies to the music. As Scott looked at Kim drunkenly swaying her butt to the beat, he wondered why the hell he was so attracted to her.

Eventually, under Scott's guidance, they made their way back to Scott's car and then his house.

They should've just fallen into sex, but somehow her inebriated state and his relative sobriety threw things out of alignment. They just weren't meshing and it bothered Scott. After Kim fell asleep, Scott remained awake. He was tuned up from the evening. He was so into her. Her drunken adoration for him should have made him feel good, right?

Somehow, however, he felt disturbed and let down by the evening. He wanted her attention, her intimacy but he'd only been with her for a couple limited hours over a two-week period. She was so foreign, he knew so little about her, yet there she was, finally, close to him in his home and staying the night.

He walked out to the kitchen to get a glass of water and just sat at the table. Her phone was right there. One of the new iPhones with a pink metallic design. Given her status as a hyperconnected mom, small business owner and social butterfly, it felt like that phone was almost a part of her. He thought about picking it up and looking at it. No, that wouldn't be right. Major creepy invasion of privacy. He went back and crawled into bed.

He eased up next to her and kissed the back of her neck, but she rolled over. He laid there for a while, thinking about the phone. She was breathing heavily through her nose, almost snoring. He was thirsty again and got up.

Sitting at the table with the glass of water, he nudged the phone and it came to life, showing the unlock screen, which required a code. Without being too deliberate about it and picking the phone up, he tried to see if he could unlock it. It seemed like he had seen her punch in the numbers.

He got it on the first try.

Taking sips of water, he scrolled through the texts, tapping on Camden's name as soon as he saw it.

> My dad is onboard

Scrolling back in time, he read a couple more.

> The pictures look amazing.

> When does it go on the market?

Then he saw pictures of the Bodenheimer place that she had texted.

Scott studied the thread of texts in more detail. He felt a surge of anxiety as he figured out what it all meant. She and Camden were going to make an offer on the Bodenheimer place, obviously with major financial backing from his wealthy family. Unbelievable.

And she was right there in the next room.

What an awful thing to do. The place they had seen together that he had talked about buying. However abstractly, they had imagined a future there together.

Scott barely calmed himself down enough to slide back into bed next to her. She still seemed completely knocked out, but he didn't sleep a wink.

Kim woke up early the next day and Scott gave her a ride home. Scott tried to act as he usually would toward her, but it was hard.

Scott had Nate and struggled to give him the attention

he deserved being hungover, sleep deprived and incensed by what he had seen on Kim's phone. Nate was pretty grumpy, too, since he had just done a sleepover at a friend's place. Scott let him watch YouTube videos for a couple of hours in the morning then they went out to the river to play on a standup paddleboard in the afternoon.

He agonized about whether he should do the deal on the Bodenheimer place. Fuck her and that rich ass boyfriend, I'm going to do it, he'd decide. Then he would talk himself out of it. It was simply too risky, too much of a stretch. Unnecessary for his life.

After cracking his first beer of the evening at 5 p.m., Scott texted Denise.

> I'm very interested in moving forward with the Bodenheimer property.

Denise texted back.

> Excellent! Mr. Chen liked what he saw of the property. His people are working on an analysis of it. Can you meet with some of Mr. Chen's associates this week?

On Tuesday morning, after Scott took Nate to his camp at the Oregon Museum of Science and Industry, he headed to downtown Portland on his bike to Lowe Dede & Warren, a law firm on the 16th floor of a high rise that he'd never really noticed before. Sitting in the posh waiting area in shorts and a polo shirt, he felt a bit informally dressed.

After five minutes or so, the receptionist showed him into a conference room with a spectacular view of the city and the mountain range beyond. The two attorneys, a middle-aged bald guy and an attractive young woman who looked to be early in her career, explained that Mr. Chen had reviewed the details of the Bodenheimer property extensively. It fit his interests well and he was eager to find a partner who could work with him to secure the use of it.

They explained the process of making the offer to Scott. A letter from the German banking conglomerate Wegner Bank ensured that Scott had the resources to make an all-cash offer on the approximately $2.2M property. The bank would pay out the cash for the sale without contingencies and would structure a special type of mortgage for Scott that he would pay off from income paid by Darden Wine Holdings.

"Please don't mention the existence of the firm to anyone in the transaction. You are the buyer. You are acting on your own. These agreements with us should remain confidential."

Scott left the office with the letter. Having a statement from a major global bank that said he was good for $2.2M felt kind of exciting. Scott had a vague recollection regarding money laundering scandals in the news connected to Wegner Bank, but Wegner was such a big name in international finance that it didn't worry him too much.

The property would be on the market on the weekend. He texted Denise to let her know that he was ready to make an all-cash offer as soon as the listing went live.

She had already been briefed by Mr. Chen's firm.

9

The Bodenheimer property went on the market on the last Friday of July. The price was $2.4 million, a little higher than Denise had expected. Denise was in touch with listing agent Barry Chisholm. He said that they were collecting offers through the weekend and would review them on Sunday night.

When seeking a starter home in Portland's competitive inner Eastside real estate market a decade earlier, Scott had been outbid on several homes. Often, the winning buyer was a big player with an all-cash offer.

The current plan was to offer $50,000 over the asking price. But on Friday night, Scott called Denise.

"Denise, I'm worried we won't get the property. This is confidential, but I know someone else is going to put in a very aggressive offer."

"Mr. Chen would be very interested in this information. Find out anything you can about the other offer," she said. "I will be in touch."

Soon, Scott got a text from Denise letting him know that one of Mr. Chen's associates would be calling him. Ten minutes later, his phone rang.

"Hey Scott, Jared here. I work for Mr. Chen. I understand that we're in a competitive, blind auction sort of situation with regard to this property and it would be helpful to see the whole picture. I can help with that."

"Right," Scott said.

"This may sound strange, but I need you to install an app on the phone of the listing agent. This will let us know what is going on."

"What?" Scott said. He was shocked.

"I will email you instructions for putting the app on."

"But how will I get the agent's phone?"

"Denise will help with that."

Scott drove out to the Gorge the next morning and met Denise at The Coffee Spot. She was dressed more casually than usual in distressed denim jeans and a summer blouse. Her usual confident tone of voice seemed a little off as she explained what to do at the open house being held at the Bodenheimer property that day.

The plan was to get Barry to show off some pictures of the property on his phone. Then they would distract him somehow and install the app.

The estate was open for viewing from 12-5 on Saturday and Sunday. Denise and Scott got there at two on Saturday and there were already a few cars lined up on the private gravel drive leading to the farmstead. On a sunny summer afternoon, the sprawling estate was as spectacular as ever. Even Denise seemed in awe as the view unfolded on the way from the car to the house.

Berkshire Hathaway Certified Agent and Broker Barry Chisholm was situated on the patio chatting with a couple in their sixties who were quite conservatively dressed. Barry had a dark-complexioned healthy look about him, with thinning brown hair and a husky physique. He sported a pink Polo shirt and designer jeans and was gesticulating with his arms as he held forth about the virtues of the property.

"Denise! How are you on this beautiful day?" Barry asked as he saw Denise approach.

"Hi Barry, nice to see you," Denise said. "Let me introduce you to my client, Scott. He's a friend of the owner, Chuck."

Barry gave Scott a firm handshake.

"Hey, I heard you had some cool overhead drone shots of this place," Scott said.

"Totally dude, hit up my website for those. It's as easy as Googling 'broker Barry.'"

"I had a question about one of the photos. I'm wondering whether one of the outbuildings is part of the estate. It wasn't clear. Can I show you?"

"Sure."

"Do you happen to have a phone to look at them?"

Barry pulled his giant new iPhone out, opened up the property listing and gave the phone to Scott to look through the photos. Meanwhile he checked in with the couple who had started to wander off from the patio. Denise had disappeared.

In a minute the sprinkler system came on. The older couple, now out on the lawn, got sprayed from head to toe by one of the high-powered sprinkler heads. While the two of them yelled expletives, Barry began rushing frantically about in search of the shutoff.

Scott had a complex set of instructions for getting the app on an iPhone. He stood on the patio amidst the chaos and dug into the settings menu. The first step was disabling the security and the next involved using a Bluetooth connection to install the spyware app. Scott started the latter step but couldn't complete it before Barry returned and he had to give the phone back.

Scott and Denise wandered around the estate for 20 minutes or so before departing. On the drive out, Scott asked Denise, "Did you see the look on his face when those sprinklers came on?"

Denise cracked a smile. It was the first sign that she had a sense of humor.

"We still need to get the app on Barry's phone. I think I know where we can find him after work. That fucker always goes for a drink after a showing," she said.

The wind was actually pretty good that day, so Scott rigged up a 4.2-meter sail and took a few fun laps at the Hatch just to mellow out his nerves.

As Scott was disassembling his windsurfing gear in the Hatchery parking lot, his phone buzzed and he answered. It was Denise.

"He's at Sixth Street Bistro, just what I expected. Lacey will meet you there for a drink."

"Okay," Scott replied.

Scott drove across the river and parked his car in downtown Hood River near the restaurant/bar. Just as he was getting out of the car, a tall, tanned woman in wedges and a short skirt approached on the sidewalk. She looked like a hot cocktail waitress, Scott thought, probably in her early thirties. Part of a botanical tattoo was visible on her upper thigh.

"Are you Scott?"

"Lacey?"

"Yes. You know this guy, right?" she asked.

"Yep."

"Let's do this."

They entered the restaurant and went up to the loft area. Sure enough, Barry was seated alone at the bar and well into a glass of chardonnay. He was chatting with the bartender like a regular.

Scott heard Lacey mutter "ugh" under her breath as they approached the bar.

Scott pretended not to notice Barry at first, but then after a moment, he reintroduced himself as one of the visitors to the open house earlier in the day.

"Oh yes, I remember you. What a beautiful property. It's a hot potato. The whole town's talking about that place." Barry looked over at Lacey and said, "I don't know if we've met?"

They chatted a bit just standing there by the bar and Barry invited them to have a seat. Lacey sat next to Barry. It wasn't long before they were all onto another round of drinks and Barry was holding forth about his latest series of real estate deals, his luck on the golf course and his prodigious kiteboarding ability. Lacey gushed at every detail and laughed gleefully at all his attempts at humor, welcoming Barry's touches to her forearms and shoulders.

"If you'll excuse me, I'm going to attend to nature's call," Barry said.

"Oh, before you go, can you show me those awesome kiting shots?" Lacey asked. Barry whipped out his phone and showed some pictures of him fully geared up and airborne on a kite.

"Oh my," she said, taking the phone from him. "These are great!"

"Be right back," Barry said, getting up off his barstool. "Oh, but I should probably hang onto this." He took the phone from Lacey. "In my line of work, I never know when someone will need me."

Barry returned to Scott and Lacey with a swagger in his step and said, "So what do you say we all go back to my place and smoke a doobie?"

Turning to the bartender, he said "I'll get these guys' tab."

Lacey gave Scott an approving glance. Barry's place was a new rowhouse just a couple blocks from the Bistro. It was totally minimalist and modern with huge floor-to-ceiling windows. Predictably, the great room spilled out onto a balcony with a spectacular view of the Gorge.

"So what's the deal between you two?" Barry asked as they settled into the white wraparound sofa. "Boyfriend/girlfriend?"

Lacey giggled, "He's cute isn't he? He doesn't mind sharing. That's one of the reasons I like him so much."

Barry cracked a bottle of sparkling wine and poured glasses for everyone. "I'd love to toke a little too," Lacey said seductively. Barry got up to fetch a joint and Scott could see Lacey putting something into his wine from a dropper in her purse.

They all got a little more drunk or at least acted like it.

Lacey was laughing at everything Barry said and touching his leg. She had him talking about some of the big real estate deals he'd closed over the past year and this had led him to show off some of the properties on his phone.

She also put a hand on Scott's leg. Eventually, she asked, "I wonder which one of you is the better kisser?" She turned to Scott and gave him a long, luxurious kiss. He had to admit that he didn't mind it. Then she gave Barry an equally long one, putting her set of well-manicured feminine hands on his corpulent body while she kissed him.

"I think Barry's got it," she said, laughing. "Show me around your place?"

Barry and Lacey got up and walked around. As soon as they made their way downstairs where some bedrooms were, Scott got back to work on the phone, which still had the screen lock disabled. This time things went pretty quickly and in about three minutes, the app was in place. Scott could hear Barry and Lacey talking and laughing downstairs.

When he got down to the bottom of the stairway, he followed their voices to a bedroom. Barry was sprawled out on the bed shirtless with a bulge in his denim. Lacey had taken off her top and was doing a kind of striptease in front of him, her pert breasts bared in all their glory.

Trying to play the part, Scott came into the bedroom and ran his finger down Lacey's bare, tattooed back and then whispered into her ear, "I got it installed."

Lacey sat down next to Barry and rubbed his chest. "Oh baby, I want me some of this. We need to make it happen another night, though. Text me."

Barry looked a little dazed and confused but gave her a weak smile.

In a minute, Lacey had her clothes back on and was exiting the house in businesslike fashion with Scott.

"You were good back there," Scott said.

Lacey just smiled and continued walking in the direction of their vehicles.

When they parted, she said, "I was lying, you were a better kisser" and winked.

THE ECLIPSE

Scott spent the night on a friend's couch in White Salmon. At 6:25 a.m. his phone buzzed with a text from Denise.

> We need to up our offer Scott. Meet me at
> The Coffee Spot at 7.

Scott got dressed quickly and made it there by seven. Denise had her hair up in a bun and was wearing a pristine pair of black Nike sneakers and a tracksuit while she sipped her latte and worked on her Dell laptop.

"Okay, Scott, we're going to make some changes to our offer. We need to increase it to $100K over the asking price.

"I also need you to write a letter to the seller."

Scott gave her a questioning look.

"I know, I know. That's what we're up against. You met Bodenheimer, right? We need to appeal to him, give him a sense that his property will be going into the right hands. You need to play to whatever is his thing."

"Windsurfing?" Scott said. "He's old school. That'll have to be it. And the natural wine thing can't hurt."

"And I need you to do this in the next few hours. Let's say by noon."

"Okay."

After Denise left, Scott remained at The Coffee Spot. He pulled out his laptop and wrote a letter to Chuck Bodenheimer and his wife.

Dear Chuck and Barb:

As someone who has known you from a distance for many years and recently became acquainted with you personally, I am extremely excited to be making an offer on your property. It was such a pleasure visiting your home a couple weeks back.

If I become owner of your current home, I anticipate spending many weekends with my son and our friends there. At 8, Nate already loves to windsurf and having this place will get us out to the Hook all that more often. I am looking forward to bringing him and his friends here. They will be the next generation of windsurfers in the Gorge.

Like you, I am a businessman. And for me, the property will be an opportunity to invest in an industry that I believe is central to the future of the Gorge: natural wine. I look forward to partnering with a young, up and coming natural winemaker who can establish a thriving vineyard on your property. The beautiful setting will be wonderful for sharing food and wine with others.

Thank you for considering my offer.

Scott Larson

Scott fiddled around a bit with the letter. Denise could have shown him the other letters, but he didn't really want to look at them. He could imagine what the letter from Kim and Camden said. Plenty of bullshit about family, wine and happy people picking grapes. If his offer was the strongest financially, he'd have a shot.

There wasn't much more to do now. It was going to be windy later out east, so he got on I-84 and headed for Biggs Junction for some windsurfing at The Wall.

It had been another busy weekend at the winery and Kim was exhausted when things started to wind down Sunday evening. They really needed more help at the tasting room on weekends. She was the owner, after all, and shouldn't need to hustle all day long like this. To top it off, Camden's parents had been in town over the past few days and she had played the role of Camden's partner with them. This was yet another irritating aspect of their ambiguous relationship.

She felt pretty guilty about the plan to purchase Chuck Bodenheimer's property. It hadn't really been her idea. She told Camden about the place after the visit with Scott and then he ran with it, convincing his dad to come in with the cash as a co-investor. Camden's dad had to come out and

THE ECLIPSE

see the property himself, of course.

Kim could get along with almost anyone. With Camden's parents being from Wisconsin, they didn't have much in common with Kim. His dad liked to talk sports, especially golf and the Packers and his mom was a high maintenance type who was into decorating their three homes, rather tackily if you asked Kim — one in suburban Milwaukee, the other on a lake in northern Wisconsin and the other on Sanibel Island in Florida.

They did have drinking in common, though. Kim was an accomplished West Coast party girl, but she had never seen 70-somethings consume like this Wisconsin couple did. She could often barely keep upright after an afternoon and evening in their company.

They had all looked at the property together the week before and everyone had agreed it was absolutely stunning. Of course, Camden's dad had a million questions about it and proceeded to mansplain real estate investing over a two-and-a-half-hour, $500 dinner at the Hood River Hotel.

Scott hadn't said much to Kim about the property since they had seen it together. In fact, they hadn't seen each other since the birthday party a couple of weeks ago. She couldn't imagine that he was going to venture into the murky deal with the co-investor that he'd mentioned.

She wasn't sure how she'd break the news to Scott that Camden had purchased the property. They still had their plan to watch the eclipse together, but for better or worse, Kim needed to cancel that. Kim's ex-husband had informed her that she had to keep the kids an extra couple days and there was really no negotiating with him. She'd extend the central Oregon vacation she'd already planned with her kids and watch the eclipse with them instead of doing the romantic getaway thing that she'd promised Scott.

She suddenly felt a pang of guilt and texted Scott.

> Hey....did you get out there for that wind today?

She didn't hear anything for an hour or so. She was tidying things up at the winery while Camden entertained his parents.

> Yes! I just got back to Portland.
>
> Darn, I'm all alone out here at the winery;)

Scott wanted to write that he missed her, but he didn't feel like he could be that openly emotional.

> I so wish I was there.
>
> Me too. Hey, we're going to have to do our eclipse getaway on another weekend. Looks like I have my kids then.
>
> Oh shoot, I was looking forward to that!

Scott felt both disappointment and a sense of relief on learning that their eclipse plans were off. He was nervous about the offer on the property and what it meant for his relationship with Kim. He turned off his phone and turned in.

10

Back home in Portland, Scott got the text from Denise at 7:45 a.m. on Monday morning. His offer for the Bodenheimer property had been accepted.

Holy shit.

Even though he hadn't talked about the property much with Kim since they had visited it, he knew that the first thing he had to do was tell her.

He would call her.

On second thought, he knew that she was in Portland. He would go over there, in person.

He got in his car and began the familiar drive toward her home in the West Hills.

His heart was pounding and his face was burning as he crossed the Burnside Bridge, drove through downtown and then headed up into the winding streets that led to her place.

It had been a while since he had made this trip and in his agitated state, he took a wrong turn in the maze of streets surrounding her place and ended up on a dead end and had to awkwardly turn around.

When he finally pulled into Kim's driveway and got out of the Saab, the morning summer sun hit him straight in the face. Her entryway was in a shadow.

He knocked on the door. Through the floor-to-ceiling window adjacent to the door, he could see a figure approach who walked a little bit like Kim. It was her daughter Sierra. He'd never met either of Kim's children but he recognized her from photos.

"Hi," she said as she opened the door.

"Is Kim there?"

Scott paced nervously.

The daughter gave him a curious look and then turned around and shouted "Mom!"

Kim arrived after a minute.

"Hi Scott, what brings you around?" Kim said with a puzzled look on her face.

Scott felt himself shaking.

"I wanted to tell you in person. I got the Bodenheimer place."

Kim's jaw dropped. "How do you mean?"

"I mean my offer was accepted."

"Oh, I didn't know that you. Wow. I mean, congratulations." Kim could only stammer out the words. Her daughter was staring at her.

"Sierra, I'm just going to go out in the backyard and talk to my friend," Kim told her. Kim exited the front door and walked with Scott across the driveway, through a gate and down a walkway to a patio with a small yard. They stood among large brightly colored ceramic planters with freshly watered plants. The small patch of grass was lush and green despite it being the end of summer.

Scott, flushed in the face, said, "I know about the offer, yours and Camden's offer that is."

Kim was quiet for a bit.

"Oh Scott, I'm sorry. It wasn't even my idea. I told him about the place and he and his parents just went running with it."

"I guess you never saw a future for us after all," Scott said. "I'd hoped against the odds that you could."

Just then, Camden entered the yard through the side gate. Unshaven and wearing a mostly unbuttoned short-sleeve shirt, shorts and flip-flops, he looked a bit unkempt.

"Hi, I'm Camden," he said, extending a hand.

"Scott."

Both men participated in a death grip-firm handshake.

"Everything okay back here?" Camden asked.

An uncomfortable silence followed.

"I think I'll be going now," Scott said, nodding to Kim and then Camden.

As Scott walked out of the backyard and closed the gate, he overheard Camden say, "Just heard from the agent that we got beat out by another offer."

As Scott drove east on Burnside Street toward his side of town, a wistful old country song by Joe Ely, "Honky Tonk Masquerade," came over the stream of KEXP radio he had playing. The song's themes of desire and deception seemed to fit the situation perfectly.

He was going to be a real estate investor now, part of the "landed gentry." But what did it matter?

That evening, he began to wonder whether he should go through with the purchase of the winery. Was this really a wise move financially? And were these partners trustworthy?

After a nearly sleepless night, he concluded that he had only been after the property because it was a way of connecting with Kim. Winning the bid for the property had given him a temporary ego boost, but he really did not need the additional complexity and risk in his life. It wasn't the right thing to do.

The next morning, Scott called the attorney's office to inform them that he was withdrawing from the deal.

They called him back 20 minutes later.

"We're so disappointed to hear that you want to withdraw, Scott. We've had a word with Mr. Chen and he insists that you meet with one of his associates to discuss the situation."

"I want to pull out of the deal. I'm not interested in talking about it," Scott said.

"You need to understand, Scott, that we're breaking a contract here, both with the seller and your co-investor. This was a no contingencies offer, remember? Mr. Visser can meet with you later this afternoon. He will text you regarding a location."

Scott's phone rang a little after 11.

"Hey Scott," a vaguely European-accented voice came on the line. "How are you? My colleague, Mr. Chen, has put us in touch. How about a beer, man? I love Portland beer. I'm flying in from the Bay Area in about two hours. Where do you like to drink beer?"

"What about 10 Barrel in the Pearl?"

"Sounds great, man."

At 2:30 p.m., Scott was seated across from Laurence Visser on the rooftop patio of 10 Barrel Brewing in Portland's Pearl District. Visser appeared to be somewhere in his late fifties or early sixties, tall with a medium build. He had thin lips and a well-chiseled face with perfectly straight, white teeth. His silver, slicked-back shoulder-length hair contrasted with his deeply tanned face. He wore a striped oxford shirt rolled up at the sleeves with a gray polo shirt underneath it.

While Scott sipped an Apocalypse IPA, Laurence explained that he was the CEO of Darden Wine Holdings, the corporate entity that encompassed the wineries owned by Mr. Chen in the United States. Darden ran six wineries in California and Washington and they planned on adding the one that Dimitri and his son would be starting up in the Gorge.

"Let's talk about this deal. You've landed the most coveted wine property in the Gorge I hear."

"I love the property. I'm just, well, not sure if this deal is the right fit for me," Scott said.

"Okay. I get it. It's a big decision. What do you do regularly as an occupation?"

Scott described the gig he had teaching European history at one of Portland's public high schools.

"That's awesome. I admire that. I'm Dutch. European history is very real to us and very recent."

"Indeed," Scott said, sipping his beer.

"You're what, 47? You've been teaching since when?"
"1998."
"Right. And you're probably wondering why me? What makes me the right guy to do this deal."

"I do wonder."

"Well, we've looked into you, Scott. We've taken stock. You're a great fit for us. Smart, stable. Perfect credit. A good citizen. Already a rental property owner."

"Thank you."

"This is an opportunity, man. It's maybe a chance to open up some new horizons in your life. You'll work up to a 20 percent stake in this investment, but it doesn't have to end there."

"That's something to consider," Scott said and then turned to the waiter, affirming that he'd have another.

"Scott, this is a smoking deal, man. You are the envy of everyone in the Gorge wine scene right now, man. I hear that they have three backup offers on the place. You're at the front of the line now, man."

Listening to Laurence somehow relaxed Scott and elevated his mood. His Dutch accent gave him a certain charm and legitimacy. The beer was putting Scott at ease and his sense of excitement about the property began to return.

"What can we do to make you more secure in the arrangement? Do you have an attorney?"

"I do, in fact."

"Have him look over the paperwork. He can assure you everything is above board."

"Okay, let me think about it. I'll let you know first thing tomorrow."

He called Mark that afternoon.

Mark was calm as they talked.

"Well Scott, this seems like a quite attractive opportunity with maybe a bit too much international intrigue thrown in. I tell you what, I'd be happy to represent you, to look over everything you need to sign, make sure it's all on the level."

"That would make me feel so much better, man. I think I'm going to do it."

"You know what my rates are," Mark said.

"Right."

As soon as Scott dropped Nate off at his day camp, he took a walk over the Tillicum Bridge. He carefully weighed the pros and cons of doing the deal. It was a potentially amazing opportunity. There were risks working with this international investor, but he'd already gotten himself in part way, so there were also risks with pulling out. The $100,000 stake they wanted wasn't really that much in the grand scheme of things and the upside potential was amazing.

He then made his way to U.S. Bank for the $100,000 cashier's check that was required as his part of the deal. He decided to use his home equity line rather than tap into Nate's college savings funds.

He met Mark back up at the law firm that afternoon. The various non-disclosure agreements, waivers and contracts that he had to sign seemed to go on and on. The next step was flying to Frankfurt to sign off on the loan.

The comforts of Lufthansa's first-class cabin permitted Scott to nod off for at least a couple hours on the direct flight from Portland to Frankfurt. A driver from Wegner Bank met him and drove him over the rain-slicked Autobahn to the bank's headquarters, an imposing black skyscraper in Frankfurt's financial quarter known as the "Bankenviertel."

In a sterile white conference room overlooking the gloomy, rain-soaked Frankfurt cityscape, the two young, impeccably dressed German bankers explained the somewhat complex terms of the loan that the bank was underwriting that depended on the legal agreements drawn up in Scott's last meeting with Mark.

Two hours later, a 7-series BMW retrieved him from Wegner. The back seat was occupied by a compact Asian man. He had slicked back dark hair peppered with gray but a boyish face with full lips. He wore an impeccably tailored charcoal suit without a tie.

"Good afternoon, Scott. I'm so glad we could meet in person."

"Mr. Chen, it's my pleasure," replied Scott.

"I've arranged for us to dine together tonight."

They were driven to Francais, a white tablecloth restaurant in the Bankenviertel. Situated in the imperial-looking Frankfurter Hof Hotel, the restaurant featured high ceilings, ornate red wallpaper, stodgy old furniture and a mostly stuffy looking, suited clientele. Mr. Chen had a regular table in a corner of the dining room.

"I do much of my banking in Frankfurt. Not the most exciting city. But I work closely with Wegner Bank on many of my investments and I have a home here."

They got into a wide-ranging discussion of politics, books and travel over a $300 bottle of Burgundy that predated the collapse of the Berlin Wall. Finally, the conversation returned to the arrangement at hand.

"I've heard you had some second thoughts about the deal," Mr. Chen said. "I want to assure you that there is nothing to worry about as long as we stay in touch. If you ever want to sell the property, to disengage, just talk to me, we will work it out."

"It's a fabulous property," Scott said. Scott's observations about the potential of the property to be a top-level estate vineyard and an excellent long-term investment seemed to go over well with Chen.

"I can tell that you've got an analytical mind like mine," Chen said. "If you'd ever like to get out of teaching, we might be able to work together."

He told Scott that he had been in touch with Dimitri about having Dimitri's son as the winemaker on the property. "We want to move forward with converting this to a winery as soon as possible and bringing on Sasha as the on-site winemaker. It will be fabulous wine. Denise and Laurence will be assisting with the permitting process and some of the construction as necessary.

"Once I visited Oregon and Washington. Amazing places. I have some visa issues traveling to the United States at the moment. I hope we will drink wine some time together in the Columbia Gorge," Mr. Chen said as they parted.

The closing for the property was slated for the morning of August 21, 2017, the day of the total solar eclipse. Signing the final paperwork at 8:00 a.m. proved to be an anticlimax. Scott was in and out of Columbia Gorge Title Company with a key to the property within an hour.

He made his way across the Hood River Bridge and drove to the junction of Highway 14 and Cook Underwood Road. Five minutes later he pulled into what was now his 70-acre Columbia Gorge estate. The place was perfectly manicured and completely deserted.

The house was just as he'd remembered it from the showings but now totally empty of all furnishings. Denise had left a gift basket on the kitchen counter and even though it was only 9:30 a.m., Scott pulled out a half liter bottle of pFriem IPA, cracked it open, then wandered out onto the patio.

At 47, he was at a place in his life where he could survey a wide swath of time that had passed. It was strange: Some things that happened 30 years ago when he was in high school still seemed like yesterday. Those years had gone by in a flash.

Even though his life was likely half over, in some ways he felt like he was just getting started on things.

He checked his watch. It was minutes to the eclipse. He could feel the buzz coming on from the warm beer and his mind drifted to thoughts of Kim.

He walked down the woodchip pathway and out onto

the lawn by the barn. The morning sun shone brightly from the southeast, like any other summer morning. He sat down in the grass and took in the spectacular view of Mount Hood.

And then it began. The sky got a deeper shade of blue and the air suddenly seemed to get cooler. The trees and the peaks in the distance took on darker hues. The dimness reached a peak and receded in a matter of minutes.

After Scott finished the beer, he wandered back into the house. His phone, laying on the kitchen counter next to the gift basket, buzzed.

As Kim was driving back south to Sunriver after viewing the eclipse at her friend's ranch, she snapped a selfie of herself and the crew in the Range Rover, which included her friend Michelle and the three kiddos in the back.

At a pitstop, she sent the photo and a text to Scott.

> Not gonna lie, it was pretty amazing. Wish we could have watched it together like we'd planned. How's the new house?

Kim waited for a reply from Scott, but she didn't hear from him.

After getting back to Portland from Sunriver, Kim was thrust into back-to-school chaos. She scrambled to get her two kids to a seemingly endless list of obligations that included doctor's appointments, haircuts, music and athletic tryouts, and social events.

Two weeks after the eclipse, the Columbia Gorge exploded in what became known as the Eagle Creek Fire. It raged from east of Cascade Locks all the way to the touristed waterfalls and hiking trails near Multnomah Falls. The fire and the ensuing smoke upended events at the Ross winery and, according to Camden, would likely destroy the grapes this year.

Scott was still on Kim's mind. She felt so bad about how things had turned out with them. About a week after the fire, Kim tried texting Scott again and heard back. They agreed to meet at Shangdong, a Chinese restaurant in Portland's Hollywood neighborhood, known for its commercial district where busy Broadway Street and Sandy Boulevard intersect and the iconic Hollywood Theater stands.

Scott waited in a booth in the nondescript building that housed the restaurant. He peered out the window. Smoke from the fire had blown into Portland and a haze lingered over the city. About 15 minutes into his beer, he saw Kim cross the parking lot. She was wearing a waistless, knee-length black dress that he liked. He could feel an ache in his stomach as she approached.

He stood up and kissed her on the cheek when she got to the table.

"Good to see you, Kim."

"You too. Isn't this smoke awful? Thanks for picking the restaurant. I can't believe I haven't tried this place before."

They settled into conversation about the fire, the start of school and the wine scene in the Gorge.

Scott told her a bit about the plans for the Georgians to get the winery up and running on the property.

Finally, Scott got the nerve to say what was on his mind.

"I thought we had something, Kim, something real. A connection. I was hoping we could build something together."

"We do have a connection. We do. I just realized I can't leave my life with him now."

Scott stayed silent.

"I still haven't really figured out what I really want," Kim continued. "But this is where I am right now."

"So this is where it ends, in a Chinese restaurant on Northeast Broadway?" Scott said, making a brief attempt at humor with a reference to the break-up scene at the end of Woody Allen's "Annie Hall."

After the meal, Scott walked Kim to her vehicle and they

parted with an embrace. Then he watched her drive west into the smoke that enveloped the city.

11

Summer 2019 started out with a few stretches of great wind in May and June, and July delivered just like it usually does in the Gorge. Having the house on the estate was awesome for crashing after windsurfing sessions. Scott was making so much money on it as a vacation rental in the off season that he didn't feel guilty about spending lots of time there in the summer.

His love life wasn't bad either. He hadn't quite turned his girlfriend Rachel into a windsurfer, but they both loved to use the place as a retreat after some Gorge trail running or backcountry skiing on Mount Hood.

Most of the time when Scott made his way out to the Gorge now, he did so in a new Toyota Tundra, which had plenty of room for his windsurfing gear plus Nate and Rachel. He still had the old Saab though and kept it at the Gorge place. It was fun to take it on solo windsurfing missions, especially those that involved winding Highway 14 on the Washington side of the Gorge.

As Scott drove the Tundra from Portland out to the Gorge one August afternoon, he'd often ponder the scars of the Eagle Creek Fire. Its damage wasn't as apocalyptic as made out to be when it was happening, but those big stretches of burnt-out gray forest amidst the green couldn't help but bring back memories of that searing late summer of 2017.

The contractors had been busy over the winter and spring building an entirely new winemaking facility on the property. The previous summer had been gangbusters for the newly founded Revazov Winery, Dimitri and Sasha's take on Georgian wine in the Gorge. The approach had been a sort of anti-marketing campaign. Word of mouth among the natural wine crowd in Oregon and Washington and the charming but makeshift feel of the place had given it an insider appeal. Throw in some artsy Instagram posts and its mystique was amplified that much further. Invitation-only tastings and parties had gotten bigger and bigger all summer.

Scott looked down on the winemaking action from his home on the property. As the owner, he acquired the financing for the expansion via Mr. Chen's associates at Wegner Bank. He also applied for various permits required for development. The funds to repay the loans came from the winery to the bank without Scott needing to intervene at all.

Occasionally he met with the Revazov team and Laurence, but mostly Dimitri and Laurence managed the construction contracts. Scott made it to a few of the Revazov parties. After he met Rachel at the White Salmon Backyard Half Marathon the previous summer, he wasn't too inclined to get drawn into social activities.

On balance, the real estate deal that he had done two years before had worked out flawlessly.

Kim couldn't believe her oldest was driving. She sat in the passenger seat of her recently acquired Audi Q7 as they made their way east on Interstate 84, just past Multnomah Falls. Kim took her eyes off the road for a second to look at the messages on her phone. Camden was coming out later that day to the winery for their August Wine Soiree, a farm-to-table dinner event. This year's theme was the release of the "Campfire Red" Eagle Creek Fire Pinot Noir. It was an estate wine made from the grapes that were affected by the fall 2017 Eagle Creek Fire. Even though they had more staff now, it was still a stressful event to plan for Kim.

"Watch out!" Kim exclaimed when she looked up from

her phone to see the brake lights of a truck in their lane quickly approaching. Everyone lunged forward in their seats as Aiden hit the brakes.

Ross Wines was a thriving business, along with the rest of the Gorge. Trump sucked, but at least the economy was good, Kim figured. Visits to the tasting room had been steadily increasing throughout the previous summer. Instead of buying a wholesale new vineyard as they had considered doing with the Bodenheimer property, Camden's dad had helped front a major upgrade to their Hood River Valley estate.

The property wasn't perfect, but the renovation project, which included a new winemaking facility and tasting room, was a major accomplishment for Kim. She took pleasure in overseeing all the logistics involved in the upgrades. She happily dealt with architects, designers and contractors. Those organization and planning skills were ones that she liked exercising.

The modern "intervention" applied to the house that she shared with Camden on the property was such a relief. It included a brand new $120K kitchen and an expanded great room with a much better mountain view. Kim was someone who just couldn't function 100 percent if her living or working spaces were dated, run down, or otherwise sub-par.

Kim was taking the two teenagers out to the Gorge in the hope that they could mix in some fun weekend activities along with her business responsibilities. Maybe some berry picking, paddleboarding or swimming? It was so hard to find family time now that they were older.

Despite the frantic pace of the dinner, Kim was able to grab a few moments for mingling. She'd had her eye on a table full of tanned Gen Xers that seemed to be having a great time. One of them, a tall, fit-looking guy with thinning hair, a well-chiseled face and sexy brown eyes, gestured to her to come over.

This group had come up from the Bay Area for a week and they were tearing through the Gorge, kiting and mountain biking during the day and enjoying the artisanal food and wine opportunities every night. It felt so good to Kim to be part of their fun week and she fell into conversation easily with them.

"So, what other wineries have you visited?" Kim asked.

A fit and well-coiffed woman wearing a colorful summer dress piped up. "Oh we had such an amazing night on Sunday at Revazov! The natural wines are phenomenal and what they've done to bring in the Georgian winemaking traditions here is amazing. Now we all want to take a vacation to the Republic of Georgia."

Kim felt a jolt of recognition. That was the old Bodenheimer property that Scott owned or partially owned or whatever. She'd been hearing the buzz about that place around town but hadn't been to visit yet. She and Camden were slightly irritated with the whole natural wine scene and they generally put Revazov into that category.

The next morning over coffee she scanned the Revazov website. She studied the photos, remembering the walk-throughs she had done on the Bodenheimer property with Scott and then with Camden and his family two years ago. She hadn't been in touch with Scott much since then. Just a text message or two. They had run into each other getting coffee one morning, that was about it. She looked at his Facebook page. He was so incredibly cute, no wonder she had gone for him two years ago.

Now that the winery was up and running and the renovations were in place, Kim had to admit she felt a bit restless. Never one to be content, she was always after the next new thing, the next challenge. She had agreed to take on coordination of the Columbia Crush, a weekend-long event at the end of September celebrating the fall harvest at Gorge wineries. It encompassed several wineries and involved tastings, parties and family-friendly activities. Revazov hadn't signed on yet so she thought it might be time to pay them a visit.

Scott was hanging out on the patio reading The Economist when Kim came walking around the house.

"I ignored the sign," Kim said, referring to the "private" sign on the driveway to the house marked for the benefit of winery visitors.

Kim was dressed in white, form-fitting pants and a silk sleeveless top, her sunglasses resting on her head.

Scott looked up and could feel his face go hot when he realized that it was Kim. He stood up to greet her with a hug.

"Kim. It's been a while."

She explained that she had just met with Sasha Revazov and signed Revazov on to be part of the fall Columbia Crush wine festival.

Scott nodded as he listened and looked her over, his eyes drifting down to a large diamond ring on her left hand. Seeing it felt like a punch to the gut. Nevertheless, he invited her to sit down on the patio and asked if she'd like a coffee.

"I've got wine, too. It's almost 11."

"Oh, I can't stay long, but sure."

Scott went in and reloaded the French press. Rachel had gone back to Portland for the week, having a regular job during the summer unlike Scott. After Scott brought out the coffee, they moved onto the Adirondack chairs on the lawn.

Their old rapport came back instantly. They stayed away from the topic of their respective love lives but shared stories about all that had happened otherwise over two years with little contact: renovating their properties, the changes in their kids' lives, the presidential race and even the downfall of Louis C.K., a comedian they both enjoyed.

Scott finally couldn't resist. "Tell me about your ring."

"I'm married again! Camden and I decided it was time. The wedding was about a year ago in September."

"'A late September wedding'? That's a line from one of my favorite James McMurtry songs," Scott remarked.

Time passed almost imperceptibly and before either of

them looked at their watches, two hours had gone by. Scott joked that it was time to open that bottle of wine and even offered to make her some lunch, but she said she'd better be going.

"We should do this again," Kim said.

"Okay," Scott said.

He gave her a goodbye hug.

Camden Ross was taking samples from a dozen barrels of pinot that he had racked the previous fall. He was in the zone and took pleasure in pursuing his craft, especially in the recently renovated winemaking facility that he had designed himself.

He finally felt like he had the life that he wanted. Well, mostly. His first marriage had disintegrated just as he discovered his life's passion in winemaking. Now he had a business and a life partner who shared the passion. Things had been rocky with Kim and sure they could still be on or off, but when they were on, they were on. With the winery renovated and production running at a higher volume than previous years, things were moving to a new, higher plane.

Camden Ross Junior was an artist, not a businessman, but financial success was important to him. His dad, Camden Ross Senior, had made millions in the freight transportation business in Milwaukee, Wisconsin. The junior Ross felt that he would never earn his dad's respect without a fat balance sheet for his own business. The fact that his dad underwrote his business endeavors made the pressure that much worse.

The summer soiree dinner had gone well, but he could tell Kim was a bit irritated at times. Now that the renovations were in place, she needed something new to focus on. Hopefully, coordinating this multiwinery Columbia Crush event would be the thing. He had little interest in thinking about marketing and festivals, especially during the push of the harvest season. He would be focused on his craft.

Kim had been gone quite a while for the meeting at Revazov. Camden was somewhat irritated that she wanted to collaborate with them. He hated the whole hip, natural wine thing. Thought it was phony, something a bunch of Millennials did as an advertising gimmick. The old school Oregon winemakers who had mentored him would have nothing to do with it.

He also didn't like it because Scott was involved, that dude that Kim had been seeing when he and Kim had taken a "break" a couple years ago. She had gotten swept up in something passionate while he was left with a string of lame Tinder dates. Okay, there had been the thing with the hot 26-year-old, but she had been just a brief distraction. She hadn't cured him of Kim.

"So, how'd it go?" Camden asked, giving Kim a light greeting kiss. "You certainly had a long meeting with them."

"Oh, they are going to be such a great partner. Sasha has so many ideas, he's such a crazy kid. I think you guys should hang out some time."

"Right on."

"I stopped downtown while I was gone, did some shopping," Kim said. "That's why I'm back so late."

Scott was in a daze after hanging out with Kim. Their conversation kept replaying in his mind. He thought about more things he wanted to tell her. Funny stories, details he'd left out of their conversation. It was as if time had collapsed and two years had just evaporated. He felt that he was almost back where he was emotionally when he had last been with Kim.

Rachel was so different from Kim. She was more like Scott: quiet and driven. They had a connection too, but it was more about them being the same than different. Rachel liked quiet evenings at home, cooking together, reading. She didn't have kids like Scott or Kim, so that in a way made things easier, but it could also lead to a gulf of experience and relatability.

When Rachel came out to the Gorge after the workweek, Scott was so relieved to see her. Thoughts about Kim washed away. They had another one of their adventurous Gorge weekends. They hiked the Timberline Trail on Mount Hood and then retreated to Scott's place afterward to cook and enjoy the hot tub under the stars.

Kim just liked the energy at Revazov. And she was still so enamored by the Bodenheimer estate that had slipped through her fingers. She was due to go back for a planning meeting for the Columbia Crush and she was sure it would conclude with a wine tasting.

Before the meeting she texted Scott.

> Going to be at your place for a meeting.
> Would be fun to pop by again.

Scott replied.

> I just might be around.

She kept thinking of the conversation with Scott. It had shocked her to see him again. God, he was so good looking. Something clicked between them and she hadn't realized how much she missed their connection.

The planning meeting put Kim in her zone. She and a group of winery managers worked on sequencing a series of events for the Columbia Crush festival. Jody Moriarty, a total control freak from one of the wineries in Lyle, tried to dominate the conversation but Kim held her own as organizer and facilitator. She loved the process of bouncing ideas around to plan an event. Sure, it was a bit chaotic, but when they called time after two hours of discussion, they had the broad outlines of a plan.

Kim wasn't sure if Scott was home. But after the planners had their little happy hour tasting, she took the liberty of walking up to Scott's house and looking around. She was buzzed and couldn't help but be a bit nosy.

Scott came upon Kim gingerly moving around his lawn, looking over the landscaping and admiring the view. He remembered her cat-like movements and how in the past he'd derived pleasure from just watching her walk about and study things. Somehow the way she took in the world just intrigued him so much.

He tried to be quiet as he approached her from behind. Suddenly she whirled around and he saw her radiant face. Her wide, stunning smile always left him a bit breathless. Even at 50 her facial features still had a striking definition to them and looking her straight in the eyes made him feel weak in the knees.

She gave him her old affectionate shoulder shove.

"You surprised me."

He could sense she was a bit buzzed.

"Checking out the property?"

"Admiring it."

They conversed for a bit about the Columbia Crush meeting. A tension was in the air. The conversation came to an awkward pause.

"So, fancy a glass of something?" Scott asked.

"I thought you'd never ask," Kim said.

Scott returned with a couple of IKEA wine glasses and a bottle of rosé and they took their places under the tree in the Adirondack chairs. The wine flowed and their old rapport returned as they conversed, this time at a deeper level. There was so much to catch up on.

Scott remembered how much he adored Kim's voice.

Time ticked by and the early evening August sun dogged down in the west while the heat of the day lingered. When the bottle was empty, they talked more. Finally, Kim rose and said she had to be off.

As they stood there, about to part, Scott gave her a goodbye hug. But somehow as the hug broke, their hands came together for a few seconds. And then almost in slow motion, Scott pulled her in and kissed her.

THE ECLIPSE

Once they started, it was hard to stop. They made out there standing up for what seemed like minutes before Kim moved away silently, walking to her car and driving away without saying a word about what had just happened.

12

After Scott and Kim's encounter, another Gorge weekend arrived. It was typical early September Gorge weather with moderate west winds and cerulean skies.

Kim had done a pretty good job of putting Scott out of her mind over the past two years, but now she was thinking about him whenever she got a free couple of minutes.

The Columbia Crush festival was coming up and the pressure was on. Kim was texting and emailing constantly to put together the massive event, which had staggered activities running from Friday through Sunday at seven different wineries.

She even got the opportunity to go onto the Portland TV news to talk about the festival. She had to dust off her old broadcast PR skills, but she put together a hot outfit and pulled it off with aplomb.

When the festival arrived on the last weekend of September, the chaos and stress of dealing with last-minute details reached a peak. But the events were extremely successful. Many more people than expected came to the wineries.

The Friday night kickoff was a fun event at another Hood River Valley winery, then there were family activities at Dierkson Cellars on Saturday. Saturday night was the big party at Revazov, which was amazing. Twenty- and thirty-somethings descended on the place. Instead of the typically pleasant but rather bland band that Kim usually hired for Camden's winery, they had a real indie rock electronica act playing. An amazing chef Kim had identified did the hors d'oeuvres and they were phenomenal.

Kim had to admit she was under young Sasha's spell.

With a mop of curly dark hair, penetrating brown eyes and sleeves of tattoos, he had a striking presence when he entered a room. He could hold almost anyone spellbound as he described the wines he was making in his somewhat broken English and charming Eastern European accent.

At the Crush planning meetings, he would always do everyone better with ideas that broke the mold of wine marketing and wine events. Kim could see he was the future and would ally herself with him despite the skepticism of some of the other winery representatives. It was his idea to go big with the Saturday night event and make it more of a real party rather than a lower key family affair that ended at nine.

During the party, Kim worked logistics as the partygoers rocked it. She and Sasha dealt with the inevitable hiccups of holding an event of that scale. The young attendees danced with the stars overhead and drank copious quantities of natural vino. As the evening wore on into the wee hours, she took a break in the bathroom and texted Scott.

> Hey there's a party on your property. Where are you?
>
> In bed.
>
> Get down here and dance with me!!!!
>
> Give me five minutes.

Scott came down, grabbed a glass of tempranillo and as Nate slept in the house above, he and Kim mingled among the Millennials and danced like they were in their twenties. Then they went up the path to Scott's house and made out right by his door.

"Oh I missed you, I missed you," Kim kept saying.

Eventually, she said she had to get back to the event and

wrap things up.

The fall was a focused time in Camden Ross' life. Summers were always so chaotic: one week camping with his daughter, the next packed with winery events and all the while trying to squeeze in a little mountain biking and kiteboarding. In the fall, things calmed down a bit. Amidst the cooler weather, the harvest and crush gave him a focus.

Some of his days, he traveled to buy grapes at vineyards in the Willamette Valley or in the Yakima, Washington area. Other time was spent on pressing the grapes and getting them into the barrels. They were often long days on his own at the winery. This was the first year with the new building and equipment and he was enjoying all the new toys.

He hadn't seen Kim much in September. After the Columbia Crush, she had headed back to Portland to be with her kids. Tonight, she was headed to their Gorge place and they were finally going to spend some time together. He was a bit irritated though that she wasn't home yet.

It was a beautiful early fall evening. He cracked a beer and wandered around out in the vineyard wishing she was there to take in the sunset. An hour later, as he was getting out of the shower, he heard the door open and Kim come in. He greeted her in a towel as she was bringing some groceries into the kitchen.

"Hey baby, it's been a while."

"Hi love," she said as she embraced Camden and gave him a perfunctory kiss. "I got some salmon for the grill."

When he returned, dressed, she had glasses of wine poured for them and the dinner going. She asked him lots of questions about his winemaking and he was happy to hold forth on all the unique qualities of the grapes he'd acquired in the last couple weeks. He did notice Kim was drinking at a pretty good clip over dinner.

Something about her was distant and it made him want her that much more. After dinner he led her straight from the table to the bedroom where they made love as ardently as any 50-year-old pair ever would, Camden surmised.

Camden felt all was restored and fell asleep quickly. But when he awoke at 2 a.m. and she was out working on her laptop in the living room, something struck him as off. He never really knew what was going on in her head and he supposed that was part of what kept him attracted to Kim.

"What are you working on? I thought the Columbia Crush was over?" Camden asked as he was coming out of the bathroom.

She looked up.

"Yes, but that project has given me some ideas that I need to work out," she said, then put her head back down.

He walked over to her, somewhat aroused by part of a breast visible in the opening of her fleece bathrobe.

"Come back to bed, baby," he said, kissing her neck.

"I'll be in there soon, love. I'm getting some good work done now."

In the morning, Kim drove to Dimitri's home in downtown Hood River for the meeting they had arranged at Dimitri and Sasha's request. Kim found the digs impressive and took Dimitri up on the offer of a latte made in his commercial-quality espresso machine.

Sasha, his girlfriend, Dimitri and Laurence all sat around the relaxed modern furniture in the living room with a cloudy but still impressive Gorge amphitheater view in the background. They let Kim know that they were impressed with her PR acumen and her connections to others in the wine industry in the Gorge. Revazov had a cult following among the young and hip natural wine crowd. But they needed to broaden their appeal and tap a more traditional clientele as well. They felt that they could use her expertise as Revazov scaled up to "the next level."

Kim was brimming with excitement as the conversation unfolded. This was what she had desired for so long after she had put her career on hold to have kids. It was one thing to have success through her partner's winery but quite another to be wanted by one of the fastest-growing, hippest new wineries in the area.

It was clear that there was a division of responsibilities within Revazov. Sasha made the wine, but Dimitri and Laurence ran the business side of things and they led the conversation. They initially proposed a consulting arrangement but let her know that they would consider the possibility of a partnership stake in their business at some point in the future. Kim demurred, pointing out that she already was a business partner in another winery. Inside, she was already thinking of how awesome it would be to be part owner of a hot, up-and-coming winery.

In her new role as a consultant, Kim started visiting Revazov for weekly marketing meetings late on Wednesday afternoons. That was a day her kids were with their dad. She had so much fun brainstorming with Sasha, his girlfriend and the tasting room manager. She was charged with implementing a new advertising and PR strategy and brought a new dose of business-like formalism to the meetings with plans and progress reports.

Kim didn't expect to see Scott around Revazov after the meetings because he was back teaching in the fall. But the last Wednesday in October, a blustery and wet day, she saw the light on in the house as she was pulling out from her meeting. She pulled back into her parking space, zipped up her parka, got out of the Q7 and strode up the walkway to Scott's house.

No one came to the door at first, but then there was Scott in an old flannel bathrobe.

Kim stood at the entry to the house in her parka, buffeted by the elements.

"Hey there! Come on in here and get dry!" Scott said.

Kim crossed the threshold.

"I got off a bit early today and thought I'd try to catch a late afternoon session at Doug's. It was blowing hard out there," Scott said.

"Was it worth it?"

"Totally."

"I'm working for Revazov now," Kim said.

"I heard. They just dropped off a couple bottles of this Georgian-style red blend and I was thinking about opening it. Join me?"

"I really need to get back to the other side of the river for dinner. But I suppose a sip wouldn't hurt." Scott looked hot in that ugly bathrobe as he walked over and flicked on the gas fireplace. He poured them glasses and they settled into the couch by the fire.

The blustery weather and the warmth of the fire went well with the dark, red wine. After a few sips, Kim lost herself in an animated description of all that was happening at Revazov. Scott listened intently.

After 15 minutes or so, Scott quieted her with a kiss and then one thing quickly led to another.

A half-hour later, Kim rose and dressed in the dim light. Scott couldn't keep his hands off her even as she clothed. He kissed the back of her neck and put his hands around her as she texted Camden.

She started moving faster.

"Sorry, I have to go," she said, pushing back Scott's advances but not without a long, sensuous departing kiss that recalled earlier times.

Camden had shifted their reservation at Solerra, a restaurant on the Hood River Waterfront, to 8:30 p.m. on Kim's request. It was 8:40 when she finally arrived. As they shared a pizza and salad, Kim explained to Camden that the meeting at Revazov had turned into a bit of an impromptu wine tasting. Camden was genuinely curious about what was happening at Revazov and peppered her with questions about their winemaking activities throughout dinner.

Camden supported this consultancy Kim had at Revazov. He knew it was important to her, but fuck, that whole place irritated him, irritated in a way that made him oddly obsessed by it.

He'd read over everything about them online. Their rise in the competitive Pacific Northwest wine industry over the last two years was impressive. They had write-ups in the Los Angeles Times and the Alaska Airlines in-flight magazine. Not to mention the 12,000 Instagram followers. He'd even gone so far as to call up one of his connections in a wine trade organization and get some of the figures they reported regarding sales and revenue. By either measure, they were now in line with the biggest wineries in the Gorge. It was unbelievable how well they were doing considering they were only a couple years old.

Sure, his operation had doubled in size in the last two years as well. But after years in business and big investments of time and money, he was pulling in about a tenth of the revenue that Revazov was.

Kim was used to keeping secrets. It wasn't exactly because she was a deceptive person. She was just fascinated by so many people and enjoyed so many connections with others that sometimes it could all get tangled up. She wasn't one for clear beginnings and endings. When it came down to it, she was close to a number of people, but no one besides her understood how it all fit together.

As the harvest season transitioned into late fall, she began the affair with Scott. When they'd been together before, it had been during a time when she and Camden were taking a "break" from their relationship. But now she was married to Camden. Their relationship wasn't open. Or maybe it was, a little bit, even if they hadn't said anything to that effect?

Likewise, Scott was in a relationship.

No, this wasn't good. She had not done this kind of thing before in her life. She'd always been true to her partner. Well, that was *largely* the case. There had been that time in her early twenties and then right after she and her ex were engaged. And she'd certainly had breaks from her relationship from Camden from time to time.

This would work itself out. But meanwhile, the affair was so delicious. And somehow it all fit into her work with Revazov that she was loving. They had a huge marketing budget and their meetings were so fun and energetic. She was connecting with journalists, launching an ad campaign and learning a ton about social media. She'd always loved the estate, too, and that's usually where she and Scott met.

On Thanksgiving weekend, she had a big family dinner at the Ross estate with her kids and Camden's. She left the house on the pretense that she had forgotten her laptop in Portland and had to drive back. Instead, she headed across the river and up to Scott's property. Scott's girlfriend was on the East Coast with family. An early-season snow had fallen and he was waiting for her with a fire, candlelight and a bottle of prosecco ready to open.

He made love to her slowly as she liked, pausing at times to increase the intensity. Afterward, they tiptoed through the snow to get into the hot tub and finish off the bubbly while enjoying the stars overhead. Later, curled up by the fire, they fell into their old banter. They had so much to say to each other and so little time.

The next day, Scott's friend Catherine and her daughter came out to the Gorge for a day-after-Thanksgiving get-together with Scott and Nate. It was a tradition that they had carried on for a few years now.

Their first task was hunting for Christmas trees. They hiked through the early season snow at Little John Sno-Park and were able to nab a couple gangly but appealing noble firs. Then they retreated to Scott's place. The kids played in the snow while Scott caught up with Cat over a bottle of Beaujolais nouveau that she had brought over.

"I can't believe the lame lines these guys give," Cat said as she showed him a message from some dude she had met on the Bumble dating app who had arranged a meeting with her but then canceled at the last minute.

Scott took her phone and read the message: "I'd love to rock your world, but my head's just not in the game."

"Gosh," Scott said, laughing. "Two clichés in one sentence. Good one. He looks a little bit like George W. Bush."

"He is cute, but what a fucking jerk. Just remember, Scott, it's not easy out here in the wild. You've got a good thing going with Rachel."

"It's going pretty well. I mean, yes, it's fine."

"Is something up?"

"No, really — it's fine."

"Seriously?"

"You'll never guess who has a job just down there in the winery," Scott said.

"Oh Scott, not her. Don't tell me she's around. Kim?"

"You guessed it."

"Stay away from that. Do you know how many sad stories I had to listen to about her two years ago?"

"We just have this connection, this spark. I'd almost forgotten about it."

"You've been talking to her? Oh Scott. Is she still with that same guy she wouldn't leave?"

"Yes, they actually got married, but I just wonder. I wonder if this time it could be different. We get each other and just click in a way that I don't with Rachel. I feel like Rachel is too much like me."

"Don't get pulled in, Scott. She's flaky. Remember 'it's complicated'?"

"Of course, I do," he said, sighing.

"We've just run into each other a couple times and talked," Scott said, looking away and blushing a bit.

Cat scowled. "Right. You're fucking her already. I know it."

"How 'bout we get the meal started?" Scott said.

13

Kim left the bathroom where she'd been adjusting her makeup for the past 10 minutes. She stood in the full-length mirror in the hallway to check out the finished product.

"As ever, you look stunning in a cocktail dress," Camden said, coming up behind her and putting his hands on her waist.

They were running a bit late.

Camden took the wheel of Kim's Q7 and they wound down the Hood River Valley on Highway 35 in the waning light of a dry Saturday in late January. Besides the two tracks of bare pavement cleared by the traffic, the road was covered with the red cinders used to provide traction on the snow and ice that had recently melted away. They were headed to the annual Gorge Wine Awards at the Columbia River Inn.

"Maybe this will be the year," Camden said.

"Could be. Seems like there is so much new talent out there every year."

"I know, but I feel like it's my, I mean, our, turn."

Kim put her hand on Camden's shoulder and squeezed.

After checking in for the event, they stopped to have their picture taken in front of one of those celebrity-style photo backdrops. Then Kim rushed over to greet one of her colleagues with whom she'd planned the festival in the fall, Julie from Savage Grace Winery. Camden headed for the bar. He got a scotch for himself and a glass of Analemma grenache for Kim, gave her the glass and then wandered over to Josh, one of the vintners he'd known since starting in the Gorge.

They were seated in a half-hour. The wine flowed freely over the course of a longish, somewhat mediocre dinner. Finally, the award ceremony got started. Kurt Mueller, a longtime Gorge winemaker who chaired the Gorge Wine Commission, emceed the proceedings.

Camden knew this was a small-time event, but it was still exhilarating to hear his name called when his 2018 Reserve Pinot won the best-in-class award. Their whole table whooped and hollered as he rose to take the prize. He recalled bagging a best-in-class and two gold medals the previous year.

The Gorge Wine Awards were mostly a promotional activity for the nascent Gorge wine scene which always seemed to be overshadowed by stuff going on in the Willamette Valley, the Yakima Valley or the Walla Walla area. But Camden did have his eye on their annual winery of the year award.

The award honored both excellence in winemaking and the wine tasting experience. Camden figured that with their recently opened estate tasting room and the consistent stream of awards that his wines had taken over the last few years, he was in a good position to take the prize. The winner of the award inevitably got a two-page article in the spring Gorge Guide and some press attention from publications further afield.

The judging panel included a wine writer and a sommelier from Portland but it was really steered by Mueller and his cronies. At last year's award ceremony, Mueller had said to Camden, maybe not in so many words, that Ross Wines was due to take the award.

After the prizes for individual wines, Mueller switched over to announcing the winners of the charity silent auction. As he worked his way through all the donated prizes, which ranged from dinners at fancy Portland restaurants to spa getaways on the coast to vacation rentals in Baja and Maui, it seemed to go on forever. Finally, Mueller moved on to the winery of the year award.

"This winery is one that took us all by surprise. Founded by a young, energetic winemaker and his father, they have brought new tastes, new ideas and new people to our small wine community. They are the first natural, all-organic winery to receive this honor."

Before Mueller could say it, Camden knew that it was Revazov. He reached for the bottle of pinot on the table and filled his glass up to the rim.

Usually Camden was the sober one who took the wheel after a social event, but this time it was Kim. As soon as she closed the door of the Audi, Camden started his rant.

"I'm telling you, Kim, there's something off base about that place. Sure, they've got 20 times the followers on Instagram as we do, but how the fuck, how the fuck are they doing 20,000 cases a year? They are among the top 20 producers in the state?"

"I'm not gonna lie, love, that place has pretty amazing energy."

"It was my year, Kim. This was our time. Revazov, it's all smoke and mirrors natural wine bullshit. I thought Mueller, if anyone, would see through that shit."

"As you've always said, babe, the Gorge is a wine backwater and the Gorge Wine Awards is a small-time affair."

Scott paced nervously back and forth at Gate C23 of Portland International Airport where the Alaska Airlines flight to Palm Springs was boarding. The gate agent had called all rows about five minutes earlier and only a few stray passengers were still entering the jet bridge.

It had taken some strange contortions of their schedules to get things aligned. A substitute teacher (a halfway decent one, Scott made sure) was teaching Scott's two AP history classes. Kim had traded days with her kids' dad and rearranged some business meetings.

He breathed a sigh of relief as he spotted Kim in the

distance, walking swiftly up the concourse toward him. She was wearing a loose-fitting white sweater, some skinny jeans and ankle high leather boots. Her recently done hair bounced with each stride.

"Let's do this," she said as she approached Scott. She looked him straight in the eyes and gave him a full kiss on the lips before turning to board the flight.

They plunked into two seats in Row 2, first class, thanks to Kim's huge frequent flier balance.

"My ex was late picking them up, as usual," Kim said. Then she turned to the flight attendant and let her know that they both would like mimosas.

The sun was shockingly bright as they exited the airport in Palm Springs. They rented an SUV and drove to their Airbnb rental, a small, single-story home with midcentury modern touches that was tucked into the eclectic Araby Cove neighborhood. The place was modest but tastefully done and had a fabulous poolside view of the San Jacinto mountains.

Upon entering the house, Kim skipped off to the bedroom to change into her swimsuit while Scott headed into the kitchen to mix up some fresh margaritas. By the time he'd whipped up a pitcher, Scott could already see Kim through the sliding door to the backyard. She was lying on a sun lounger next to the small pool.

"God, this feels heavenly," Kim said as Scott walked outside with margaritas in hand.

"I think we're dying up there in Oregon for lack of vitamin D. Can I put on some sunscreen?"

"I'll take some of that coconut oil there. I'm not worried about a burn. I was just in Maui a couple weeks ago."

Scott kneeled on a towel next to Kim's lounger. The reality that Kim had done a tropical getaway with Camden just a couple weeks before stung, but also sort of aroused him.

Kim lay there with her eyes closed, her lightly tanned

skin reflecting the midday sun. He slowly massaged the coconut oil all over her voluptuous front side. Then she flipped over and he did her back, the back of her arms, then her legs, starting with her feet and working his way up to her thighs, where her skimpy bikini bottom cut into her buttocks.

As Scott's fingers wandered, Kim uttered a pleasurable moan. The backyard was very private and that made it easy. They spent the rest of the afternoon and evening in a sensual haze of poolside decadence.

Scott had booked the Airbnb with the knowledge that it was in the same neighborhood as the former Palm Springs home of his favorite actor, Steve McQueen. Apparently, McQueen and his second wife Ali MacGraw had spent a lot of time in the midcentury modern love nest. As Scott headed out for a trail run the next morning, he made sure to catch a glimpse of the place.

When he returned he was on a runner's high. Kim had done her morning pilates by the pool and she was in a good mood as well. They went out for a leisurely brunch, then drove out to Joshua Tree to look around a bit before retreating to poolside mode in the afternoon.

Scott had never been to Palm Springs, but Kim had an aunt and some cousins there, so she was very familiar with the area. By late afternoon, Scott was feeling pretty spent from all the sun, tequila and sex. But Kim insisted that they rally and go to a favorite restaurant for dinner, a fancy steakhouse sort of place.

Scott ordered a martini and Kim went with the bar's variation on a margarita as they waited at the bar for their table to be ready. Given the afternoon decadence by the pool, the drinks didn't elevate their moods like they usually would at cocktail hour. Instead, Scott could sense a headache coming on.

A diminutive woman in her mid-forties with impeccable SoCal grooming approached them at the bar.

"Kim, I thought that was you. I had no idea you were here! I haven't seen you since the wedding I don't think!"

"Deb, this is Scott. Scott, Deb is one of my cousins who lives down here."

"Hi there," Deb said, giving Kim the eye as she shook Scott's hand.

"He's an old college friend. We're catching up," Kim said somewhat perfunctorily.

They chatted a bit about various family news and then Deb said she had to go.

"Have fun … catching up," Deb said with a wink.

"We will," said Kim.

After they were seated at their table, Scott got a text from Rachel asking how his weekend was going. Scott relayed a fictional anecdote about the trail run that he had taken with the friend he was supposedly visiting.

The deception ate away at Scott. It took him back to the compromised relationship he'd had before with Kim. With an afternoon and early evening of drinking working against his better judgment, Scott turned the conversation to the topic that they'd been avoiding all weekend: their relationship.

"I don't like this place we're in, Kim. It's not right."

"Scott, remember, I'm married."

"I want to make this real."

"Scott, this is amazing. Don't get me wrong. But my life is so intertwined with …" She paused. "Him and the winery. We've built a business together. I can't just walk away from that."

The waiter approached the table to take their orders.

"But we could build something new, something for ourselves."

Kim turned to respond to the waiter.

They neglected to return to that topic for the rest of the evening.

Two weeks after the Gorge Wine Awards, Sasha and

Dimitri Revazov announced to their employees and friends that they were hosting a big bash at the winery to celebrate the winery of the year award. When Kim asked Camden to go, he immediately agreed. Did he relish the idea of hanging around that crowd? No. But it'd be bad form to retreat and lick his wounds. Besides, he was somewhat curious about the place.

The party was held in Revazov's "Wy'east Room," a spacious meeting room with a spectacular view located on the second floor of the newly constructed Revazov wine production facility. It felt wild and festive compared to the award ceremony at the Columbia River Inn. Furniture had been cleared to make room for a DJ and a dance area, which was already occupied by a couple of young Revazov tasting room attendants when Camden and Kim arrived.

Among the crowd mingling at the other end of the room, Camden noticed Charlie Albrechts. What an asshole. The guy was narrating an apparently hilarious story to three 20-something girls. They were practically doubled over laughing.

Albrechts was in his forties and the third-generation chairman of the Pacific Northwest's largest wine distributor. With a full head of disheveled bleached-blond hair and a permanent tan, he had a look of casual excess. He wore a shiny pink silk shirt that flowed over a dad bod gut and down to distressed denim designer jeans. His wine distribution company was connected to all the right restaurants and wine stores in Oregon and Washington and had turned up their nose at Camden's small-volume winery.

Camden fell into conversation with a couple who owned another vineyard near Revazov while Kim bounced around, chatting with some of her connections. Going to refresh his drink, Camden couldn't help but wander a bit. The recently built structure, gigantic by the standards of Gorge wineries, had extensive wine making and bottling facilities on the first level and offices and meeting rooms on the second.

He strolled down the hallway to the offices, which were

mostly locked up. Then he went down the back stairway to the warehouse-style first floor. The digitally secured doorway to the industrial-looking wine making area was propped open with a wooden wedge. The equipment, which Camden knew well, was all top-end stuff. Hundreds of barrels were neatly arrayed in a sophisticated racking system.

Camden noticed what appeared to be a bottling process that was underway. He examined the bottling line. It was a top-of-the-line model built by an Italian manufacturer. It appeared that the bottling operation had been going on recently, maybe even today. Nearby was a pallet loaded to the hilt with bottles that had a label that he didn't recognize from the tasting room: "Northwest Kvevri Syrah - 2018."

What the fuck, he thought, grabbing one of the bottles and dropping it into the inside pocket of his down parka. He wanted to find out what all the fuss was about.

When he got back to the party, Kim was out on the dance floor with some of her 20-something coworkers. Camden didn't like electronic dance music. Indie rock was more his style. The whole scene was a bit annoying, but he knew better than to encourage an early exit. Let her party, he thought. That might put her in an amorous mood.

He took the bottle outside to walk around the estate. It was an unusually starry night in February and the sky was spectacular here high above the Gorge.

His feet crunched on the seven-day-old snow as he walked out to the picnic area adjacent to the tasting room. He found a bench and uncorked the wine with the corkscrew he almost always kept on his person. Though in a way he hoped the wine would disappoint, he was looking forward to an illicit drink out here by himself on this beautiful night, toasty in his $850 Patagonia down parka.

After popping the cork, he was puzzled as he took in the stale aroma. When he took a sip of the red liquid, he uttered an involuntary "blah" and spit it out, leaving a violent red splatter on the snow. This stuff was awful. It tasted stale and sweet like a boxed wine from Costco. This was what all the

THE ECLIPSE

fuss was about? He knew this natural wine stuff was overrated but really?

Just then he heard some footsteps approaching.

"I think you've got the right idea. I like it much better out here. What are you drinking there?"

"Trust me man, you don't want this toxic waste."

"Well in that case, I've got a flask of something perhaps more fitting for this weather."

It was Scott, Camden realized. They'd met in passing a few times.

"I could use a shot of that if nothing else to clear the palette." Camden took a sip from the flask. Uncomfortable silence followed for a minute.

"You're a backcountry skier, right?" Scott asked.

"I am," Camden said.

"Living in this place part time over here in Washington, I've been exploring Mount Adams more. Ever been up to Adams at this time of year?" Scott asked.

"No."

"When we had that clear set of days in early February, my buddy and I skied up into the Mount Adams high country and camped out two nights. It takes some time to get in there but in the winter, it feels so remote and beautiful."

"I skied off the Hood summit last week," Camden responded.

"That's a little too steep for me," Scott said. "I usually park my gear on the Hogsback. I did ski off Middle Sister last spring and that was awesome."

The back-and-forth on backcountry skiing continued for a few minutes until Scott's girlfriend Rachel came out to get Scott. She wanted him to come in and talk with one of their trail running friends they both knew who lived in White Salmon.

Camden thanked Scott for the drink and then said, "Let's get out there one of these days."

"I'm always up for a tour," Scott replied as he and his

girlfriend walked back to the wine production building, their feet crunching in the snow.

When they were gone, Camden took the wine bottle, poured it out behind a bush and then hurled it as far as he could out into the vineyard. He sat there for a while wondering how it was that this fancy bottle of wine tasted so shitty, then finally went in to retrieve Kim.

Kim was feeling the party the next day. She didn't have her kids that weekend and the tasting room was bound to be quiet, so she relished the chance to sleep in. Camden already had heated up some croissants and had a fresh French press ready for her as she sauntered out of bed close to 10. He seemed in a good mood and said that he might go up to the mountain for a few runs since it was supposed to be a sunny afternoon.

She wasn't prepared when he told her that he'd hung out with Scott outside the party the night before. For some reason he'd omitted that detail as they were driving home. Kim was afraid that she was blushing as he told her that they'd shared a flask of bourbon. She gulped down an extra swig of coffee. He also confessed to filching a bottle of the Kvevri Syrah.

"The wine from that bottle was terrible. How the fuck are they making money with that?"

Kim just sipped her coffee and let him continue.

"And I saw Albrechts there. That fucker. I know they're using him as a distributor. They're in New Seasons and high-end restaurants in Portland and Seattle. And working on an East Coast distributor. How did they pull that off?"

"It's good wine and good energy," Kim said. She came up to him and gave him a playful kiss. "But they don't have the artistry of your wines," she said in a somewhat teasing tone.

After Camden left, Kim couldn't resist texting Scott about the night before. She'd seen him at the party with Rachel and been so jealous.

14

It was a typically dreary February Wednesday at the Ross Wines estate. Kim was back in Portland with her kids and Camden felt a bit restless. He made some adjustments to a few of the barrels he'd racked in the fall and then put in some time pruning out in the vineyard.

He couldn't stop thinking about that funky bottle of Revazov wine. He went on the Revazov website and searched around for it. He was curious as to how much they were charging for that nasty stuff. There was no sign of it on the website so he called the tasting room.

"Hey, a friend was telling me about a wonderful wine you guys make. It's called the Northwest Kvevri Syrah, 2018 vintage. I was wondering where I could get a bottle of it and how much it is?"

"Okay, no problem. Let me check."

The phone went silent for a while.

"Sir, that's one we don't have available anymore, unfortunately."

"Are there any wine stores that would have it around?"

"Let me check. "

More silence.

"I'm sorry but I can't help you. I'm told that the 2018 is not available now. Our 2019 Syrah is wonderful though, I'd recommend it."

"Well, do you know what the price of it was when you did have it available in the tasting room."

"Actually, I don't think we ever did."

"I'm in the wine industry, do you have a wholesale price

for it?"

Camden heard some keyboarding sounds through the phone.

"$550 per case."

"Wholesale?"

"Yes, that's correct. You can work through Albrechts if you'd like to place an order."

"Thanks for checking."

As the afternoon wore on, Camden still felt restless. He invited his buddy Todd McKinley, a winemaker who worked for one of the bigger Gorge wineries, Hermann Creek Cellars, out for drinks that night.

A few hours later, they met at the "river shitty," Todd's affectionate name for the River City Saloon, a longtime downtown Hood River drinking establishment that served as a lively venue for bands on weekends, especially during the summer.

"Sure, I'll take another," Camden said to the waitress as they settled into the booth after a game of pool. The place was pretty much dead with six or so other people there.

"Hey man, maybe you'd have some insight into this. What's up with Revazov?"

"That place is fucking on fire," Todd said.

"I think there's something weird about it. I was poking around in their shop during the big party they had a couple weeks back and I filched a bottle of their most expensive stuff from the bottling line. I swear it tasted like Ernest and Julio Gallo. I mean it was bad."

"I've heard some funny things about them," Todd said.

"Like what?" Camden asked.

"You know Chip over in Yakima, right?"

"Yeah, my syrah guy."

"He was telling me that they paid him in bitcoin for his grapes. They gave him an extra 20 percent for taking crypto."

"Well, I don't think they were using those grapes in this vintage," Camden said. "But most of their stuff is at least halfway palatable wine."

"Why do you even care that much about this place?"

Camden explained, probably being more honest than he otherwise would have because of the beer in him. He told Todd about being outbid for the Revazov property and how annoying it was that Kim was being drawn away from their winery for the consulting gig. He explained how he'd looked into the corporate structure of Darden Wine Holdings and discovered that they owned a few other wineries on the West Coast, but that the ownership details were murky.

"Fucking natural wine bullshit," Camden said, taking a sip from his third draft.

"Well, you should figure out what's up with that two buck upchuck," Todd said. "Somebody is getting screwed in that deal."

A few days later, Camden called his dad.

"Hey Dad, good morning."

"Camden! Always great to hear from you."

The gravely sound of his dad's voice was familiar and also slightly discomforting to Camden.

They did the usual small talk about what had been going on in their lives. Then Camden brought up what was on his mind.

"Dad, Kim's been working for this newish winery in the Gorge. Actually, it's located on the property we bid on a couple years ago. I've been looking into them a bit. I think there's something strange about their business practices."

"Well, what do you mean?"

"It seems like they are way too successful given the size of their operations and how new they are. I was in their production area at a party awhile back and came across a strange pallet of wine. Crappy, almost undrinkable, red wine they are selling for $45 a bottle."

"Well, you know, the wine business is mostly marketing. Just because they're selling some mediocre stuff doesn't mean that they are doing something wrong."

Camden hated that line about wine being mostly about marketing. His dad said it way too often.

His dad continued, "Is somebody actually buying the stuff?"

"I don't know, I suppose they must be. How would you figure out what was going on?"

"You'd need to find out where that funny wine is going. I suppose if it's not drinkable, there might be some kind of scam going on. They might be recording the wine as being sold and doing something else with it."

"Why would they do that?"

"Well, maybe they are trying to inflate their business on the books to impress an investor or secure a loan."

"Got it."

"Take care of yourself, son. Remember, you've got your own business to concern yourself with."

"True. Very true. Thanks for talking."

"Have a good week, Cam. My best to Kim. Talk to you soon."

A week and half later, on the second Sunday in March, Kim told Camden that she had a meeting up at Revazov. Camden decided to surprise her and drive up to the winery while she was at the meeting, figuring that they could have a drink in the tasting room after she was done.

As Camden pulled his truck into the familiar driveway of Revazov, he noticed a white Sprinter van parked next to the garage door of the big winemaking building where the party had been. Camden continued to the customer parking area, got out of his truck and walked into the tasting room building, which had been created from the old barn on the property.

A 20-something girl in an Oregon State hoodie was seated at the bar chatting with the tasting attendant, who Camden recognized from the party. She was a statuesque young woman who was wearing skinny jeans and a loose wool sweater that revealed a bare shoulder. Besides a couple of retirees at a table, they were the only ones there.

Camden's arrival forced an interruption to the conversation that the two young women were having. The tasting attendant floated over to Camden, who had taken a seat at the bar a few stools away.

"Hi, welcome to Revazov. How are you this afternoon?"

"You know, I'm good. I was wondering if I could try the flight of reds."

"Excellent choice. Let me get that put together for you."

She got out a wooden tray and six mini carafes and began filling each carafe with a couple of ounces of wine.

When the tray was complete, she did her spiel, introducing each varietal as if it were a person she knew.

"The Georgian-style red blend, this one gets along with everyone. The pinot, on the other hand, is reserved and kind of keeps to itself when it first hits your palate, but then opens up with this sensual blackberry and spice."

After she was done with the lineup, she added, "All of these wines are naturally fermented. Sasha crushes the grapes, filters them and they go into the kvervi and stay there, completely undisturbed. There are no additives or adjustments."

She continued. "Natural wine always has its own character. I get so excited when a new vintage comes out, it's like meeting someone new!"

"Sounds a bit unpredictable," Camden said with a friendly but questioning look.

She was an attractive girl and so effusive about the wine that Camden was almost buying it. He took his time with each one, swirling his glass, peering through the liquid and then taking in the scent before taking a sip.

The Georgian-style red blend wasn't bad. But the two pinots were way too acidic, almost vinegary and the Georgian saperavi tasted a bit off. So he asked for a full glass of the red blend.

Eventually, the other woman wandered over and the three of them began conversing. Delilah, the tasting room attendant, had moved out to the Gorge to get into the wine business after graduating from Lewis & Clark College the previous fall. The girl in the hoodie, Madison, was the driver of the van that Camden had seen on the way in. He talked with them a bit about the late February Gorge weather and the ski season. They both knew Kim from Revazov. He confessed that he was a winemaker himself and they gossiped a bit about the Gorge wine scene.

Kim lay flat on her stomach on Scott's bed, her voluminous hair fanned out on the pillow. Her well-manicured fingers were splayed on the headboard of the bed as she braced herself, arms extended. She moaned rhythmically.

Scott slipped his hand around her neck and tightened his grip slightly, just as she liked. He gazed out the window in his bedroom at the cloudy overcast view of the Gorge, distracting himself from the intensity of the sex for a second.

After a minute or two, he paused and shifted her onto her back. Their eyes met for a final moment of passion.

After lying still for a few minutes, Scott got up to refill their wine glasses while Kim checked the phone that she had been consciously ignoring for the last hour. She saw a text from Camden.

> Hey babe, thought we could meet for a drink at Revazov after your meeting? I'm here at the tasting room.

"Holy fuck," Kim exclaimed, "Camden's here!"
"Fuck, fuck, fuck," Kim said as she scrambled to put her clothes back on. "I need to go down there and meet him."

Camden left the tasting room and walked out on the picnic area. This was the spot where he had hung out with Scott a couple of weeks earlier, but now it was free of snow. He checked his phone. No message from Kim yet. He wandered down toward the winemaking facility. The pathway to the building said, "Winery Staff Only." Camden noted the security cameras mounted on the light posts alongside the walkway.

Instead of going to the main entrance to the winery offices, he wandered around the building to the loading area where the Sprinter van was parked. Madison was there and two guys were loading wine cases into the back of the van.

"No sign of my wife, guess she is still in that meeting," he said to Madison.

Camden peered in through the garage door to the production area that he'd explored during the party. Pallets of wine cases were stacked near the garage door. There were a couple of younger dudes working the bottling line.

"I'd love to look at that bottling line," Camden said as he stepped forward into the production area. He walked over to the bottling line and awkwardly greeted the young men working the bottler.

"Hey guys. This is quite a machine you have here."

He could see they were bottling more of that '18 Kvevri Syrah that he'd tasted at the party.

"So how is it you load the labels in?" he asked one of them.

As the kid turned to explain over the hum of the machinery, Camden slipped the tracking device into a half-filled case, pretending to examine the label on one of the bottles.

"Cool, cool," he said as the kid showed him the labeler.

"I don't think you're supposed to be in here, by the way," said the kid.

"Oh right, my bad," Camden said. He walked back out of the winemaking area and around to the office entrance of the facility and then rang the doorbell to get in. No one answered.

Then his phone buzzed with a message from Kim.

What a nice surprise, I'm in the tasting room!

Camden walked back to the tasting room and there was Kim at the bar.

"Hey babe, I was just up at the production building looking around for you."

"Oh we must have missed each other. This place is big!"

They sat at the bar and got two glasses. Camden went with more of the red blend while Kim tried an orange wine.

"I'm surprised to see you out here. I thought you weren't such a big fan of this place," Kim said.

"Maybe I'm coming around," Camden said.

Kim seemed unusually interested in hearing about his day.

"Would you two like another pour?" Delilah asked them. "This may be your last chance for a while. The governor just announced that all bars and restaurants are closing tomorrow due to the coronavirus."

Just then, Sasha and some of the winemaking crew showed up in the tasting room.

Sasha spoke to everyone in the room, announcing the order from the governor and adding, "I can't predict what the next days or weeks will hold. What I do know is that at this moment of uncertainty, we can enjoy some wine and company together." Delilah opened a couple of bottles and everyone, employees and the few customers that remained, drank and conversed about the pandemic that was upending life around the world.

Camden had purchased the tracking device online and then picked up a prepaid SIM card at a Plaid Pantry. There was an app on his phone that showed its location.

The next day, he could see the wine being picked up from Revazov. It was delivered to a location that proved easy to identify as one of Albrechts' wine distribution warehouses in Portland. There it sat for just a few days before moving to another location.

He could see from the Google Maps-enabled app that

the wine was in a building in Portland's outer NE industrial area that ran along the Columbia River, east of the Portland airport. Some internet sleuthing on various directory websites did not reveal the occupant of the building.

A day later, Camden drove to Portland with three hours to spare before he was supposed to pick up his daughter. He took the NE 181st Avenue/NE Airport Way exit, following Google Maps directions that wound him through a maze of warehouse and industrial properties. He'd been in this area once or twice to pick up some heavy equipment for his winery but really didn't know his way around. The address was one unit in a pale yellow, sheet metal industrial building that occupied an entire block. Each unit had a large garage door and an adjacent entry door.

He pulled into the wide parking lot, designed to accommodate semi-trucks and parked his pickup a few units away from the one where he'd located the tracking device. He walked over to the doorway. Besides the street address number plaque above the door, the unit had no other signage and the venetian blinds on the door window were closed.

He got back in his truck, started it up and planned to head for his house. But just as he got moving, he had another thought. He drove the truck around to the street on the other side of the building.

There was no entry point on this side. Instead, there was a sidewalk and a setback with landscaping. Some of the units had windows. He drove along slowly, using the navigation on his phone to locate the unit that interested him. It had windows with some shrubs in front of them. He parked the truck a little ways away.

Camden walked down the sidewalk and into the shrubbery to stand next to the windows of the unit in question. The shrubs weren't very well trimmed and partially obscured the windows so he wasn't that conscious of being seen.

He could see the inside of an office through the windows

and noticed that one of them was cracked open for ventilation.

He looked around behind him. The street was quiet. He got his fingernails under the screen frame and pushed up and pulled and it popped right out. He slid the window open and hoisted himself inside headfirst, dropping onto the carpeted floor with his hands. The tiny office was nearly barren save for a stack of papers on a desk and a shredder on the floor.

Beyond the office was a cavernous garage-like industrial space. There were empty pallets stacked in the corner and two large recycling dumpsters. A quick examination revealed that the dumpsters were filled with empty Revazov wine bottles and broken-down wine case boxes. Near the dumpsters was a white plastic slop sink stained red in the basin.

A cursory glance at the papers in the office revealed that they were invoices or bills of lading from the pallets of wine. Camden snapped pictures of a few invoices and the inside of the garage space.

Then he paused and looked around the office. There it was, sitting on the desk: the tracking device he had placed in the wine case. He put it in his pocket.

He walked back out into the main warehouse area and then he saw it. A security camera. Fuck.

He could try to trace it to a recording device and destroy that. But it looked likely that it was connected via Wi-Fi to the internet. Probably recording to the cloud. Hopefully they wouldn't detect the break-in and look at the footage.

The next day Camden called the New Seasons corporate office and asked to speak to the wine buyer. Cheryl Middlebury called him back in 30 minutes. He explained that he had some sensitive information about their wine purchases and asked to meet her in person.

"Well, they're advising us to avoid in-person meetings with this coronavirus thing, but I suppose I could make an exception."

In a half-hour, Camden dropped by New Seasons' modern, industrial chic office space located in Revolution Hall. He recognized Cheryl from various wine events in the area. She was probably close to Camden's age but had an edgy, hip style. She wore slip-on Vans, skinny jeans and a halter top that showed off the ink on her shoulders. Camden noticed a faint shade of purple in her dark, short-cropped hair.

"Nice to see you, Camden. How is Ross Wines getting along?"

"Not bad, all things considered. Alright if we talk somewhere private?"

She motioned to the fishbowl conference room in the open floor plan office.

"I know this may seem strange," Camden said, "but I have some information to share with you about Albrechts. I think you're being charged for wine that you didn't buy."

"What?"

"Unless you buy wine to throw away, that is."

She gave him a confused look.

"If I share this with you, will you promise to leave me out of it?"

"Okay, fair enough."

Camden showed her picture of the invoice with the charges listed for Revazov.

"Do you recognize this delivery location or this wine label?"

Cheryl pulled out her laptop and logged into some kind of business software. "I don't see a record for that charge, or evidence that we've ever purchased any of that Kvevri Syrah label. I don't see this charge anywhere either.

"Let me call Albrechts."

Cheryl got on her phone and immediately reached someone at Albrechts. Camden heard her report the invoice number and the wine label. She went back and forth with the person on the phone and then waited a bit before saying thanks and ending the call.

"She found the invoice and told me it had been paid," said Cheryl. When I told her that it wasn't in our system, she checked with her boss who said that the charge was misassigned to our account. Nothing for us to worry about."

"Okay," said Camden. "I'd watch those charges carefully. I think something strange is going on with Revazov."

"They are actually one of our more popular new wines."

"Wonderful," Camden said, a bit sarcastically. "Thanks for looking into this, Cheryl."

"Take care of yourself, Camden. Stay healthy!"

15

Laurence had to wait 10 minutes after their appointed time for Mr. Chen to finally appear in the Zoom room. They began with the usual pleasantries. Then Laurence gave some updates regarding the ever-expanding Darden Wine Holdings portfolio. So as not to seem alarming, he waited to bring up the most urgent matter on his mind.

"We've got a jealous vintner here," Laurence said as he shared the shots of Camden at the winery, then the shots of him at the warehouse. "He's Camden Ross, the husband of Kim Marseilles, a consultant at Revazov. He's a small-time winemaker in the Gorge."

"What does he know?"

"We got a call from Charlie Albrechts, who said one of the wine buyers approached them about a charge for our wine that was under their account. I suspect Ross was the one who tipped them off.

"Albrechts covered it fine," Laurence continued, "and it doesn't sound like anyone's alarmed. Charlie says that he's got a better way of doing the accounting, a different way to pass through charges. Something about subaccounts. It'll still pass an audit, he says."

"Albrechts has been such an effective way to move my assets into our businesses. I'd hate to upset that arrangement."

Laurence said, "I do know that if the heat came on Charlie Albrechts, he'd sell us out to the feds in a second."

With the screen share still on, Laurence switched to a shot of Scott and Kim, taken outside Scott's home on the

Revazov vineyard. And then a fuzzier shot of them inside the house. "Something else you should be aware of: Our man Scott Larson is fucking Ross' wife."

"Oh my," Mr. Chen murmured as he examined the pictures. "I didn't know Larson had it in him," he added, pausing.

"Let them fuck. I like that. They both work for us and if we know their little secret, that could have advantages. In fact, we've talked about a bigger role for Larson and I don't see that changing this."

"This whole thing seems a bit volatile. Maybe we should cool things down with Revazov given this extra scrutiny." said Laurence.

Laurence could see Mr. Chen light up a cigar on the Zoom call. He loved to smoke as he expounded on grand strategy.

"Laurence, I don't want to cool things down. I see opportunity in this virus. In fact, I just talked to my broker in the Cayman Islands. The put options I bought in February have paid off handsomely. I want to deploy those funds to expand Darden."

"How do we handle Ross?" Laurence asked.

"Let's watch him. We can apply technology to do that. At the same time, let's see if we can bring him inside our operation, get him on our team. This could work out to the benefit of all parties. He's obviously agitated by his wife's involvement with us, but maybe we can make him see things our way," Chen said, exhaling a puff of smoke from his cigar that completely obscured him on camera.

Scott ran his hands along the contours of Kim's naked body.

It was 11 a.m. on a Tuesday in the first week of May and they were lying in Scott's bed.

"I had a conversation with Laurence yesterday," Scott said. "They want me to come in as part of a new real estate partnership they are creating and acquire more vineyard land to develop."

Kim's eyes widened. "Really? Tell me more."

"Well, I don't know a whole lot more, but he said it could be 'lucrative,' that I could potentially quit my day job to do it."

"That sounds like it could be amazing, Scott."

Kim began massaging Scott's chest.

"I'm going to think about it."

"Scott, you've been teaching for what, 20 years? You've told me yourself you're ready for a change."

"For some reason, I don't really feel like I have much choice when I'm talking to Laurence. He knows about us, Kim."

Kim sat upright.

"What the fuck?"

"Yep, I guess somebody saw us on the estate. He's worried about Camden finding out about us and it blowing up."

"Oh fuck."

"Laurence said we should quote unquote 'bring Camden in.' That I should befriend him so that he doesn't come to suspect anything. And they'd like to get him involved with Darden Wine Holdings, too. They believe that he's been talking bad around town about Revazov, spreading false rumors."

"It doesn't surprise me. He hates the place," Kim said.

"I suppose I could ask him to go backcountry skiing," Scott said. "I think the trailheads on Mount Hood will reopen soon."

"Right," Kim said, in thought.

Scott sighed. "Kim, I really don't want to keep up this deception. I want to break it off with Rachel. I want us to be a real couple this time."

"Scott, in case you forgot, I'm married. And at a time like this, with a pandemic and all, well, it's not a time to make a change."

"I'm not like you, I can't do this polyamorous thing."

She glared at him. "I'm NOT polyamorous. But to put it bluntly, I'd need to know there's a future if I were ever to leave my marriage. That we'd have a real partnership and the means to pursue our dreams."

The next day Kim gave Scott Camden's number and Scott texted him.

> Hey Camden, Scott Larson here. The Hood backcountry is reopening on May 8th. How about a ski tour? Maybe we could find some spring corn snow on Saturday? Weather looks good. Scott.
>
> Hey there Scott. That sounds good. What did you have in mind?
>
> How about Cooper Spur?
>
> Wy'East could be even better.

Scott knew of the Wy'East Face, a steep snowfield high above Mount Hood Meadows ski resort. He had read about it and seen plenty of shots on Instagram but had never skied it. It had been on his list, sort of, but it was known to be a dangerous slope in all but the most optimal conditions. Despite his hesitation, he couldn't back down from Camden Ross.

> I've wanted to try that for a while. Wy'East it is.

If the surface were hard and unforgiving, a fall could mean a high-speed slide down the 2,000-foot face, terminating in exposed rocks. However, on a sunny spring day, the surface would probably soften up to "corn snow" conditions which would make for satisfying and relatively easy turns.

THE ECLIPSE

Scott drove from Portland and Camden came from Hood River on Saturday morning. They met at the Mount Hood Meadows parking lot. The forecast was for partly cloudy skies, moderate winds and a high near 55 at the top of the mountain.

Camden led as they ascended along the border of the ski area with climbing skins on their skis. Scott had telemark gear whereas Camden had a lightweight alpine touring setup. Scott could feel an aggressiveness in the pace set by Camden but he didn't have any trouble keeping up.

Eventually, they popped out of the trees and onto the Vista Ridge, which runs along the top of the ski area. It was windy above the trees and they both stopped and added a shell. The snow was hard and icy. Hopefully, it would soften up, Scott thought.

As they skinned higher, Scott periodically looked up at the mountain towering above. The Wy'East Face was a giant white wall dropping down from a 10,500-foot ridge connected to the mountain's summit. There was a little notch above a rock band that Scott had scoped out from pictures on the web as the termination point of their route and he kept eyeing it nervously as they climbed.

After they passed the Cascade Express lift, they headed up the ridge above the Dallas Bowl. Eventually, it got too steep to move up the mountain on skis and climbing skins, so they stopped on an island of exposed rock to put on crampons and pull out their ice axes.

"God this wind sucks," Scott said.

"Yeah, maybe it'll back off as we get up higher," Camden said.

"Still pretty firm snow, too," Scott said.

"Just let the sun do its work," Camden replied.

They continued straight up the face. The horizon to their right was defined by the steeply angled slope and a cobalt blue sky. The vast Eastern Oregon desert stretched out below.

As Scott watched the back of Camden's legs confidently

kick steps into the icy slope, he thought about the weekend in Palm Springs with Kim. The freckled skin of her chest as she lay in her bikini by the pool. The sophisticated, sexy way she looked lying there with her Côte d'Azur sunglasses on.

And this man was her husband.

The thought gave him a surge of adrenaline and he moved past Camden, taking the lead. He front pointed his crampons as he picked up the pace and approached the band of rocks that flanked the final pitch.

Scott reached the ridge first with Camden a couple of minutes behind. The view to the south of Mount Jefferson and the distant Three Sisters was spectacular.

"Beautiful morning up here," Camden said understatedly as he made the ridge.

The wind was slightly mellower on the ridge. They took some time to gaze down at the South Climb route where they could see dozens of climbers making their way along massive Crater Rock and up the spine known as the Hogsback that leads to the final pitch to Mount Hood's summit.

"I'm a little worried that the snow's still on the firm side. This wind is keeping it hard. Wonder if we should wait a bit for it to soften?" Scott said.

"Ahhh, I think it's pretty much there," Camden said. "And if it's a bit firm up here, we'll get to enjoy the corn window lower down."

Scott could tell that the snow was still icy in the steepest part of the descent.

"Okay, let's do this," Scott said.

They made the transition to ski gear in a few minutes.

"After you," Scott said.

"As you wish," Camden said.

As he dropped onto the face, Scott could hear the scraping of Camden's skis on the icy surface of the face, which started at a gentler angle then rolled onto a steep pitch. Camden quickly carved a few aggressive turns and then stopped and waited for Scott next to a rocky outcropping.

Scott's heart and head were pounding. His launch was more cautious, lurching and he made a couple poorly formed survival turns between long traverses. The snow was super icy and fast. He eventually made his way over to Camden and stopped.

Camden then dropped into the steepest part of the descent, carving beautiful turns at controlled speed.

Scott waited, then followed. He moved cautiously but got more confident as he sensed the snow softening. When he was about a third of the way down the face, he began to move faster, attempting to mimic Camden's more aggressive set of tracks.

But the speed was more than he was used to and one of his edges lost grip on an icy patch. In an instant, he slammed down on his hip and started sliding headfirst down the slope.

"Oh shiiiit!" Scott exclaimed.

He flailed about, picking up speed, trying to arrest himself with his poles and skis.

Somehow, he managed to catch an edge of his ski and slow down, but not before having descended more than a couple hundred feet. When he came to a stop, he was shaking with fear and shock. He waved to Camden who was a quarter mile away or so.

"Everything okay, buddy?" Camden asked, when Scott skied over to him.

"Just a little slip on the ice."

They returned to the cars without saying much and had a beer on the tailgate of Scott's truck.

Scott heard Camden's phone buzz.

Camden answered it and talked for a minute.

Then he asked Scott, "Feel like coming over to our place for dinner? Kim reminded me we've got some steaks we could throw on the grill. You could bring Rachel over. As far as the virus thing, well, we can keep our distance."

This was a weird proposition, Scott thought.

"Sure," he said, pausing, "Rachel is in town. Let me check with her and get back to you."

"Sounds like a plan."

A few hours later, Rachel and Scott were at the threshold of Kim and Camden's place at the Ross Wines vineyard. It was a doorway that Scott knew all too well.

Kim wore a loose-fitting wool sweater and Camden a flannel shirt and jeans. They made a good-looking couple, thought Scott. Camden initiated some pandemic-style elbow bumps as a greeting.

"Well, Kate Brown says gatherings of up to two households are okay so we're just coming in under the wire I guess," Scott said.

They chatted awhile at the bar in the kitchen, sipping some vino and munching on nuts as the dinner came together: Tuna steaks and one of the Ross pinots.

At the dining table, Kim and Rachel initiated a conversation about the pandemic. Scott and Camden eventually turned the conversation toward off-piste ski vacations.

They retreated to the living room next to the fireplace with glasses of bourbon for the men and wine for the girls.

As he sipped the bourbon, Scott recalled the first time he made love to Kim next to that fireplace and thought about the strange course of events since then.

"Scott, you really hooked up with a winner there with Revazov," Camden said.

Still in his own head, Scott took a minute to respond.

"Yes, thanks to Wine Jamie," Scott said, "I'm now part of the property owner class out here I suppose."

"I just can't believe how well that place is doing. The fucking Millennials love that biodynamic wine. I suppose I should embrace it."

"I'd say you're hitting the mark with this," Rachel said, holding up her glass of pinot.

"The thing about the natural wine movement is that

there is no coherent philosophy or approach. Is it environmental? About technique? Terroir? You can't pin it down. It's so woo-woo. It's almost a denial of the winemaker's craft, an excuse to kind of let things take their course and remove the artistry of winemaking."

Kim put her hand on Camden's shoulder and smiled. "This is his favorite topic, debunking natural wine. And now I'm doing marketing for it." She laughed.

"I bet you guys are sore from that skiing this morning. The stars are out. Anyone feel like dipping their toes in the spa?" Kim asked.

"Sounds delightful," Rachel said, "but we didn't bring swimsuits."

"Oh, you're friends, we don't need to worry about those. Have a shower in one of the bathrooms downstairs and put on a robe."

Scott and Camden changed first and headed out to the hot tub. Camden brought the bottle of Bull Run bourbon that had been in the freezer and their glasses.

Camden was on a roll about natural wine.

"When I talk to these college kids who come out here and want to work on a winery for a summer, they want to learn more about stuffing cow horns with shit than the process of making wine. It's unbelievable."

Scott sipped the bourbon and listened.

Then he saw the lights go off in the house and the light on the deck as well. It was almost totally dark. Kim and Rachel walked out on the deck at the same time in the white bathrobes.

Scott kept his eyes on Camden as Kim disrobed in the darkness, her voluptuous figure faintly silhouetted in the near darkness. She slipped in next to Camden and cuddled up to him. Rachel revealed her slim, toned runner's body and Scott thought he could see Kim and Camden looking her up and down.

Kim relayed an anecdote about a time on a ski getaway with Camden when she'd shocked another couple by entering the hot tub in the buff while the others had their suits on.

"Nakedness itself isn't sexual, you know. People make such a big deal out of it."

Just as she made the remark, Scott could feel her foot run up the side of his leg.

Rachel told a story about how comfortable her coed Hood to Coast running relay team was with getting naked in front of each other. Scott was cuddled up next to Rachel, but Kim kept touching the inside of his leg with her foot. He was starting to get an erection.

"I really am only good in a hot tub for 15 minutes," Scott said.

"Do you mean with sex?" Camden said and then emitted a guffaw. "Hell, I'm just getting started," and he took another pull from his bourbon.

Scott got out of the tub and toweled off.

"I'm going to go get a sparkling water, anyone need anything?" Scott asked.

"There are plenty in the beverage refrigerator," Camden said.

"Thanks," Scott said, realizing that he should have asked where they were.

He walked back into the house and headed to the bathroom before the kitchen. Just as he was closing the door, Kim slipped in.

She kissed him lustily. He felt her hard nipples as she opened her robe and they embraced. They both looked at themselves in the mirror as she played with him until he was fully aroused.

Then she announced it was time to return to the tub.

Scott emitted a sigh and said, "I want you now."

"Soon. I promise," Kim said, closing and tying Scott's bathrobe and then giving him a lusty full-mouthed kiss. "Camden goes to Portland on Tuesday."

Soon enough, Scott and Rachel thanked Kim and Camden for the hospitality and said it was time to head home.

When Scott and Rachel got back to Scott's place, she was totally turned on and Scott was thinking he should be too after all that erotic build up. As their bodies came together under the sheets, Scott wanted to make it happen but couldn't. All he could think about was Kim.

Camden slept better than he had in weeks. He hadn't had sex like that with Kim in a long time. It seemed like she was so unavailable recently especially living with all the kids in the Gorge house.

While the teenagers were still asleep, Kim came into the master bedroom with a couple of cups of joe and they read on their tablets and enjoyed the coffee. Kim usually didn't like her coffee interrupted but something about the vibe this morning was different. Kim looked sexy in that nightgown and one thing led to another.

Afterward, they lay there.

"Last night was fun," said Kim.

"Totally, I enjoyed myself."

"You know, I've been doing pretty well with this Revazov work. And I know you, well, are skeptical about the place. But I wonder if you'd consider talking with them about some ideas."

Camden could feel his neck tighten.

"Who do you mean by them?"

"I mean, well, the Darden Wine Holdings people, Laurence Visser perhaps. They are interested in your winery."

"Why?" Camden said, irritation creeping into his voice.

"Well, I'm not sure, but maybe they could offer us some support, some of that huge following they have in their network."

"I don't need them."

"Will you at least take the meeting, Camden, hear what they have to say?" Kim said, running her finger down his chest.

The slightly erotic tingle relieved the angst just a bit and brought his mind back to the good state it had been in before this topic.

"Okay," Camden replied after thinking about it for a minute.

Camden didn't like the idea of having his business anywhere near Darden Wine Holdings, but on the other hand, maybe if he took this meeting, he could find out a little more about the operation.

A few days later, Laurence Visser pulled up his Mercedes-Benz CLS four-door coupe to Ross Wines and got out. Kim and Camden greeted him at the front door of their home. Laurence wore his usual outfit of billowing khakis and an untucked oxford shirt, but two months into the coronavirus pandemic, he had grown a new beard.

"I've heard so much about you, Camden. Thanks for taking the time," Laurence said.

"Should we start with a tour and a tasting to warm things up?" Kim suggested.

"Absolutely! So is the tasting room back open now that the governor has lifted restrictions?" Laurence asked as they walked from the house to the tasting room building.

"We just started to take tasting appointments as of May 12th and we plan to be open for walk-ins starting in June when we can mostly operate outside," answered Camden.

When they got to the tasting room, Kim poured Laurence samples of a few of their reds, while they continued to talk about the pandemic and its effect on the wine industry.

Laurence took a sip from the first sample, a 2017 pinot noir. "Very impressive," he said, putting his nose in the glass and inhaling before a sip. "I love how the aromas pop." And then after a swallow, "Ahh yes, delicious. I'm getting cherry and blackberry and a hint of pepper."

"Sounds about right," Camden said, unable to restrain a satisfied half smile.

"This is phenomenally fine stuff, my friend."

"Thank you," Camden said.

"I was wondering if this was the pinot that I saw on the web site. I was so intrigued by that description."

Laurence fumbled with his phone but said he wasn't getting a connection.

Camden pulled his phone out and pulled up the wine listings from the Ross Wines website. He handed his phone to Laurence.

"Ah yes, there it is," Laurence said, studying the wines on the site for a minute with Camden's phone.

"Do you by chance have any of the 2018 Reserve Pinot that won the award recently? That sounds phenomenal."

Kim had run up to the house to get something so Camden went behind the bar, found the appropriate bottle and poured Laurence a glass while he continued to study the Ross Wines website on Camden's phone.

"Kim said that you had a proposal to share and that's why you are here," said Camden as he handed Laurence the glass.

"Yes, I do. Can we have a look at the production facility first?" asked Laurence.

"Absolutely," Camden said, getting up.

Laurence put Camden's phone on the bar and they made their way out to the winemaking building. Kim rejoined them on the way.

They entered the wine production facility. "You've done an impressive job here," Laurence said, admiring the barrels, tanks and other high-end winemaking equipment.

Eventually, they all sat at a table in a corner of the large room. Laurence said, "Camden, we feel that there is so much potential in Ross Wines. We see a partnership opportunity. Your wine with our marketing and distribution apparatus."

"Really?" Camden said with a contemplative look on his face.

"We have the reach and the connections to get your

product out there, to vastly expand your sales. We also have preferred access to grapes."

"Could you get me into Albrechts?"

"I think we could."

"That is something to consider," Camden said. "I'm basically dependent on my wine club these days."

"If you can share some of your internal production and distribution figures with us, we can do a serious meeting in the next few weeks."

"Wonderful," Kim interjected.

Camden stayed silent.

"Thank you so much for having me," Laurence said. "Kim, can I have a word with Camden?"

"Of course. I need to run back to the house anyway," Kim said.

Camden was already on his feet, in anticipation of Laurence's departure, but Laurence motioned for him to sit. Camden did so with an annoyed look on his face.

Once Kim had left, Laurence said, "We know you've been curious about our operations."

Camden gave a mock confused look.

"Our surveillance cameras have you in the Revazov production facility and visiting, well, another one of our properties."

"Okay, you got me, I've been looking around. I've been curious about your success."

"My lawyers call what you were doing trespassing. But I appreciate the initiative, the willingness to take a risk and find out a little more about the competition. We could use people like that in our corner. Think about our offer."

Laurence stood up and extended his hand.

Camden slowly shook it, looking straight into Laurence's eyes.

After Laurence got back in his car, he messaged Jared to make sure that the app that he had installed on Camden's phone during the wine tasting was active.

Once Laurence left, Camden returned to the wine production area to take care of a few things. The meeting with Laurence had sent his brain spinning. The confrontation at the end was a shock. But it wasn't entirely unexpected, either.

Camden was still sitting on that info that he had discovered at the warehouse. He'd tipped off New Seasons and that hadn't resulted in much, as far as he could tell, but he also wondered if he should go a step further. Maybe report them to the authorities. The fact they had him on camera as an intruder made him wary of doing that.

There was something attractive about their offer. There was so much tension between his vision of Ross Wines and Kim's at Revazov. Could this resolve that tension? He contemplated what had been unthinkable: joining forces with Darden Wine Holdings. Getting into Albrechts' distribution network would have great advantages. Maybe he could write off what he'd discovered in the warehouse as some harmless accounting shenanigans.

Kim's kids and his daughter were away that day and the house was quiet. Camden needed to run back to Portland and pick up his daughter. Kim made him lunch before the drive and asked him some gentle questions about the prospect of the partnership with Darden but didn't push it. She sent him off with a double Americano for the road, just as he liked.

When he got about 10 miles west of Hood River on I-84, however, he realized that he had left his phone back at the house. He pulled off at Viento and headed back east on the Interstate, then got off at the Highway 35 exit.

Ten minutes later, as he approached the Ross Wines property, he just barely caught a glimpse of silver from a vehicle that he knew wasn't Kim's in the driveway. He drove up the long driveway and then recognized the vehicle as Scott's Tundra.

His body was shot with adrenaline as he approached his front door and entered.

"Hello, anybody home?"

Silence. He wandered into the kitchen and the open dining and living area. He saw his phone on the desk where he often left it. There was an open bottle of white wine on the dining table but no glasses next to it.

Then he heard a faint sound from down the hall that led to the master bedroom. He began walking that way and then recognized what it was. He stopped, breathless.

He turned around, took his phone and left the house.

As Camden drove back to Portland, he stayed in the right lane of I-84 and passively followed the truck in front of him. His mind raced.

Kim was fucking Scott.

He'd even heard, somewhat distantly, the sound of Kim having sex. Was it different than it was with him?

What would he do now?

He would call Kim as soon as he got to Portland and tell her to move out of the Gorge home. He'd buy her stake out of the winery and cut her loose.

And Darden Wines, they could fuck off as well. He would detonate that, too. Call the authorities and tell them everything. Forget the worries about breaking into their property.

After he picked up his daughter, he told her that there was a change of plans and headed to their Portland house in the West Hills. She didn't seem to mind that they weren't going to go out to the Gorge.

As soon as they got in the house, he called Kim.

As the phone rang, Camden's heart pounded with the prospect of confronting her.

Kim answered on the third ring, "Hi Cam."

"I'm in Portland, I think we're going to stay here for the night."

"Really?"

This was when he was going to do it. Confront her.

He paused.

"Are you still there?" Kim asked.

"Yeah, I just don't feel like beating back there tonight. What are you up to?"

Kim fell into normal chit-chat. He let her talk.

Camden managed to sleep an hour or two that night. Emma was 14 now and didn't need much attention in the morning. He made himself coffee, made her breakfast and then she went off and did whatever she did on her phone.

He took a walk in the neighborhood.

This had been Kim's house originally and they had shared it on and off for the last decade. She'd probably want it back.

His mind shifted between hurt and rage. In their 9 years together, they'd been through a few breakups and had at times seen other people. They were married now though and this was beyond the pale.

He'd started thinking about the very concrete matters of how they would unwind their intertwined business and financial lives.

Ross Wines was complicated. They were co-owners of it, but the property and the business had benefited from large infusions of cash from Camden's family over the years. It was his damned winery, his idea and his life's work. If they split, she could be entitled to half of it and that wasn't fair.

Kim was always after something new and shiny and glamorous. What she saw in Scott, besides him being someone different, Camden wasn't sure. It was probably the association with the success of Revazov and Darden Wine Holdings. The simple aspirations of a small winery just weren't enough for her.

He would play it cool. He had the ability. That's the only reason that he was still with Kim. He knew how to ride out her fickle moods. To be the patient one with the long view while she followed her whims and then soured on them. He would do that one last time and then crush her and Scott and Revazov and Darden Wine Holdings.

When he got back to the house, he got on his laptop and visited the anonymous tip form on the federal Alcohol and Tobacco Tax and Trade Bureau website. He detailed the knowledge that he had about Revazov moving undrinkable wine through Albrechts' distribution channels. He left his name off the submission.

He also contacted Bill Curtis, his attorney in Portland. The one he'd used in his previous divorce. Curtis had recommended a prenup when he married Kim last year but Camden had ignored his advice. He knew any mention of such a thing would have sent Kim into a rage.

Laurence saw the pastel colors of Mr. Chen's coastal Montenegro home as he came up on Zoom. He had shifted to his estate there during the outbreak. He looked relaxed, seated outside in the evening light in a white linen shirt with a glass of wine.

"Good morning, Laurence. How are things?"

"Things are interesting. We reached out to Camden Ross to see if we could do a partnership with him. At first, he seemed interested. But now he's turned us in to the TTB."

"Who?"

"The feds. The Alcohol and Tobacco Tax and Trade Bureau."

Mr. Chen's eyes widened. "What? How did — "

"Don't worry," assured Laurence. "We hacked his phone and were also able to get into his laptop. We saw him visiting a TTB website where people can turn in evidence, a whistleblower kind of thing. So my guy spoofed the site in anticipation of him actually turning stuff in."

"So you're saying that we snagged the transmission?" Mr. Chen asked.

"Yes."

"Brilliant. What do we do now?"

"I suggest we make him think that Revazov is getting punished by the TTB. We wind things down a bit and then we're back to expansion plans in a few months to a year."

Mr. Chen paused, evidently in thought. After a minute, he spoke.

"I don't see us slowing down now. We need to move this summer to expand and to legitimize the business. Now is the opportune time. We've been incubating Revazov and we're ready to leverage that. I want to use our sales volume there to secure a loan from a bank in the United States to purchase interest in another winery. We need to build out our footprint within U.S. financial institutions. If he gets us under any kind of investigation, we'll have a huge setback."

"He also might have found out about Kim and Scott's affair. He contacted a divorce lawyer," Laurence said.

"Really? Sounds like the situation is more volatile than before." He paused and thought for a few seconds.

"We need to remove him from the picture," Mr. Chen said.

"Let me remind you that this is the United States. It's not Azerbaijan or Malaysia," Laurence said.

"What if there was an accident?"

"Well, then, I suppose that could resolve things."

"I think we know someone who can make accidents happen."

"Do we?" Laurence asked.

16

June 6th. Gerhard was seated in the first-class section of a SWISS flight from Frankfurt to San Francisco. The flight was about a third full, mostly of Americans returning home due to the pandemic. He wore a full-body Adidas tracksuit and a black cloth face mask. He was traveling under a passport that identified him as Dr. Ingo Merz, a German scientist employed at AnschutzRNA, a German pharmaceutical company collaborating with an American firm on a coronavirus vaccine.

Gerhard didn't like transoceanic flights. Taking one inevitably meant that he missed a workout. After the evening meal, Sauerbraten with some roasted vegetables and a glass of Burgundy alongside, he washed down an Ambien with a double Dewar's. The next thing he knew he was deplaning in San Francisco. From there, he would fly to Portland, Oregon.

He had been to the Columbia Gorge before, but it had been more than a decade. This was a place where he could do many sports that he liked, including kiteboarding, windsurfing and mountain biking. At the airport he rented a GMC pickup and pointed it east on I-84.

The Airbnb he had in downtown Hood River was in a new section of townhomes and was clean and modern. After dropping off his things in the unit, Gerhard headed out toward the Ross Wines vineyard in the GMC. He could go in for a tasting, but something told him not to. He drove a little ways past the entryway to Ross Wines on Highway 35 and pulled over to the side of the road. He looked at his phone and studied the satellite view of the area.

Then he took the next turnoff on the left to a road that skirted the back side of the property. He drove down a quarter mile or so, parked and walked in along some pear trees until he came to a wooded spot that had a view of the house compound.

He observed the property for about 20 minutes. A couple of guys came and went from a warehouse-like structure on the property. Then he saw Camden Ross wheel a bike out of the building and put it in the back of a pickup and take off.

The firm already had software on Camden Ross' phone that allowed Gerhard to monitor his whereabouts. Gerhard watched the dot representing Camden move along the digital map of the area rendered in the tracking app.

Camden Ross and Todd McKinley met for an afternoon mountain biking session in Post Canyon, a hilly, wooded trail system the west end of the Hood River Valley. The early June dirt had a perfect tackiness to it. They followed it up with a Jersey-style pie and pints of India Red Ale at the bar at Double Mountain Brewery in downtown Hood River.

Once Camden was about halfway into his beer he asked Todd, "Can you keep something quiet?"

"Sure thing, dude."

"Kim is having an affair."

"Fuck, that's terrible."

"It is. You know we've been on and off before, but this is different. We're married and in our early fifties for fuck's sake."

"Who's the other guy?"

"Scott."

"The high school teacher? The one with the property in Underwood?"

"The property that's really owned by a crime syndicate."

"Really?"

"We've talked about this, remember? Well now I know

more. I found out that they are dumping that bunk wine but still taking payments for it through Albrechts."

"They are washing money?"

"I think so."

"It kind of lines up with their meteoric rise. So what are you going to do about it all?"

"I want to break it off with Kim, and I want to take this Revazov operation down."

"How do you plan to do that?"

"I reported them to the feds, the Alcohol and Tobacco Tax and Trade Bureau that is."

"And?"

"Well, I used an anonymous tip form. I'm not sure what's happening."

"Dude, if you think they are laundering money, you might want to contact someone in law enforcement directly. I'd be worried about protecting your own ass."

As Todd said that he looked over at a man clad in a track suit seated a couple stools away. He was lean and had bronze skin, short brown hair shaved on the sides and a scar on his neck that was noticeable from across the room. His age was unclear: somewhere from late thirties to early fifties.

The man raised his glass and looked at them. Todd and Camden returned the gesture, then turned back to each other.

"Yeah, you are probably right," said Camden. "I should get in direct contact with someone. I'm just a little unsure because some of the things I did to get this information weren't exactly kosher. I mean I sort of trespassed on their business to get it."

"Well, it sounds like you have some good intel and they'd probably like to know about that even if they can't use it in court. What about Kim, have you confronted her?"

"I'm not saying anything to her yet. I don't want her to know that I know. I'm having an attorney prepare some papers for her to sign that will change our business partnership agreement."

"Well man, all things considered, you seem in pretty good shape. Well done on the bike ride."

"Thanks," Camden said.

They ordered another round and talked for a while longer before heading their separate ways.

It was an unusually warm day in early June. Scott drove from his Portland place out to Forest Grove, a sleepy college town nestled in the farmland between Portland and the Oregon Coast Range. He was the first to arrive at the coffee shop in the old Foursquare house. He got an iced mocha and found a table on the shaded patio.

Real estate agent Denise showed up next. It had been a while since Scott had seen her. She was dressed casually for the heat in white pants and a pastel blouse and wore a cloth face mask that coordinated with her outfit. Scott offered to get her drink and she requested a matcha iced tea.

Laurence arrived about 15 minutes later.

"Hi team," he said in his Dutch accent, his disposable face mask dropping down below his nose as he spoke.

"Can I get you a drink?" Scott asked. "My tab is open."

"Damn it's a warm one. I could use a lager."

"No alcohol, I'm afraid."

"Double espresso and a club soda chaser, then."

Scott came back to the table in a few minutes.

"I'm confused," Denise said. "What are we doing going to Dougherty Vineyards? It isn't for sale."

"No, it's not," Laurence said. "But it's a fucking amazing property."

"I looked at the website," Scott said, "and it's been in the Dougherty family since the fifties."

Laurence's drinks arrived. He downed the espresso in one gulp then sat back in his chair.

"The Dougherty family has been under some strain recently. The elder Dougherty, the one who really converted the family farm into a successful winery in the eighties, well he's had his eye off the ball. His son Steve has stepped in and tried to take over, but he's in way over his head."

"I read a blog post about the place by Wine Jamie from last fall and she didn't sound too fond of the place," Scott added.

"They are up to their eyeballs in debt. And our distributor, Albrechts, just cut them loose. The COVID thing hasn't helped matters as they get a lot of revenue from weddings and that sort of thing."

Denise took a deep breath and straightened her posture. "As usual, Mr. Chen likes to be well informed," she said.

"I've booked a tasting for the two of you. You should go as a couple."

"Okay. So what exactly are we doing there?" Scott asked.

"I'd like you to develop a relationship with them, Scott. And Denise, you can size up the property."

"How am I supposed to do that with a tasting room attendant?" Scott asked.

Laurence smiled, the sun now shining in his face, and looked at Scott through his aviator sunglasses. "That's your new job, mate. Figure it out."

The arrival of summer in the Gorge was usually a pleasant time of year for Camden Ross. He loved the long days as well as all the wine events that let him showcase his work and connect with friends and admirers.

This year was different. The coronavirus had brought all winery events to a halt and his business was in a precarious place. Kim's kids were living almost full time at their Gorge property and that made the place feel chaotic. And now there was the stress of navigating his relationship with Kim given her affair with Scott.

The occasional mountain bike ride and kiteboarding session provided a bit of relief. Once they reopened the beaches in May he was getting out there with the kite once or twice a week. His go-to launch spot was the Hood River Event Site, a centrally located beach with a big grassy rigging area. One Tuesday during the second week of June, a cool frontal system pushed in from the coast and lit up the Gorge wind machine. With most of the wind sport tourists yet to arrive in Hood River, he was enjoying a section of river off that beach almost exclusively to himself.

After about 30 minutes, another kiter joined him on the river. Had he seen this guy before? He wasn't sure, but he was good. He'd just hit the smallest ramps and floated 30 feet in the air. The guy wore wraparound purple sunglasses that were almost as large as ski goggles.

Camden started going for it too, so much so that he pushed it a bit too far and had a crash landing and his board got away from him. No problem, as he was able to keep the kite under control and retrieve the board.

They were both blasting back and forth, boosting higher and higher with each jump. On every reach, the dude seemed to get closer and closer to Camden. This made him nervous but it was also playful and fun.

As Camden was carving a turn at the end of a reach, the man came up behind him and Camden felt a violent jerk backward as the lines of their two kites intersected and began twisting.

"Ahh fuck," Camden uttered involuntarily as he released the bar to depower the kite. The two kites were spinning around each other as they fell to the river. The other dude was about 15 feet from Camden.

"Sorry about that, man! My bad!" yelled the man as he raised his hand to acknowledge his mistake.

They were still being pulled along by the partially powered kites.

"Release and go to safety!" the man yelled.

They both popped their chicken loop, which released a lot of tension from the lines and put the kites in safety mode. Soon the lines were submerged in the water in a confusing mess.

"Hang on, stay there, let me see if I can get this," Camden said.

Camden began to try to sort out the tangle by moving

up along his lines to the point where the lines were crossed over and got to a spot where he thought he could work through the mess. He unhooked his leash and, periodically sticking his head under water, began to pass his lines over the man's. It was a pain and took his full concentration.

After a minute or two had past, Camden was surprised when he heard the man behind right behind him. "Thanks dude, I think we're close. I think if I can just get this one around you, we'll be good."

The man went underwater next to Camden and he could feel him messing with kite lines around his body.

Suddenly, Camden felt a strange tension around his legs. Then they were locked together and he couldn't kick to tread water, which was essential as he wasn't wearing a life vest. He moved a hand down to feel what was holding his legs together while he tried to use the other arm to tread water and keep his face above water.

Then he felt the man grab each of his arms simultaneously and push a knee into his back. Camden's face went underwater.

Adrenaline surged in Camden and he twisted violently and dove forward deeper into the water away from the knee, getting one arm free and wresting whatever was holding his legs together loose.

When he popped up above the water surface, Camden gasped for air and looked around. To his side was the man with the purple glasses and behind him was someone new, a guy with a wing foil who had stopped close by.

"Oh man, I'm sorry," the man with the purple glasses said to Camden in his accented voice. "I got the lines wrapped around your legs by accident and I was trying to work you out of it."

Camden was in shock from the momentary terror and just treaded water for a second. Before he knew it, the man who he had collided with was able to get his kite airborne again and he ripped off across the river.

The wing foiler floated over to Camden. "Are you okay,

dude? It looked like you two were really tangled and struggling."

"That was fucked up," Camden said, still trying to catch his breath. "The guy was trying to drown me, I swear. Do you know him?"

"Actually, I've seen him at the beach. It's hard to miss him. He likes to rig up in a Speedo."

"Right," Camden said, with a vague recollection now of seeing the guy on shore.

Camden's lines were still tangled, but eventually he relaunched his kite and headed back to shore.

17

There was an early summer chilliness in the air when Camden got home from kiting. Kim was inside sitting at the dining table working on her laptop.

"It's cocktail hour," he said.

"I'll go along with that," Kim said. "What would you like?"

"I need something stronger than wine. I'm lucky to be alive."

"Oh dear, what happened?"

Camden relayed the harrowing kiteboarding episode.

"Who was he?"

"I don't know. It was just so fucked up."

Kim made Camden a strong old fashioned and she poured herself a glass of chardonnay. Then they sat opposite each other, him on the big leather chair and her on the sofa.

"Strange times," Camden said after a long pull from his drink.

Kim got up and began massaging his neck.

Her touch felt pleasant as the alcohol kicked in. But in a minute, he thought of Scott and winced as she dug her fingers into his shoulder muscles.

"Everyone has gone a little mad in this pandemic," Kim said, sitting back down.

"Yes," said Camden.

He paused for a while.

"My dad must have too much time on his hands. He insists that we sign some paperwork about the business. Just some formalities."

"About what?" Kim asked.

"Oh, about how the equity in the business is divided up."

"Oh," Kim said, "I thought it was our business."

"It is. Of course it is. But as you know he's invested in it over time and feels he has a stake."

"I thought those were gifts."

"They were, Kim," Camden said in a somewhat exasperated tone. "This is just a formality. It would make things a whole lot easier if you just helped me take care of this. Especially, as I'm entertaining this partnership proposal with Darden Wine Holdings."

"Okay," Kim said.

"Speaking of that, have you heard anything about the next steps?"

"Laurence said to expect a meeting soon," Kim said.

Camden stood up, took another drink and peered out the window at Mount Adams illuminated by the early evening sunlight.

Gerhard found the speed and the power of kiteboarding sensational. He had learned to windsurf on the Chiemsee in Bavaria in the eighties, but for the past 15 years or so, it was all kiting for him.

Kiteboarding had worked well a couple years ago in the Canary Islands. His target, the CEO of a French construction company who was competing with Mr. Chen on a project in Malaysia, was doing reaches off El Cotillo beach on Fuerteventura. Gerhard dropped his lines in front of the man and nearly severed the guy's neck. The collision was so violent that Gerhard himself was almost knocked unconscious. Gerhard slipped away from the scene and the man's death was declared accidental by the police.

But the Columbia Gorge kiting areas were relatively small and visible. His attempt on Camden had almost worked. But that wing foiler had approached and he had to bail. It was unfortunate, because Camden had seen Gerhard and this limited his options and approach.

He had another idea, however. A Google search revealed that a fatal mountain biking accident had happened about a decade ago at Syncline, a trail system located on a desert plateau on the Washington side of the Gorge. According to an online article published by the Columbia Gorge News, in 2005, the mountain biker had fallen to his death off the volcanic cliff band on the west end of the trail system known as Coyote Wall.

One morning before dawn, Gerhard drove to the Syncline trailhead with a mountain bike that he had rented at Discover Bikes. He ascended the plateau on the switchbacking Old Ranch Road and then traversed over to the intersection with the Coyote Wall trail that ran along the cliff edge.

He stopped at the intersection to take his bearings, standing over the bike's top tube. He could see his breath in the cool morning air. The view was amazing. It was just getting light and looking to the south, he could see the morning sun illuminate the east side of Mount Hood.

When he was ready to go, he clicked his seat into the downhill position, grasped the handlebars and dropped in.

The trail swooped back and forth as it descended the plateau. Many sections of the trail were deep ruts a foot or two below the level of the surrounding ground. The speed was exhilarating as he weaved his way down the wide-open expanse.

Pretty quickly he reached the Little Moab section, which featured many areas where the riding was over rock. It was slower going than the upper section. When he got to the bottom of the Little Moab Trail, he traversed back up to the intersection where he had started.

He dropped in again. When he descended this time, he studied the areas that got close to the cliff edge, paying attention to his speed and the trajectory of his bike. The hairpin turns were natural places to slow down, but some of the sections that swooped back and forth next to the cliff

THE ECLIPSE

could actually be taken at pretty good speed and the videos he had watched indicated that experienced riders did just that.

He found a couple of possibilities and marked them on his phone's navigator app.

This time, he didn't drop into Little Moab. Instead, he ascended again to that same intersection at the top, dropped in and rode to the most promising spot. He got off his bike and inspected the trail. It was a deep rut that ran about five feet from the cliff.

He walked to the cliff and looked over the edge. It dropped straight down to a pile of volcanic scree about 200 feet below.

He got back on his bike and descended the trail to his truck.

Gerhard tried to eat meals in his rental as much as possible. It helped him keep a lower profile. But he couldn't really get the food he liked in the Hood River grocery stores. The sausages weren't like those in Germany. And he got sick of cooking for himself.

The Pancake Hut was up in Hood River Heights, the less-trendy area of town lacking spectacular views of the river. Gerhard liked to frequent the place in the mornings. It was in a building that had once been a chain restaurant and was constructed as a circle with the booths on the edges and the kitchen in the middle. He'd even gotten friendly with one of the waitresses there, Chantelle.

She was in her late twenties or early thirties and always took care of his table. She wasn't the prettiest gal but she was young and had the kind of voluptuous figure that he liked. She always seemed to give him the eye and he began joking around with her. He'd say cheesy things like "Good Morning Beautiful" in his German accent and she'd giggle.

When he finally asked for her phone number, she apologized and said that she had a boyfriend. Gerhard replied by just saying, "That's okay." Then he just waited and smiled at her. It didn't take her long to scribble her number out on Gerhard's breakfast check.

They met at a bar a couple of nights later and quickly shifted to Gerhard's rental townhouse. He took a couple Viagras and they worked on a bottle of vodka and had sex on and off for four hours, binge-watching "Game of Thrones" on Gerhard's laptop between fucking sessions.

A week after giving Scott and Denise an impromptu tour of his family's winery, Steve Dougherty called Scott. They met for a beer at Walking Man Brewery in Forest Grove. Soon, Steve brought up the "investment and expansion opportunities" that Scott had briefly mentioned at the winery.

"My dad would never forgive me for even looking into this but tell me about them."

"My colleagues at Darden Wine Holdings are building a portfolio of investments in small wineries and vineyards in the Pacific Northwest. They are interested in partnering with established wineries and working together to expand sales and reach. They have capital ready to deploy."

Scott found it surprisingly easy to fall into this business speak.

"What could that mean for my family's winery?"

"We could help you grow the business, make things sustainable," Scott said.

"What's the catch?"

"No catch, we're looking to expand and you are looking to sustain and grow. This could be a win-win situation."

God, what a cliché, Scott thought just as he said the phrase "win-win." But Dougherty was buying it.

"It's an intriguing prospect. Let me talk to my family and get back to you in a bit," Steve said.

As the summer days wore on, Camden held off on confronting Kim. He told himself that it was because he had to get the pieces in place before he broke it off with her. As soon as Kim signed the papers, he would divorce her and pay out what little was owed to her for her interest in Ross Wines.

Part of him wondered if he was just making up excuses to avoid the confrontation. It pissed him off that she had this parachute in the form of a career with Revazov and Darden Wine Holdings. He wanted to take them down too but his tipoff to the TTB didn't appear to have gone anywhere.

Though he was worried about the breaking and entering incident at the warehouse, he finally decided to make a direct contact with federal law enforcement about his suspicions regarding Darden by sending an email to the Portland Field Office of the FBI.

To his surprise, Special Agent Grant Peterson returned the message the same day and set up an appointment with Camden at the FBI's Portland location for the following day.

Camden drove out to the office, located near the Portland airport, but just as he was walking toward the building for his appointment, his phone rang. It was Agent Peterson.

"Mr. Ross, I'm sorry to do this to you, but due to COVID we've just put a new procedure in place for talking to leads. We're now using a secure version of video conferencing to take these meetings."

"Okay, no problem," Camden said.

"Great, well, can you talk soon, say in an hour, over your computer?"

"Sure," Camden said.

Camden returned to the West Hills Portland house for the Zoom conversation.

Soon enough, the special agent appeared against a Zoom background with the FBI seal on it. Peterson was a tall, corpulent man, almost totally bald, who wore a somewhat ill-fitting navy blue suit and tie.

Camden told of his curiosity about Revazov's

unbelievable sales figures and of tracing the suspicious wine to a warehouse where it was being dumped. He also revealed to Peterson that Darden was interested in partnering with his own winery.

Agent Peterson asked many follow-up questions and took copious notes. As he moved his body and handled a notebook, Camden could see glimpses of his real surroundings as the Zoom software became unable to distinguish between Peterson's body and the background setting. For just a split second, Camden saw what he thought was a window with bright sunlight outside. He thought that was strange, considering the current gloomy weather in Portland.

Peterson said, "Mr. Ross, it's of the utmost importance that you keep these suspicions that you have confidential. We need you to help us find out more to build a case."

Peterson said that the partnership proposal was particularly interesting. He asked that Camden respond positively to any overtures that they made about the partnership and gather as much information as possible. He also instructed Camden to install a recording app on his phone to record conversations with the Darden Wine Holdings people.

Camden agreed to follow the instructions and stay in close contact with Peterson as things developed.

Gerhard drove out to Syncline a few days after his first visit there. This time, he arrived even earlier than his previous pre-dawn visit. From his truck he pulled out a backpack loaded with equipment: a folding shovel, a battery-powered hammer drill, two-part epoxy, 30 feet of 1/16-inch wire rope, two threaded metal anchor stakes and various small fasteners and rock-climbing gear.

He rode his bike up the trail in the darkness, relying on the moonlight to make out the contours of the trail. He located the area that he had identified on his previous trip. The trail was already a fairly deep trench of a little more than a foot. He found precisely the spot he wanted and used the drill to drive a threaded anchor into the ground on the side of the trail away from the cliff edge.

Then he rode back up the trail to a spot where there were big boulders and picked one out that was probably around 80 pounds. He lugged it back to the spot where he had placed the anchor and set the boulder next to the edge of the cliff. He used the hammer drill and a masonry bit to make a hole in the boulder.

He blew out debris from the hole and squeezed in some of the two-part epoxy and set an eye hook in the epoxy. The epoxy took 15 minutes to cure.

The anchor he put in next to the trail was set about an inch below ground level. He used a compression ferrule to make a three-inch loop in one end of the wire and then, clearing the dirt away from the head of the anchor, slipped the loop over the anchor.

He paid out the wire, running it down into the groove of the trail and out to the cliff edge. He made a couple loops in the wire using ferrules: one at the end and one a few feet from the end. Using a carabiner, he attached the loop at the end of the wire to the boulder's eye hook. He pushed the boulder over the edge of the cliff and it dropped until the wire caught it. It hung next to the cliff about four feet down from the edge. The wire was taut above the trail.

Gerhard straddled his bike and bounced the front wheel against the wire to see if it gave. The wire had seated itself on the uneven, rocky ground and was surprisingly taut. Positioned at this spot on the trail, his bike was pointed straight at the edge of Coyote Wall, which was about eight feet away. From the point where the wire was set, the trail curved to the left and continued down the Wall parallel to the cliff edge.

He put on gloves and pulled the boulder back up using the middle loop and set it on the ground next to the cliff edge. He took a second anchor stake and attempted to screw it in near the cliff edge, but it wouldn't go in all the way because the ground was too rocky. Instead, he took out a set of trad climbing anchors and leaned over the edge of the cliff and tried some in the cracks of the rocks on the cliff face.

Once he got a climbing anchor in place, he attached a remote release mechanism. Holding the boulder with the carabiner, he lowered it off the edge of the cliff and clipped it onto the loop at the end of the wire that was attached to the remote release.

It was still dark and there was no sign of anyone else around.

He stood back and pulled out the electronic controller for the release mechanism and then depressed the button. The boulder dropped with a crunch and a clunk, yanking the wire taut over the trail.

Gerhard then hauled the boulder back up and disassembled the setup. He left the two anchors in place, making sure there was dirt over the screw-in ground anchor. He left the boulder adjacent to the cliff and rolled it over in a way that obscured the eye hook. He also retrieved another rock from up the trail and left it next to the anchor on the trail.

Then he headed down the trail and into town for some early morning pancakes.

Scott's phone buzzed and he saw Laurence's name come up on the screen. He answered.

"Hey Scott, how are you? Do you think you could help me arrange a little business meeting on Saturday?"

"Sure, I'm basically free that day."

"I'd like you to help us land the Ross Wines partnership agreement. Charlie Albrechts would like to meet with Camden and talk about getting Ross Wines into the Albrechts distribution channel. Charlie loves mountain biking whenever he gets out to the Gorge. So I'd like you to organize a bike ride with him, Camden and you. His favorite spot is the Syncline Coyote Wall trail. Do you think you could put together a ride with the three of you out there? Then I can meet you all at Syncline Winery for a tasting and conversation to wrap things up. And I suppose Kim should come to that meeting as well."

"Alright," Scott said. "I can do that. I don't know much about the Darden-Ross partnership proposal. Do you have some details that you can share with me."

"Of course, of course. I'll have my girl email you," Laurence said.

"Sounds good."

"I'll text you Charlie's number and you can get things rolling from there. Sound good?"

"Sure," Scott said.

It was starting to get uncomfortably warm in the sun as Camden adjusted the trellises in the recently planted section of pinot. It was late Thursday morning and he'd been out in the vineyard for a couple of hours. He headed back to the house and into the kitchen. The papers from the attorney were on the counter. Kim had signed them.

He felt relief, but then a sinking feeling in his stomach. This was it. The last obstacle. He would confront Kim tonight.

Then he looked at a text message on his phone.

> Hey Camden, Scott here on behalf of Darden Wine. We've spoken to Charlie Albrechts about getting your winery into his distribution network and he'd love to meet you. He's a big mountain biker and wondered if you'd go biking with him on Syncline on Saturday morning?

Camden replied.

> Sure, I'm game. What time and where to meet?

> 9 am on Saturday at the Syncline parking

> lot?
>
> Works for me.

Charlie Albrechts and Scott Larson? The summer was getting stranger by the day, Camden thought. He'd love to kick both of their asses on a mountain bike though. And this would be an opportunity to find out more information about Darden to feed to feds.

Camden could see Kim out the living room window. She was straightening the outdoor furniture outside the tasting room before it opened up that day. He walked out to her.

"Hey, do you know about this meeting this weekend about the partnership proposal with Darden?"

"No!"

He relayed the plan about the bike ride and the meetup afterward at Syncline.

"Sounds like a delightful way to move this forward," Kim said.

Camden went back into the house.

He looked out the window and thought for a minute. He would hold off on confronting Kim about the affair, at least until he let this meeting play out.

On Saturday morning, Camden woke up early while Kim remained asleep. He put on his bathrobe, went out to the kitchen, popped a bagel in the toaster and made up some coffee. He scrolled social media on his phone for a while, checking out the latest pandemic news. Then he brought a cup of coffee into Kim as she liked.

"Hey sexy," Kim said.

"Hey there," Camden said.

"Come here."

Camden slowly walked over to her, then sat on the bed facing her.

"You look good," she said, putting her hand on his chest.

She moved her hand down to his abdomen and then

lower.

Camden had kept his distance from her since finding out about Scott. They hadn't had sex in weeks.

She's trying to manipulate me, he thought. Soften me up for the Darden deal.

He started to twist his body away.

God, it felt good though.

She eased his bathrobe open.

The morning sunlight from the east-facing window filtered in through the blinds and onto their bodies as they made love.

Afterward, they lay there on the bed, intertwined. Neither said a word.

Camden wondered, would he really leave Kim, even if she wasn't entirely faithful?

Scott saw Camden's F-150 pull into the Syncline parking lot shortly after 9. Camden was clad in some sporty looking loose mountain biking shorts and a blue bi-color jersey. Scott had an old shirt from a trail running race and some stretched out spandex road biking shorts on. Scott's steel mountain bike from the nineties contrasted with Camden's $10,000 carbon fiber one.

"Dude, with this new job you have, you should invest in a better bike," Camden said.

Scott smiled slightly and replied, "You're probably right."

This was the first time that Camden had seen Scott since that afternoon he'd discovered him with Kim. The sex that morning with Kim had momentarily erased the reality of Kim's infidelity, but now he was staring right at it in the form of Scott.

Soon Scott got a text from Charlie Albrechts. Scott relayed to Camden that instead of making the nearly 2,000-foot climb with them, Charlie was getting dropped off by his girlfriend on Atwood Road at the top of the trail system so they should look for him up there.

"What a fucking pussy," Camden said.

"I guess we should hit the trail," Scott said.

They departed the parking lot and began grinding up the ascent. As they pedaled up the switchbacks of the Ranch Road, they made some awkward conversation about the pandemic and its effect on the wine business. Soon they fell into silence as they tackled the uphill.

Scott took the lead and set a pretty good pace. Camden was sucking air harder than he would have preferred as he watched Scott's muscular calves flex with each pedal stroke. Inside, he began to fume as he thought about Scott with Kim.

When Scott reached the intersection with the Coyote Wall trail, he stopped and waited for Camden.

Camden got there in a minute, dismounted his bike and then walked up to Scott.

"Where's Albrechts?" Camden said.

"This is where he was supposed to meet us. I just texted him but I'm not getting a reply," Scott said.

"So what do we do?" Camden asked.

"Let's hang here a bit," Scott said.

Scott laid down his bike and they stood there not saying much for a couple minutes.

"What can you tell me about this partnership deal?" Camden asked. "Seeing that that's why we're here."

"You'll learn more at the meeting afterward, but I think Albrechts could be a real boost to your sales."

Camden nodded. Scott began to go on about the potential benefits of Ross Wines partnering with this larger entity.

"I know you are fucking her, Scott," Camden said, interrupting Scott.

Scott opened his mouth like he was about to say something, but nothing came out.

"No comment?" Camden asked, adding, "Well, I have one. FUCK YOU." He punched Scott in the face, dropping him to the ground.

Scott lay there on his back on the dusty ground. His mind was spinning and pain began to radiate from his face.

He leaned on his elbows and looked at Camden.

Camden was getting on his bike. "I'm not sure what's going on with this meeting with Albrechts, but I'm going to ride now," he said.

Camden rolled onto the descending Coyote Wall trail. That little confrontation with Scott hadn't been part of the plan, but he'd been unable to control himself.

He tried to focus in on the bike ride. He'd reassess his next move at the bottom of the trail, he figured.

Just a minute after starting the descent he heard the crunching sounds of another bike on gravel behind him as he made one of the sweeping turns. He looked back to discover it wasn't Scott but another dude who must have gotten between them.

Someone else was gaining on him? Was this Albrechts? This was irritating and it caused him to push harder, both on the straightaways and coming out of the turns.

The trail was now winding along the cliff edge. Camden usually took this part pretty easy but with the guy behind him, he picked up the pace.

Gerhard could sense Camden pushing hard. As he looked down the expansive plateau and the winding trail, he could see the designated spot approaching in the distance. He backed off and depressed the remote release to put the trip wire in place.

Camden kept riding well ahead of him in an aggressive manner.

When Camden's front wheel hit the wire, the back of the bicycle lifted into the air and he catapulted forward in spectacular fashion. Camden landed with a thud on his back, his legs splayed over the cliff edge and his bike next to him.

Gerhard brought his bike to a stop right before the wire and quickly dismounted.

Camden lay there for a second on his back looking at the sky. He could feel his legs dangling and then he realized they were hanging off the cliff. He reflexively pushed up with his arms and back from the edge. God his back hurt like hell. Slowly he began to get to his feet.

Then he felt a hand on his upper arm and heard a voice behind him. "Hey are you alright?" the man asked, as Camden began to stand up.

He looked over his shoulder and saw those purple wraparound sunglasses. Suddenly Camden recognized the man from the river.

At that moment, the man shoved him hard and he fell free.

Just as Scott got to his feet following the punch, another biker had gone bombing through the intersection from some point above.

Scott's cheek hurt like hell and his head was in a fog. There wasn't much to do but head down the trail.

Navigating the single track required Scott's full concentration so he mostly kept his eye on the trail straight ahead of him.

After Scott had ridden a couple hundred feet more down the trail, he looked up and saw Camden and the other biker who had passed a few hundred feet ahead. They were both off their bikes. Camden was on the ground and the man was walking toward him. Scott's concentration returned to the twisting trail, but when he looked up again Camden was gone.

A coldness came over him as he approached the other biker and then dismounted.

"He crashed. I tried to help him up from the edge and I lost him," the man said in a German accent.

Scott looked over the cliff and saw Camden's still body

THE ECLIPSE

on the rocks below, his biking jersey a splash of color on the otherwise dark volcanic rock.

"Camden!" Scott shouted.

"I'm going to call 911," Scott said, pulling his phone out.

The man approached Scott at the edge of the cliff, putting his hand on his shoulder. "Scott, I need you to listen. This is important. When others ask, you found him. Forget about me. You never saw me. Laurence will call you to explain."

"Wait, are you Charlie Albrechts?"

"I'm not. I'm no one," the man said.

He got on his bike and was gone.

Scott stood there next to Camden's bike. Before he could process what the man had said, two other mountain bikers approached. They stopped and joined Scott, looking over the edge.

Scott explained to the bikers that he'd been following Camden from aways behind and then had come upon the accident without actually witnessing the fall.

One of them called the authorities. Scott called Kim and told her about Camden's fall. She left immediately for the Syncline trail.

Then Scott and one of the bikers began making their way down to the trailhead while the other one stayed behind.

On the way down, Scott's phone started buzzing. He ignored it.

When he got to the parking lot an ambulance and two Klickitat County Sheriff patrol cars had already arrived. One of the Hood River Crag Rats, a wilderness rescue volunteer group, was heading up the rocky embankment with two paramedics to find Camden.

Scott's phone buzzed yet again. This time he answered it. It was Laurence.

"Scott, I'm so sorry about the accident."

"How did you hear about it?" Scott asked.

"I know you must be in shock. I'm calling to tell you something important, though. I know you met a man on the trail, at the scene of the accident. Please do not mention him to the authorities."

"I don't understand. Was that Albrechts?" Scott asked.

"It was a different associate of ours who was hoping to meet you and Camden. He's in the country on a special visa and well, it would be very helpful to keep him out of any law enforcement reports. Let's not make this tragedy an even more difficult situation, Scott."

Scott was speechless.

"Does that make sense, Scott? I'm sure as someone who's very, shall we say, close to Kim, you can understand why we don't want ... questions arising related to this tragedy," Laurence said.

Scott paused and then said, "I got it."

"Thank you, Scott," Laurence said, "I know I can count on you."

At the parking lot, Scott spoke to a sheriff's deputy about what happened. He described seeing Camden at the cliff edge in the distance and then seconds later seeing him on the rocks below.

"Looks like you might have taken a fall yourself," the deputy said, pointing to Scott's cheek, which must have looked swollen.

It took Scott a second to realize what the deputy was talking about. "Yeah, I did. Truth be told, I'm not a particularly confident rider and I was going kind of slow over a rocky section and just biffed it."

When asked if there were any other cyclists or hikers that might have seen what happened to Camden, Scott said that he didn't think so.

Scott offered to join the search and rescue team. They were already on their way to find Camden and the deputy declined Scott's offer to help.

In 15 minutes, Scott saw Kim's SUV careen into the parking lot. She double parked her vehicle and rushed to him and the deputy he was speaking with. Scott waited with Kim among the first responders and onlookers for what seemed like forever.

In 10 minutes, word came over the radio that Camden was dead.

After Gerhard left Scott, he descended about a quarter mile and then cut up the climb trail to a spot where he could observe the scene of the accident. After Camden's fall, Gerhard had been able to cut the wire trip line loose with a dikes and push a rock into the trail to make it appear to be the cause of the crash.

Bikers and hikers kept stopping and talking to the biker who had stayed behind at the scene of the accident. After about 45 minutes the spot was clear and he rolled in and retrieved the climbing anchor and remote release mechanism. Then he climbed back up to Atwood Road, where his truck was parked. From there, he took the back roads above the Gorge to White Salmon, avoiding the commotion at the Syncline trailhead.

He drove back to the Syncline trails that night, again parking above the trail system. He rode his bike with a light, down to the spot where he'd set the wire trip line. Using a drill, he extracted the anchor stake from the ground.

The boulder with the wire attached was long gone, fallen down the cliff at least 200 feet below onto a steep volcanic scree slope that dropped another 100 feet or so. By Gerhard's design, its trajectory was different than where Camden had ended up.

Gerhard had planned to retrieve the boulder and remove the eye hook and the wire, but now the task didn't seem so simple. The area below the cliff was not accessible by trails. It would mean bushwacking a long way in the dark.

He could drop in from the cliff with climbing gear, but that came with a host of logistical issues, especially in the dark. He could hike in from the bottom and look around, but that would appear suspicious right after the accident. He would be visible by any hiker or biker up on the trail.

He would just have to leave it be, for now.

18

July 9th. Kim looked over at gate D5 from Deschutes Brewery's outpost in the Portland airport. Her Delta flight to Minneapolis wouldn't start boarding for at least five minutes. One more glass of wine couldn't hurt.

It had all happened so fast. Camden's accident. The Ross family descending on Portland and Hood River. The grief of Camden's daughter, his friends. And guilt, an overwhelming sense of guilt. Would this have happened if she hadn't been having the affair?

She wasn't looking forward to spending five days in Milwaukee with Camden's family. They wanted her to stay indefinitely, but she pleaded that she needed to get back and take care of the winery.

The funeral was held in a large Catholic cathedral in downtown Milwaukee with a Zoom broadcast. Only 20 or so close relatives attended in person. Camden's daughter and his ex were there. Kim was the grieving partner and spouse and she played the part well, consoling others and breaking into what were genuine tears herself.

On the third day that she was with the Ross family, Camden's father asked if she'd come into his office and chat for a bit. It was an unusual request. He didn't usually direct too much attention to Kim. The retired multimillionaire kept an executive office suite in one wing of his sprawling home for his post-retirement business activities. It was outfitted in gaudy overstuffed leather furniture from the nineties.

Kim entered and took a seat.

"Thanks for taking a minute, Kim. I can't say how much it means to us that you've been here with us over the last few days. It's unbelievably difficult for everyone."

The Ross' assistant followed shortly with a latte for Kim and a regular coffee for the senior Camden Ross. Then in came another man. He was a tall, burly looking fellow, probably in his mid-sixties. He wore pleated khaki slacks, an untucked golf shirt and a pair of black orthopedic-type shoes. He had thick, gray-brown hair that was combed back, a large red nose and alert, steel blue eyes.

"This is Ralph Podowski, a long-time colleague of mine. He was in charge of security for my trucking business for many years. We wanted to ask you some questions about Camden's life."

"Pleased to meet you," Ralph said in a thick upper Midwest lilt, extending a hand.

"You too," Kim said.

Camden Senior said, "We know Camden's death was an accident."

He paused, then continued, "At least that's what the officers on the scene say. I'm sure they are right, but I'm not sure I understand what was going on in my son's life when he died."

Kim's face betrayed a distraught look. She started to cry a bit.

"Oh Kim." The senior Camden walked over and put his hand on her shoulder. She patted the tears from her eyes.

"Just a minute, I'm sorry."

"It's okay, take your time."

She fortified herself with a couple sips from her latte, which wasn't quite up to Stumptown Coffee standards, but would have to do.

"I think it's just, well, a difficult time," Kim said. "And I don't understand what your concerns are. Camden was dealing with this pandemic like all of us and trying to keep everything together."

"Kim," Camden Senior said, adopting a somewhat

sharper tone, "I heard from one of Camden's friends, Todd McKinley, after the funeral. He told me about some things that I find, well, somewhat disturbing." He turned to Ralph and asked, "Ralph, would you mind giving us a minute?"

As Ralph got up and walked out, Kim looked at Camden Senior with a strained expression on her face.

"This is a fairly delicate topic," he said, pausing. "Were you and Camden having some problems in your marriage?"

"What do you mean?" Kim asked, a confused expression on her face.

"Were you seeing someone, Kim? Someone named Scott?"

"No, no, Scott and I are just friends. I mean we did date at one point when I was separated from Camden before we were married. But most recently, we've been friends and co-workers of sorts at the same winery."

"Really? I need you to be honest, Kim."

"I know," Kim said.

Ross continued. "The other thing he mentioned was that place, the Georgian winery ... revavazov? I'm not sure how you say the name. Camden was concerned that they might be up to something, well, not kosher. I never found out much about that."

"He didn't like them very much."

"No, he didn't."

"He was such a skeptic of natural wine," Kim said. "And their instant success, well, it kind of irritated him. But ironically, we were in talks with them to partner with Ross Wines. In fact, Scott was part of that discussion. That might explain some of this confusion."

They talked a while longer and eventually Ralph returned and explained that he'd be visiting Oregon soon to perform a "review of the facts" around Camden Junior's death.

It was 10:30 and the sun was starting to feel uncomfortably hot. Scott's feet ached as he hiked along the trail, which was now going mostly downhill. He was

THE ECLIPSE

sweating under the 65-pound backpack. Just a few more switchbacks and they'd be back to the car.

"No need to rush, babe," Rachel said. "Let's savor this last bit of trail goodness."

"You're right," Scott said with little enthusiasm.

Nate and his buddy Ethan were further ahead. This was about the only time that had happened on the trip. The two 12-year-olds were eager to get back to the car, phone service and the other amenities of civilization.

It was the last day of a four-night backpacking adventure in the Eagle Cap Wilderness in northeast Oregon. The four of them had summited Aneroid Peak, swam in ice-cold mountain lakes, hiked up to Polaris Pass and so much more. Each evening they would ascend to the ridges above their campsite at Dollar Lake to behold the amazing sunsets in this area dubbed as Oregon's "little Switzerland."

At nightfall, Scott would make sure the kids were situated in their tent. Then he and Rachel would partake in cups of whiskey they had set out before hanging the bear bag. They'd savor the bourbon and the night sky, then get cozy in their tent and eventually, drift off to sleep.

Two hours later Scott would be wide awake. The back molar on the upper left where he had taken the hit from Camden would be throbbing.

As Rachel contentedly slept, Scott would stare up at the tent ceiling. He'd think about that man. And Camden, still on the rocks below.

He couldn't help but wonder if the authorities would come to him with more questions, questions about the man he had seen with Camden before the fall.

It didn't take long to load the car up and head out of the wilderness on the winding gravel road. Soon they were on the blacktop bound for Joseph, Oregon. Scott's phone was now off airplane mode and before long it lit up with email messages and texts. As Scott drove, he glanced at the phone, scanning for any hint of an inquiry about the accident.

Their first stop was the R&R Drive-In restaurant in

Joseph. The boys ordered chicken strips, fries and shakes while Scott scanned his phone for messages about the accident. Then he ordered a burger for himself and a veggie burger for Rachel.

There was a voicemail on his phone from Steve Dougherty that, transcribed by Google Voice, said:

> Scott, Steve here. Remember, we met a few weeks back? I got to thinking about what you said about a partnership. I would be interested in talking more.

There were no messages about the Ross bike accident. Scott, Rachel and the two boys stayed a night at the Wallowa Lake State Park before heading home.

Once Scott got back to Portland and had a free minute, he called Laurence to tell him about Steve Dougherty's interest.

"Excellent news, Scott. This could be a big opportunity for you, for all of us."

"How would it work?"

"I think you can help us develop a real estate partnership agreement with Dougherty Vineyards. We'd work with Wegner Bank to finance a complete renovation of their property: a new tasting room, new production facility, upgrades to irrigation, the whole nine yards. All the while, Darden Wine Holdings would engage in a contractual relationship with their winery business operations, extending marketing, distribution and technology services."

"Sounds too good to be true," Scott said.

"Well, there are some complexities. And you're going to help us out with those. You're going to be setting up a new corporate entity and using some capital, some of it from the equity in the Revazov estate, to invest in Dougherty. Call it Larson Development Ventures."

"I'll need to think about that," Scott said.

"Of course, of course," Laurence said. "There will be plenty of time for that. When you talk to Dougherty, keep it casual, don't reveal all the details of the arrangement we'd like to make. Hint at the broad outlines of it, the possibilities."

Kim's return flight from Milwaukee via Minneapolis got into Portland at 8:30 p.m. on Monday, July 17th. A week after returning from the backpacking trip, Scott was still hardly sleeping a wink. Worries about the accident and its consequences pervaded his thoughts. He hadn't told Kim exactly what he'd seen at the scene of the accident, but for some reason, he craved intimacy with her.

They'd stayed completely clear of each other as she had immersed herself in the role of grieving spouse and widow. Scott had gotten Kim's flight information from her, but they had made no immediate plans to meet up.

A half-hour after her flight arrived at PDX, he drove to Kim's place in the West Hills and parked his truck on the street. After Kim's friend dropped her off and departed, Scott got out of his truck and knocked on the door.

"Hey stranger."

"Oh my God — Scott!"

"I couldn't wait. I had to see you."

"It's been a difficult week, to put it lightly," Kim said.

They entered the dark, empty Portland home of Kim and Camden. Scott took Kim's luggage in and tossed it in the corner. Kim started for the kitchen to get a bottle of wine, but Scott stopped her.

"Come here," he said, putting a hand on her shoulder.

With her back against the wall in the entryway, he began to kiss her on the lips and the neck and then began to undress her.

"I should shower."

"I want you now, as you are."

Something in her released and she kissed him more deeply, more intensely.

Afterward, they lay in Kim and Camden's bedroom. Strangely Scott felt more at ease than he had at any time since the accident. He had really been longing for her affection.

In the dim bedroom light, Kim turned to Scott and said, "Hey, let me see your face." She flicked the light on the bedside table and examined Scott's face.

"Looks like your handsome face is back to normal," Kim said.

"That's good to hear. One of my teeth is still bothering me."

"Oh, that should get better," Kim said.

Scott said, "I'm working on another winery deal with Laurence and Mr. Chen."

"When did this come together?"

"While you were gone. This one will be structured a little differently. A real estate partnership agreement."

"I like the sounds of this. Who would have thought, Scott Larson, big shot real estate guy," Kim said as she rolled over and began to stroke Scott's chest. "You know, we need to keep this, I mean us, a secret. Right now, especially. Camden Ross Senior is watching us. In fact, he's going to be sending an investigator."

Scott's whole body stiffened. "To investigate what?"

"Camden's death. He thinks it might not have been an accident. And I think he has an idea that there's some connection with Revazov."

"It puts me in a strange position," Scott said, sitting up and rubbing his jaw. "I was the last one with him up there on Syncline."

Kim hesitated. "I'm sure you'll be fine."

19

August 7th. Ralph swallowed the last of the coffee in the eight-ounce paper cup. He was seated in the air-conditioned customer waiting area of the showroom of Vern Eide Lincoln in Mitchell, South Dakota. The showroom was comfortable and recently renovated and the coffee was decent, but this repair was taking longer than he had hoped.

He walked outside onto the blacktop and felt a blast of heat as he made his way over to the service area of the dealership. At the counter, he asked the receptionist for a ride to someplace where he could get something to eat.

Five minutes later, a teenaged kid pulled up a Lincoln Navigator SUV. They cruised along the wide streets past chain stores toward downtown Mitchell. The kid started talking about food options, beginning with McDonalds and Subway. He pointed out the Corn Palace as they drove by. Ralph asked for a "sit down" restaurant and the kid drove him to the Cattleman's Club Steakhouse just off the Interstate.

It was almost like they'd never heard of the pandemic in central South Dakota. No masks, regular seating in the restaurants. It had been a long drive from Milwaukee and Ralph allowed himself to relax a bit. He had a chicken fried steak and washed it down with an Old Style, had another, then switched back to coffee. After almost two hours, his phone buzzed. His vehicle was ready.

He kept his 2002 Lincoln Continental meticulously clean and met or exceeded all the regular servicing requirements, but this head gasket failure was something he couldn't have predicted. Mr. Ross would take care of it. Luckily, he'd been close to this dealership when it had happened. And because he was in South Dakota where firearms laws were permissive, he wasn't worried about what was in the trunk.

After they finished the repair late in the afternoon, Ralph drove until well past nightfall and took a room in a motel in eastern Wyoming. He would make the Columbia River Gorge by this time tomorrow.

It wasn't clear where the best place to start was in this case. Camden Ross Senior was uneasy about the circumstances around his son's death and his suspicions that something was off had risen as the weeks had passed. The conversations that the father and son had, brief and vague, indicated that Camden was looking into something that might be criminal. And there was the call from Todd McKinley to Camden Senior about Kim's alleged affair.

There had been no autopsy, no investigation of foul play. Camden's body had already been cremated and, according to his wishes, his remains were going to be dispersed in a favorite vineyard in the San Fernando Valley next summer.

Ralph pulled into Hood River at about 9 p.m. the next day and made his way to the Lone Pine Motel on the western end of town. Mr. Ross had suggested the Columbia River Inn on the river, but Ralph preferred a motel to a hotel where he had his own entrance. Nestled between a Safeway and a self-storage facility, the Lone Pine wasn't fancy, but it would do just fine for Ralph.

The next morning, Ralph drove into downtown Hood River for breakfast. He picked out Bette's, which seemed to have a pretty solid breakfast menu, though was a bit on the pricey side. Afterward, he wandered around a bit to get his bearings. Hood River was clearly an upscale small town with a good deal of tourists and fancy shops.

Ralph wasn't really a bicyclist, but figured he could learn something about the accident by going into a bike store, so he went into Discover Bikes in downtown Hood River.

THE ECLIPSE

As he was looking over some of the new mountain bikes, many with price tags that Ralph observed were higher than a decent used car, he got to chatting about Camden Ross' accident on the Syncline trails with one of the store employees.

"That was a freak accident, man. People ride that trail all the time. I don't know how you unintentionally go over the edge. I guess it's happened a couple times now," the guy said.

Kim's life was in complete chaos after her time in Milwaukee. Her kids had been with their dad while she was gone for the funeral and now she had them full time sans normal summer activities due to COVID. And she had the Ross winery to run.

Wine Jamie helped her connect with a number of winemakers to interview who could step in at Ross Wines for the fall harvest. Eventually she settled on a bearded hipster in his mid-thirties who had just moved up from Napa. Kim kept telling herself it wasn't because he was also the best looking of the lot.

Camden Ross Senior was attempting to involve himself in Ross Wines. He wanted to know all about what was happening with the business. She wasn't sure he'd approve of the new vintner who had a natural wine approach that would have clashed with his son's winemaking philosophy.

Strangely, Camden's dad didn't seem to have any idea about the papers she had signed that would have given Camden's family a much larger stake in the winery.

Kim had indeed signed them. On the day Camden died they were sitting in an envelope on the desk in the kitchen. But when Bill Curtis, Camden's attorney, asked about them a few days following Camden's death, Kim lied and said that she hadn't yet signed them. Then she shredded the documents.

The P.I., Ralph, showed up at her Gorge place shortly after she got back from Wisconsin, wanting to talk and examine Camden's effects, particularly his phone and his laptop.

There was no way she was going to let him get a look into Camden's devices before she did, so she denied him that request, explaining that even she didn't have the passwords to the devices. She did let him have a look around the house and the winery. He spent some time examining the bike that Camden was riding when he took his fatal fall.

After Ralph's visit to the Ross Wines estate, he decided to visit Revazov given the interest that Camden Ross had shown in the place and Kim's work there. From his laptop in his motel room, he looked over the Revazov website. Under the "Visit Us" section, it said "by appointment only due to social distancing guidelines." With a phone call, he discovered that they had a slot for a wine tasting at 2, right when the place opened.

Ralph drove the Continental over the Hood River Bridge and up Cook Underwood Road to the turnoff to Revazov. As he walked from the parking lot to the tasting room, he marveled at the view of Mount Hood. A tall, young woman with flowing dark brown hair, high-waisted shorts, white sneakers and a halter top greeted him at the entrance to the tasting room and adjacent outdoor seating area.

"Hi there, you must be Ralph. I'm Delilah."

Delilah gave him a choice of outdoor tables. They were spaced apart to facilitate social distancing and spilled out from the patio onto the lawn. Ralph took one considerably shaded by the sail-shaped awnings that were suspended with cables attached to trees above.

He ordered a flight of wine and when it arrived, he was surprised to find out it came with a 10-minute introduction by Delilah.

"The thing that's amazing about Sasha's wines is that they are so different every year. Take that pinot gris, I mean last year's was so sophisticated, like ... classical music. This

THE ECLIPSE

year's is like jazz. It's playful and unpredictable."

She continued, working her way through each offering.

"And the grenache, it's just easy. You know some nights when you want to just have popcorn and wine instead of dinner?"

"I can't say I've ever done that," Ralph said, "though it sounds like you have."

"Well, if you ever do, this is your wine," Delilah said with a good-natured smile.

She left Ralph to attend to some other customers and he slowly worked through the wines, trying and mostly failing to think about what he was tasting in each pour.

Eventually, Delilah came back to Ralph to check on him. It looked like she didn't have any other immediate demands so Ralph asked, "Have you heard about that bike accident up on the mountain bike trail up near here?"

"Oh yeah, that was awful. I hike up there sometimes. I know something like it happened once, a long time back."

"Right, that's what I understand as well. I'm working for the Ross family, wrapping up some loose ends."

"Well sometimes Camden Ross would come up here and meet his wife, Kim. She works for us. I saw him at a couple Revazov parties."

"Do you know anything about his opinion of Revazov then?"

"No, not really."

"How about his wife Kim, what can you tell me about her?"

"She was friends with the guy who owns this property, Scott. Sometimes she would park here and walk up the path to his house."

"Oh, and where's that then?"

She pointed to the path from the winery up to the residence — the one marked Private Property.

Ralph wandered around the winery grounds a bit. He was feeling the wine tasting. The scenery here was surreal. Looking to the south, Mount Hood kind of floated in the sky with just a few strands of white left on its flanks.

He walked over to the private pathway to the residence but decided not to go up it. Instead, he drove to the Klickitat County Sheriff's office in White Salmon. The masked lady behind the counter was able to retrieve and print a four-page accident report filed by the sheriff's deputy on the scene at the time of Camden Ross' death.

Then he drove back to his motel room and scanned the report which was filled with names and brief testimonials from several individuals at the scene of the accident. Nothing jumped out at him as particularly revelatory, though he looked over the notes about Scott Larson's interview carefully.

Ralph laid down on the bed and put on the ball game for a couple of hours, eventually dozing off.

When it was dark, he drove over to Ross Wines. The lights were off in the residence, which could be seen from a spot on the road. Then he drove across the river and up to the Revazov winery again. There was no direct view of Scott's home from the road. Ralph parked at a turnout, walked a quarter-mile down the road, then walked down the drive that led to the winery. He took the path to the private residence. The renovated farmhouse, nestled in a patch of trees, was dark and appeared unoccupied.

He walked behind the house and found a spot in the trees that afforded a view of the house and grounds. Then he bushwhacked through the trees back to the road, taking note of where he exited.

Scott was on his way to the Gorge place, just about to Multnomah Falls, when he saw the 414 area code that he recognized as Milwaukee's come up on his phone.

"Scott Larson."

"Hiya Scott, Ralph Podowski here. I'm an associate of Camden Ross' father. I'm out here in Oregon, in the Hood River area, trying to tie up some loose ends around that terrible accident he had. I was wondering if we could meet for coffee or something and talk?"

"Of course," Scott said reflexively. "If mornings work, how about the White Salmon Baking Company tomorrow?"

"A bakery? That sounds like my type of place," Ralph replied.

"They have a damn good cinnamon roll," Scott said, not really knowing why he added that detail.

"It's a deal, I'll see you there at 8."

Scott pushed the call end button on his phone.

As he continued to drive east on I-84, the thought pattern that had been repeating itself in his head over the last several weeks returned.

By following Laurence's directions in those minutes after the accident, he had made an irreversible choice. He had taken a fork in the road and there was no returning to it.

It was true that he hadn't seen anyone kill Camden. And it certainly was true that Camden had crashed his bike. The other biker's presence and Laurence's intervention into the situation certainly were suspicious, however.

If there was foul play in Camden's death, the affair with Kim would make him a prime suspect and that could be a very hazardous, messy situation for him, even though he was innocent. There was nothing he could do to bring Camden back. Therefore, it was probably best to keep to a simple version of events and not complicate the narrative around the accident.

But was that really the right thing to do? And what if more facts emerged around the accident? He couldn't help but worry about what the future held.

For a long time, White Salmon, Washington was much lower key than touristy Hood River, Oregon on the other side of the Columbia River. But in recent years, White Salmon had become a tourist destination in its own right. It now boasted a substantial lineup of restaurants and shops including the White Salmon Baking Company, which offered delicious artisan pastries five days a week, even during the pandemic.

Scott arrived there at 8:35 the next morning. It was a typical Gorge summer morning with just a hint of coolness in the air, blue skies and the promise of a spectacular day ahead. The outside seating area was occupied by moms in yoga pants looking after their kids, kiter dudes in board shorts and trucker hats talking about the day's wind forecast and retirees focused on a book or The Wall Street Journal.

Podowski stood out in his golf shirt and slacks. He was reading a copy of "Matterhorn," the Vietnam War novel by Karl Marlantes, with a cup of drip coffee and about a third of a cinnamon roll remaining on a small paper plate. He stood up to greet Scott.

"Thanks for meeting me, Scott. I'd shake your hand but, well, you know. You were right about those cinnamon rolls." Scott went up to the window and ordered an Americano and a cardamom bun and sat back down at the small table. His stomach was in knots.

"Scott, let me tell you a little bit why I'm here. The Rosses just lost their only son and they need closure. They want to understand a little more about what happened to Camden. I'm here to make sure there aren't any important, unanswered questions about their son's death."

"Okay," Scott said.

"So how did you know Camden then?"

"Well, I'm friends with Kim. I met Camden a couple times in passing and well, I had a conversation with him at a party in February. We figured out we like to do some of the same things, especially backcountry skiing."

"So how did you come to be ... friends with Kim?"

"We dated a few years ago, while Kim was split up from Camden."

"Ya, that's what I heard. Were you seeing her recently?" Ralph asked.

"No, I mean, yes, we were friends. She would come by to say hi sometimes when she was at the winery."

"So you were seeing each other romantically?"

"No."

"How about now?"

"We're friends."

"Just friends then?"

"Yes."

"Tell me a bit about the bike ride then."

"Well, it's a popular mountain bike ride. It's wide-open and treeless and the scenery is amazing. Pretty nice, technical single-track trail."

"It doesn't look like an accident has happened up there since 2005? Why would something like that happen to Camden given that he's such an experienced biker?"

"You know, I'm not sure. He liked to go fast, he liked the adrenaline rush. To tell you the truth, I couldn't keep up with him going downhill on a bike. That's why I didn't see it happen. He was way out ahead of me."

"So you're a little more careful rider than Camden then?"

"I'd probably say that," Scott said, "but he generally is in control, from what I observed."

"The Sheriff's report said that you had a bump on your left cheek from a fall that same day. Kind of strange that both of you would crash your bike the same day, or no?"

"Mountain biking is kind of extreme," Scott said.

"You're sure that your injury was a biking injury? You know, if you hadn't said otherwise, I might have thought he clocked you one."

"No, no, no. I can only blame my poor riding skills," Scott said.

Ralph paused a bit, taking in Scott's response.

"So tell me about what you saw of Camden's accident."

"I was concentrating on the descent so much I wasn't being very observant."

"So what was the last thing you saw?"

Scott paused. This was the part he had rehearsed in his head.

"I mean I saw him riding in the distance and then I came

upon his bike and he was gone. His bike was there but he wasn't. And then I looked over the cliff and he was down there."

"What do you think caused him to crash and go over?"

"There was a rock in the trail. Kind of odd that it was there. I think it must have caught him off guard."

"What a terrible accident," Ralph said, shaking his head. "Would you be willing to show me where it happened?"

"Absolutely, we can head up there right now if you like," Scott said. "It's only a 10-minute drive from here. Though there is a pretty long hike involved."

An hour later, Scott pulled into the Syncline parking lot. Clad in camouflage hunting boots, cargo pants and a wide-brimmed safari hat, Ralph was easy to spot. Scott parked a few cars away from Ralph's Lincoln.

It was still in the low 70s and there was a west wind blowing as they started on the trek. Scott was impressed by Ralph's fitness as they ascended the Old Ranch Road trail up to the higher trail system where the accident had taken place. As they hiked, they talked about various things having to do with the Gorge, their mutual background in Wisconsin and the pandemic.

When they reached the spot in the trail where Camden had fallen, they paused. Ralph walked up and down the trail. He stood aside as mountain bikers passed through. He appeared to be studying their trajectories carefully. He walked around on the trail surface, kicking the dirt around a bit.

As this was an area where there weren't too many loose rocks, it was easy for Scott to identify the rock that Camden must have hit. It was sitting a few feet from the trail.

"Any chance that he hit something other than a rock?" Ralph asked.

"Well, what do you think it could have been?"

"I looked over his bike at Kim's place. The front tire was sliced into just a bit in one area. It wasn't easy to see but it made me wonder if he ran into something sharp like a wire. Something that would have been hard to see."

"That's a theory," Scott said.

Ralph peered down the cliff.

"How do you get down there?"

"Well, you don't really. There aren't trails that go through the wooded area to the base of the cliffs. And those volcanic scree slopes at the bottom would be really hard to climb."

After the hike with Scott Larson, Ralph returned to his room at the Lone Pine.

He studied the Klickitat County Sheriff's report again. The sheriff's deputies had spoken with a few bikers and hikers who they had encountered on the trails and down at the parking lot during the rescue and recovery effort. There wasn't much detail about what they said but the report did give about a dozen names and phone numbers. The report concluded that the accounts of witnesses at the scene and the coroner's report had all pointed to an accident.

Ralph made a pot of coffee in the motel room and got his phone out and started calling the people in the report.

They all had pretty much the same story. They'd been out enjoying the Syncline trails and had learned about the accident by speaking to bikers or hikers along the Coyote Wall or when they'd come upon the scene of law enforcement vehicles, fire trucks and an ambulance at the trailhead. Some had stayed around a bit to watch the rescue effort.

Ralph asked each of them if they had traveled down the upper trail section where Camden's accident occurred. A good handful of them had. He talked to one of the two fellows who had come upon Scott at the cliff edge.

"Was there anything strange that you noticed as you approached the scene of the fall?" Ralph asked.

"Well, we slowed down a bit, seeing the bike turned over by the trail, and there was that rock in the trail."

"Was the rock hard to spot?"

"Not if you were paying attention."

"Was there anyone besides Camden's friend Scott there?"

"No there wasn't. It was just him. Though in the distance before we got there, you know I could swear that there could have been someone else."

He asked everyone with whom he spoke to send him an email with any photos they had of that morning.

The photos came into his email over the next few days. Links to Apple iCloud, Google Photos, Facebook albums, and a couple of GoPro files. They were the typical snapshots and videos people took with their phone on an outdoor excursion: scenic views, action shots and group photos. Ralph collected any photos and videos that had identifiable people in them and put them in a folder on his laptop.

There was one shot timestamped at about 15 minutes before the accident had been called in. Two teenaged girls plus mom and dad had been out for a hike. They'd stopped along the trail that traverses from the Old Ranch Road to the Coyote Wall trail for a group shot.

Ralph zoomed in on the photo on his laptop. In the distance he could see two riders descending the Coyote Wall trail. He identified the rider in front as Camden by the blue bi-color jersey and loose black shorts that matched the photos of Camden's body in the accident report. There was a guy right behind Camden wearing a black cycling jersey and purple wraparound sunglasses. That was strange, thought Ralph, as Scott said that he was far behind Camden on the descent.

He combed over other shots from that day for any sign of the second biker. After looking through what must have been 300 photos, he stumbled upon a shot taken along the Coyote Wall trail. It was taken by a family of four with grandparents. They were posing next to the cliff but a biker with the same black jersey could be seen descending the trail. In this photo, with some zooming in, the biker's facial features were somewhat identifiable.

Ralph texted the two photos to Scott and asked for any insights that he might have regarding the biker right behind Camden.

Scott didn't reply for a half hour.

> You know now that I think about it, there was a guy that passed me after Camden and I started descending. That must be him.
>
> But you didn't see him again?
>
> No
>
> He wasn't at the scene of the accident?
>
> Not that I saw.

Ralph pounded the pavement in Hood River with the photo, asking around at a few different spots about the man. One of the guys at Discover Bikes in downtown Hood River recognized the man from the photo. They'd rented a bike to him and even had a name on file that they produced with the help of a couple of Benjamins from Ralph: Dr. Ingo Merz.

Gerhard, impeccably dressed in a Hugo Boss suit, was enjoying a macchiato at the Prince Coffee Shop on the main floor of the Grand Hotel in Prishtina, Kosovo. He was on contract to assassinate the owner of an upstart construction company that was underbidding the work of his client. It would probably be a car accident given how crazy driving was the norm in this tiny Balkan country. His phone vibrated on the table and he looked at the text message. There was a problem with the Oregon job.

He called Laurence Visser.

"This is unacceptable," Visser said, "We have a private eye from Wisconsin poking around in our business. He's even managed to latch onto the identity that you used when you were in Oregon for the job."

"I agree that's a problem," Gerhard said laconically. "I will go back and clean things up."

"I think this is a situation where we show some force. Keep it clean, but take him out hard. We need to send a message."

20

When Ralph started on the job, he'd considered it a fool's errand, an assignment based on the irrational suspicions of a father in grief. He'd planned to take a couple of weeks, carefully investigate and report back. That would be the end of it.

But a little more than a week into the job, his mindset was changing. He had the scent of something amiss around Camden Ross' death and his old bloodhound instincts were kicking in. In his career as a security consultant and private investigator, he'd encountered this feeling before but it was a pretty rare thing.

It was like a switch flipped and then all you could think of was the investigation 24/7. You got obsessed with it and that was good and bad. You worked harder, maxed out your brain and really followed your instincts. But you also were prone to taking unnecessary risks.

Ralph was too close to retirement to be doing that.

Next year, he would trade in the Continental for a new motor home. The Ross job would take care of the down payment. His former girlfriend Darla was widowed and living in Arizona and they'd been emailing and Facebooking. He planned to take delivery of a 2021 Jayco Redhawk in October and then drive from Milwaukee to Arizona to pick her up. Then they'd be off for the adventure of a lifetime.

After looking through the photos one morning, Ralph returned to the site of the accident. He kicked around the trail in the vicinity of Camden's fall and thought about the small incisions on the bike tire. He looked over the edge and at the scree slope below. If there had been some device that had triggered the fall, there was a possibility, perhaps a remote one, that part of it had gone flying off the cliff. The news story about the fall had emphasized the difficulty of reaching the body by paramedics, noting that it had taken a half-hour of hiking through thick vegetation and rocky terrain to get there.

A skinny, bearded young man hiking with poles and wearing a relatively large backpack came walking by. He looked like a kind of independent loner type.

"Hey, I wonder if I could ask you something?" Ralph queried.

"Sure," the young man said.

"You look like an experienced hiker. What do you think it would take to get to the bottom of that cliff there."

The hiker stood and surveyed the area. He seemed happy to have been asked.

"Interesting question. Well, either a serious rappel down this cliff or a lot of bushwhacking from the bottom. I don't do rock climbing, so I'd probably bushwhack it."

"I'm looking to examine that area," Ralph said. "A friend may have dropped something down there. I need to get there. I wonder if I paid you, if you'd come with me and help me have a look?"

"Interesting offer," the hiker said.

"There's three bills in it for you."

The hiker's eyes widened. "Now that's a *very* interesting offer. I'm in!"

Ralph met the hiker, Mike, at the Syncline trailhead early the next morning. They walked through a tree-filled area alongside the cliff using a navigator app on Mike's iPhone to plot the way.

After about 45 minutes, they reached the bottom of the scree slope below the cliff section where Camden had taken the fall. Next came the hard part. They needed to ascend the scree to the base of the cliff. Ralph let Mike take the lead.

"What exactly are we looking for?" he asked Ralph.

"I'm not sure. Something mechanical, a wire, a device. Any kind of hardware."

The going was tough on the scree. One step up and they slid half a step down. Ralph held his own behind Mike.

Soon they reached a rock wall that wasn't quite to the base of the cliff. Mike free climbed it at a spot that wasn't too steep and Ralph followed his lead. They scrambled up another section of steep, loose rock to the base of the cliff. The GPS revealed that this was the location where the fall had taken place and it seemed to match the pictures of the body in the Sheriff's file. They searched the ledge where Camden had landed to no avail.

The platform on which they were standing ended on one side where a band of the columnar basalt cliff jutted out. Ralph said he wanted to have a look on the other side so they climbed back down off the ledge and onto the scree slope.

Then they ascended the scree toward the cliff on the other side of the band. They reached another rock ledge at the base of the cliff and looked down at the scree below.

"Do you see anything?" Mike asked Ralph.

Ralph took his time, squinting.

"Do you see that glint of metal down there? Let's climb back down onto the slope."

They went back down to the scree and Ralph slowly and purposefully walked down the slope, a bit off the path where they had come up.

"This is it," Ralph said, kicking a rock with his foot.

"What do you mean?"

"You see the wire connected to that rock. This was what I was looking for."

Mike examined the boulder.

"Should we carry it out?"

"I'll take a picture of it," Ralph said. "Better to leave it here, as evidence."

Gerhard wasn't in vacation mode this time around. After picking up a rental SUV at the Portland airport, he drove out Northeast Sandy Boulevard to 82nd Avenue, Portland's "Avenue of Roses," a long north-south thoroughfare on the city's far east side lined with chain stores, used car dealerships and locally owned businesses that include pawn shops, massage parlors and Chinese restaurants.

Gerhard met his contact in the parking lot of an Asian grocery store. The man supplied Gerhard with a Glock 9 mm and four loaded magazines. He offered an automatic weapon, which Gerhard declined. He also gave Gerhard the address of a person who could provide him with assistance.

Gerhard then made the two-hour drive from Portland to Goldendale, Washington, a small working-class community in the eastern Columbia Gorge that had fallen on hard times in the decade and a half since the closure of an aluminum smelting plant powered by the nearby John Day Dam.

The property must have been a 10-acre parcel and was littered with the carcasses of cars and trucks exposed to the relentless sunlight and wind of the eastern Washington desert. The two operable vehicles looked to be a dusty 2000s Jeep Cherokee SUV and a lifted Ford F-350 with a giant grill guard.

Gerhard knocked on the door of the rundown manufactured home and a young woman answered. She was probably in her mid-twenties with a neck and sleeves of tattoos. Gerhard could see that she was an attractive girl but she had a tired look about her. Jake took a minute to emerge from the house.

He was an inch or two taller than Gerhard's 6 feet, 2 inches but skinnier and fully tattooed like the girl. He wore a white T-shirt, some sweats and a pair of basketball trainers. He had intense brown eyes and his tall skinny body seemed to twitch with nervous energy.

He smiled to reveal some broken front teeth but didn't offer a hand.

THE ECLIPSE

Gerhard said, "Hello Jake, nice to meet you."

"Nice to meet you too, Aahh-nold?" Jake said, speaking slowly and mocking Gerhard's German accent.

"It's Gerhard," Gerhard said, not getting the Arnold Schwarzenegger reference.

"So you got a job for me, brah?" Jake said as they walked out to the large sheet metal garage on the property.

"Yes, there's a man who's in the area. He's doing an investigation, so he moves around quite a bit. We'll let you know when he's in a good spot. It should look like a drug deal gone bad. You're going to be the one that got away with the drugs and the cash but we're going to leave some drugs behind to make it look like that's what this is about."

"Is he going to be packing?"

"We don't know. But he shouldn't be expecting you."

Gerhard took the Glock 9 mm out and handed it to Jake, along with the magazines of ammunition.

"I got my own piece, brah," Jake said.

"This is the one you're going to use," Gerhard said. "And you use this phone to be in touch" he said as he pulled out the burner phone.

Gerhard explained to Jake how to dispose of the weapon and the phone when the job was completed and handed him an envelope with $10,000 in cash.

"The other two-thirds comes when you finish the job."

Jake pulled the cash out of the envelope and examined the bills.

"I will contact you on the phone when we have a place and a time. I need you to be available," said Gerhard.

Looking up from the money, Jake grinned with his broken teeth. "Not a problem. I got this, brah."

Gerhard turned to leave.

"Hey brah, where are you from?"

"Germany."

"Ah, fuck yeah, I knew it by the accent. Feel like getting a little foiled with me?"

"I don't do that shit," Gerhard replied.

As Gerhard walked back to his vehicle, he could hear kids in the vicinity of the house.

August 19th. Scott sat in the shabby back office of Dougherty Vineyards. At 1 p.m. it was already over 90 and the window-unit air conditioner struggled to keep the small room cool.

Scott and Steve Dougherty huddled around a laptop. Soon attorneys from Lowe Dede & Warren and an officer of Wegner Bank appeared on the screen. Scott recognized the attorneys from the signing for the Bodenheimer property. Laurence also popped up in one of the boxes on the screen.

After they had exchanged pleasantries, the attorneys explained the agreement that Steve was about to sign.

"This is the real estate partnership agreement that you will be signing with Mr. Larson. Under this arrangement, Wegner Bank will provide the financing for a series of upgrades to the Dougherty property. The real estate investment trust will then have an equity stake in the property equivalent to the investments. This initial loan of $1.5 million will kick off the upgrades but there is a potential to expand the financing as needed."

The attorneys listed off plans to upgrade the Dougherty tasting room and winery production area as well as other equipment and buildings supporting the vineyard.

"But we have the right to buy our stake out of the trust and return to full family ownership, correct?" Steve asked.

"Yes, that is possible," an attorney said.

Laurence interjected, "This is going to be a dynamite deal for you guys. It's a new beginning for your family. A fresh start."

Steve Dougherty sighed and said, "Okay."

The attorneys explained that a notary would be delivering the papers to sign within hours.

Ralph had developed a rhythm during his time in Hood

THE ECLIPSE

River. During the morning, he did some investigative work. In the late afternoon, he got a takeout meal from a local restaurant and ate it back at the motel with a couple of beers he kept in the mini fridge while watching a game. Then he'd read or take a nap for a couple of hours. About 11 o'clock, he'd get up and be moving again.

He usually drove out to the Ross Wines complex and checked up on the house. If there was nothing going on there, he drove up to the Revazov estate, parked a quarter-mile away and walked to the vantage point of Scott's house that he'd scouted out.

He didn't particularly like spying on romantic liaisons. But he'd done these types of jobs before for jealous wives and husbands and knew the tradecraft. It took a number of agonizingly long sessions but he finally got the shot he wanted: Kim's SUV parked in Scott's driveway. The two of them silhouetted together, Scott standing behind Kim, his hands on her shoulders in the living room window. It wasn't the most damning shot. They weren't in bed. But it would have to do.

When Gerhard got word that the P.I. had been out to the Syncline trails a few times, he packed a backpack full of tools and bushwhacked to the area where he suspected the rock that had weighted the trip line would have fallen. After a frustrating half-hour of searching in the early hours of the morning, he found it.

There was no way he was getting that eye hook out of there without some serious equipment, so he lugged the rock a quarter-mile aways and hid it in a pile of similar-looking boulders.

When Ralph was trying to identify the man who turned out to be Dr. Ingo Merz, he showed the photo of him around to a number of people. A guy that he spoke with in the line at Rosauers grocery store said that he'd seen him at a nearby restaurant called The Pancake Hut. Ralph took lunch there one afternoon.

After the waitress brought over a BLT, Ralph pulled up the picture of Dr. Merz on his phone and asked her if she'd ever seen him.

"I think you might want to talk to Chantelle, she usually waited on him."

A younger woman with a generous figure approached Ralph.

"Oh that's Ingo. Yeah, he was my customer here."

"I'm wondering if you'd have a few minutes to chat about him?"

"Well, I'm not sure that's okay," she said, blushing a bit. "I mean I don't know him that well. I was so surprised to see him the other day. I thought I'd never see him again."

"You saw him recently?"

"Oh, I'm not going to say anything more."

"Well, thanks anyway. Could I have the check please?"

Ralph realized immediately that the man being back in the area was potentially a hazardous situation and that he should probably clear out as soon as possible.

He was planning to head back to Milwaukee and provide a summary of his findings to Mr. Ross soon anyway. But he wanted at least one more day. He had a chance to talk to a Klickitat County sheriff's deputy who was on the scene at the time of Camden's accident.

He finished up his lunch and drove the Lincoln north of town out on Tucker Road to a gravel pit. Then he started scouring the car.

He found the tracking device inside the front fender. He pulled it out and set it on the front seat next to him and returned to his motel.

He packed up his things and left the Lone Pine without checking out, setting the tracking device in the bushes near the spot where he parked his car for his motel room. He drove across the Hood River Bridge to the Washington side and waited in the Park and Ride to try and ascertain that he wasn't being followed. He timed it so that he got back on the bridge before a long line of cars and trucks turning from the lane that fed traffic in from the east. As soon as he crossed the bridge and paid the toll, he drove under I-84 and took the eastbound on-ramp, eyeing his rearview mirror the entire time.

Soon Ralph was passing through The Dalles, driving by the Google data centers, chain restaurants and then the massive Dalles Dam. In another 20 miles, he pulled off at Biggs Junction — more of a truck stop than a town — on the Oregon side of the Sam Hill Bridge where Interstate 84 intersects with U.S. Highway 97. While gassing up the Lincoln, he stood in the sun and warm west wind and took in the vast landscape of grassy plateaus and basalt cliffs that surround the mighty Columbia.

He thought about staying in the little motel in Biggs but something about that felt exposed. He decided to drive south on Highway 97 to the nearest town. The two-lane road took him up a canyon and onto a plateau where he could see an array of spinning wind turbines off to the east. Soon he arrived in Moro, Oregon, population 325.

Ralph spotted the Tall Winds Motel to his right on Moro's main drag as he entered town but he continued on past the city park and out to the opposite end of town where the high school was and then turned around.

As soon as Gerhard saw Ralph pull up at The Pancake Hut on the tracking app, he realized it had been a mistake to be in touch with Chantelle.

On the app, Gerhard watched Ralph drive out to the gravel pit. He suspected he was tampering with the tracking device, so he put a replacement one on Ralph's car when Ralph showed up again at the Lone Pine.

When the new tracker showed Ralph pull off at Biggs, then head south to Moro and then pull into the Tall Winds Motel, Gerhard was relieved that Ralph wasn't leaving the area.

Gerhard called Jake and gave him Ralph's location. It

was just a 30-minute drive from Jake's place in Goldendale. Gerhard then headed east on I-84. He didn't trust Jake to get this job done right.

The Tall Winds Motel was an L-shaped structure with a total of 10 units. Except for a short two-story section, most rooms were at ground level with pull-in parking. Ralph could see two guest vehicles parked near the office.

He went to the office and rented two rooms at the far end of the building.

Ralph backed the Lincoln into the parking spot in front of the room farthest on the end, turned on the light in that room and closed the door. Then he walked to Husky's Market just down the road and got himself a turkey sandwich, potato chips and a six-pack of Rainier.

When he got back to the motel, he got the pump-action 12-gauge from the trunk of the Lincoln and entered the room second from the end. He sat at the small table and ate his meal. When he was done, he placed the shotgun on the floor next to the bed, settled down on the paisley bedspread and flicked on the small flat-screen television with the remote to watch some baseball.

At 8:41 p.m., as the daylight was fading, Ralph heard the knock on the adjacent room. There was a pause. He picked up the shotgun.

Another knock came, this time a little more insistent.

Jake turned the knob on the door and it opened. The room looked totally unoccupied. He walked to the back of the room to check the bathroom. Then he heard the door of the next room opening and a vehicle starting up outside. He ran back out of the hotel room and saw the lights of the Lincoln Continental pulling out onto Highway 97.

Jake ran for his truck, which was parked on the highway. He hopped in the cab, started the engine and then peeled out as he headed after the other vehicle.

THE ECLIPSE

It was dusk as Ralph drove north on Highway 97 back toward the Interstate. The Continental's 4.6-liter V-8 easily pulled him up over 90 on the open road. If he could just get to I-84 he'd have cover, other people, other vehicles around him.

However, after 10 miles or so he found himself behind a semi-truck in a curvy No Passing zone. Soon, he saw lights approaching from the rear.

A big pickup loomed a few feet behind Ralph's Continental, the headlights at the same level of Ralph's back window. It stayed there on his ass for minutes.

Soon, the highway got quite curvy as it wound its way down the canyon toward the Columbia River.

When the highway briefly straightened out, the truck pulled alongside Ralph's Lincoln and slammed into its side, sending the car off into the shoulder. Ralph struggled to get control of the vehicle as it bounced and bucked over the uneven surface.

The truck slammed into the Lincoln again, causing the car to smash into a guardrail and go into a high-speed spin. Ralph wrestled the steering wheel and the car came to a stop facing the opposite direction of travel on the road.

Dazed, Ralph stayed low and took a couple of seconds to recover his bearings. From the driver's seat, he could see the front of the car was crushed. He kept his head down and tried to start the engine but nothing happened when he turned the key.

He could hear the sound of the truck's loud exhaust as it continued down the road a bit and slowed down.

Ralph exited the driver's side of the car with the shotgun and headed for the ditch. He could now hear the throaty sound of the truck's engine as it was coming back toward him.

In seconds, the lights of the truck appeared from around a curve and barreled toward Ralph's car. Kneeling and taking cover in the ditch, Ralph aimed the shotgun squarely at the truck cab and began firing, using the pump action to reload the chamber as rapidly as possible.

As the F-350 was battered with shot that broke the windshield and blew out a front tire, it turned off its initial trajectory toward Ralph's car, then slowed and swerved, a flat tire making a whooping sound. Ralph couldn't tell if he'd taken down the driver. The truck continued down the road veering back and forth.

Gerhard had followed the chase from a distance and pulled over when he saw the Lincoln spin out.

After waiting a couple minutes, he'd heard shots and then saw Jake's truck weave uncontrollably and crash in a ditch just a bit past where he was parked.

"Verdammte Idiot," he said as he opened the door of the truck to reveal the bloody, slumped over body of Jake. He retrieved the handgun from the floor of the truck. He also rustled around in Jake's pockets and found the meth.

Gerhard got back into his car and drove a few hundred yards to the bashed-up Lincoln. He pulled in behind it, hopped out and shouted into the darkness. "Anyone need any help?"

The authorities would be here soon, he figured. He tossed the cylinder of meth into the Lincoln and drove about a quarter-mile down the road where there was a wide shoulder and parked his car.

After unloading his shotgun on the truck, Ralph had tossed some unspent shells in his pocket, called 911 and then ascended the ridge above the road, getting into a position where he was out of sight from the road but had a view of his car. He suspected that the man in the truck might return and wanted to be ready.

After a minute, a vehicle had pulled up behind his Lincoln. A guy had gotten out and asked if anyone needed help. Something about his approach seemed off and his accented voice had brought to mind Ingo Merz, so Ralph had remained quiet and held his position.

THE ECLIPSE

The car continued down the road and Ralph waited.

A couple minutes later, as a semi roared by, he heard a shot and felt a sting in his left shoulder. He dropped low and looked along the ridge. There was the silhouette of a man's figure against the sky.

The pain from the wound began to radiate but he still could move his arm enough to return three blasts from the shotgun.

The figure dropped to the ground.

The burn intensified in Ralph's shoulder but he stayed down and held his position.

After what seemed like ages, he heard sirens and saw lights.

In five minutes, it was a complete shit show. There were 12 state troopers and an ambulance on the scene. Ralph announced himself, put his hands up and worked his way down to the cops. His injured state meant that he was taken in an ambulance to the Mid-Columbia Medical Center in The Dalles accompanied by a state trooper.

Gerhard was shot in his gut but he made it back to his car. Seconds after he started driving north on 97, he saw the state troopers headed the opposite way. His wounds were serious so he used the burner phone to make a call to the medical service.

They told him to drive west on I-84. In The Dalles, a text appeared with an address in Mosier, a rural township five miles east of Hood River.

Gerhard followed the directions as they were dictated from Google. Soon he was pulling into the gravel driveway of a ranch-like property. The driveway went on for a while and he came to the house. He keyed the code they gave him to the electronic lock and he was in.

Camden Ross Senior texted Kim the story from The Oregonian the next day.

> **Sept. 8, 2020**
>
> **A shootout involving three men on U.S. Highway 97 four miles south of Biggs Junction, Oregon, has left one dead and one injured with another suspect at large.**
>
> **Jake Clark, 29, of Goldendale, Washington, was found dead of gunshot wounds in his Ford F-350 truck, which Oregon State Troopers came upon at 9:36 p.m. last night.**
>
> **Ralph Podowski, 64, of Milwaukee, Wisconsin, who troopers found at the scene, sustained gunshot wounds. Podowski was transported to the Mid-Columbia Medical Center in The Dalles.**
>
> **A third unidentified man involved in the shooting remains at large.**

Kim texted the link to the story to Scott.

After Gerhard arrived at the safe house, the service had examined him using a video feed from his phone. About an hour later a medic had shown up with pain meds, antibiotics and an IV drip.

The doctor, an older Vietnamese man, arrived the next day to perform the surgery to get the shotgun pellets out of Gerhard's abdomen. The man assured him that he was a very experienced combat surgeon, though not formally licensed to practice medicine in the United States.

He set up a makeshift surgery space in the bedroom that was a combination of equipment from Home Depot — shop lights, a tool box, a portable work table — and real medical gear.

The anesthetic wasn't hospital grade. In fact, it wasn't even an anesthetic, it was just pain killers. But this wasn't Gerhard's first experience with field surgery. He'd had a couple bullets removed in Angola in the nineties when he was employed by a private military outfit. A lifetime ago. This was the Mayo Clinic compared to that.

Now he was patched up and stuck in this place for another day or two, recuperating. Brooding on this job gone bad.

The all-stone exterior and classical details of the Wasco County Courthouse in The Dalles gave it a weighty, historic look from a distance. But as one got closer, the peeling paint on the window frames revealed a more neglected structure. The interior of the Sheriff's Office, which occupied the lower level and had an entrance at the rear, was a drab, fluorescent-lit space redone sometime in the eighties.

Ralph was seated in a nondescript conference room in that office. He'd been released from the hospital the day before and was eager to get the questioning over with and get on a plane back to Milwaukee.

The conversation began with an introduction by the Sherman County Sheriff, Dean Paschild, who explained that the shootout on Highway 97 was being investigated by a law enforcement contingent known as the Mid-Columbia Major Crimes Team.

A young detective from the Hood River County Sheriff's

Office, Meghan Crowler, led the questioning.

"So Mr. Podowski, your usual residence is in Milwaukee, Wisconsin, correct?"

"Yep, that's correct ma'am."

Ralph knew what she was going to bring up next. The break-in at the office building. That job where he had to get some evidence for a client and the alarm had gone off. He'd taken the fall, done a little community service and been paid handsomely.

"And I see you are a convicted felon."

"Yes, that was many years ago."

"And, I might add, you have a distinguished military record. Your occupation is listed as security contractor and private investigator. Is that the capacity you were acting in out on Highway 97 two days ago?"

"Yes, the reason I'm in Oregon is to pursue this investigation."

"So explain to me what caused you to shoot a man on Highway 97 last Tuesday."

"Ma'am, I was run off the road by that F-350. The man driving that truck was attempting to do me harm. I shot at his truck as it was barreling toward me."

"Mr. Podowski, what were methamphetamines doing in your vehicle?"

"I don't know anything about that."

The sheriff spoke. "Do you know how much meth and fentanyl come up from the south on that highway? How do you think it looks that you have a few grand worth of the stuff in your car? And this man you shot. He was a convicted drug felon. Were you making some money on the side during your investigation, Mr. Podowski? Was there some kind of exchange involved that went bad?"

"Sir, I'm not involved in the drug trade."

"I want to understand why you had a 12-gauge pump in that Lincoln of yours. Why you fired multiple rounds into the vehicle of a meth dealer."

"Sir, with all due respect, you folks need to widen this

investigation. You need to understand this was part of something bigger. I was attacked to cover up another killing."

Ralph went on to explain what he had discovered so far in his investigation of Camden Ross' death.

In the second week of September, easterly winds picked up speed across the state of Oregon. They caused existing forest fires to explode over a vast expanse of the central Oregon Cascades. Dense, choking smoke invaded Portland and the Columbia Gorge, putting Portland's air quality at the worst of any city in the world and closing down the already half-shuttered COVID-19 economy.

Kim hunkered down in her home like other Portlanders. Keeping her two kids on top of online school was nearly a full-time job. She also had to deal with a number of logistical challenges at Ross Wines. The new winemaker may have been a gifted vintner, and easy on the eyes, but he was terrible at logistics. Kim had to be involved at every step of the way to keep production moving and the shipments to wine club members in place.

Just as Kim had begun to put the debacle around the private investigator out of her mind in favor of more pressing matters, Camden Ross Senior messaged her a link to a story in The Oregonian.

> **Sept. 21, 2020**
>
> **Authorities from the Mid-Columbia Major Crimes Team have widened the investigation into the Sept. 8 shootout on Highway 97 to include the alleged murder of Gorge winemaker Camden Ross, who died in a mountain biking accident on Syncline Trail near Bingen, Washington, in June.**
>
> **Photos assembled by Ralph Podowski, a**

private investigator, place German scientist Dr. Ingo Merz in the vicinity of Ross at the time of the mountain biking accident.

Podowski believes that Merz was likely hired to murder Ross in June and suspects that Merz also made the attempt on Podowski's life in the Highway 97 incident. Podowski had been investigating the Ross death for three weeks at the time of the shootout.

Podowski suspects that the motivation for Ross' murder is connected to his relationship with his wife and co-owner of Ross Wines, Kim Marseilles. Ross was unhappy about Marseilles' other employer, Revazov, a winery located in Underwood, Washington. Podowski has also pointed to Marseilles' relationship with Scott Larson as a source of tension that could be part of a murder motive.

Larson, a Portland high school teacher and owner of the vineyard where Revazov is located, was riding his bike with Ross on the Syncline Trail system when Ross fell to his death.

Because Ross' death occurred in Klickitat County, Washington, Klickitat County Prosecuting Attorney Samuel Mann is working closely with the Mid-Columbia Major Crimes Team to decide if charges will be filed regarding Camden Ross' death.

When Kim arrived at Scott's Portland home, dressed down in a pair of trainers, yoga pants and a zip sweatshirt top, Scott led her into the kitchen, where he poured glasses of wine for them in silence, and then down the stairway into the basement. It had been a while since she had been over to the duplex and it recalled their earlier days. The basement was converted into a kind of rec room and TV watching area.

They sat far apart, Scott in a club chair and Kim on the futon couch. The IKEA track lighting gave Kim's face a shadowy look to it.

She stared at Scott, silently.

"This is bad," Scott said.

"I assume they've been in touch with you," Kim said. "I'm supposed to go in for questioning in The Dalles next week."

"Yes, I got a call from the Wasco County Sheriff's Office yesterday."

"Same."

"Can you believe that they even put pictures of us in the article?" Scott asked.

"At least they picked decent photos," Kim said, taking a drink of her wine and giving a slight smile.

"I need to tell you something, something I've been holding back about Camden's death," Scott said.

"Scott, that's over and done with."

"I saw something, someone. I saw that man whose picture is in the article, Ingo Merz, as I was coming down the trail."

"Scott, stop."

"He was helping Camden up and then, Camden was gone. I didn't see him push Camden over the edge but that's what must have happened. Laurence called me right after it happened and said that I couldn't mention seeing that man."

Kim was shaking her head.

"Now that it's come to this, I'm thinking I should come clean, tell law enforcement everything I know."

"Scott, you need to stay the course. Changing what you've said is not going to bring Camden back to life and it's not going to get us where we want to go."

"But don't you see Kim, what this means, who we are working for? They could have killed Camden."

"Scott, in my former life, I lived among wealthy people. Powerful people. I know how this story ends. Camden's dad and this private investigator are messing with forces bigger than they understand. If you, if we, want to disengage from Darden, we need to do it peacefully, quietly. Over time. And once we have the resources to do so. Don't blow this up."

"But Kim, I can't just lie under oath."

"Don't you see? If you encourage the idea that Camden was murdered, you could be implicated. You're his wife's illicit lover, remember. Don't go down the rabbit hole."

Kim stood up, walked over behind Scott's chair and massaged his shoulders for a while.

She sat back down and drank the rest of the wine in her glass. "Laurence has set us up with excellent attorneys. Trust them. Follow their guidance. It's all going to go fine. Now I need to get back to my kids."

Scott got zero minutes of sleep the night before his questioning at the Klickitat County Courthouse in Goldendale.

He had clear counsel from the attorneys on what to say and what not to say. But Scott didn't know if he could do that: blatantly lie, or at least deceive, officials under oath. As he tossed and turned, his mind went through a series of contorted epistemological questions. For some reason, a line from President Bill Clinton when he was being questioned about Monica Lewinsky in 1998 kept repeating in his head: "It depends on what the meaning of the word 'is' is."

Things had worked out okay for Slick Willie. Would they for him?

Now he sat on a bench in the Klickitat County Courthouse. It was a nicely renovated Art Deco building. The hallway was dimly lit and the freshly waxed floors reflected the light from a window at one end. He'd dressed a bit up. Put on a pair of khakis and an oxford shirt. He had a nervous sweat going and he could feel his face already flushed as he sat there and waited.

Detective Meghan Crowler asked Scott to come into the conference room. The room kept the character of the building's Art Deco design but with modern lighting. Four other detectives were there for the questioning.

They eased him into it, going over a lot of background information. Then they got into the topic of how he knew Camden and Kim.

Crowler pulled out a printed picture, no doubt provided by Ralph Podowski, of Kim and Scott in the Gorge house. It was taken at night, looking in through a window. He appeared to be leaning over and touching Kim.

"Like I said, we were just friends, at that time."

"Friends with benefits, perhaps?" Crowler asked.

"No benefits," Scott said.

"Hard to believe, a good-looking guy like you, Scott, and an attractive woman like Kim. Are you gay?" one of the male detectives asked.

"I've got a girlfriend," Scott said defensively.

Eventually, the questions made their way to the bike ride. Scott stuck to the story that he had given the Sheriff's deputy on site.

"Scott, this is about the alleged murder of a man. I need you to tell us the truth."

"That's the truth," Scott said.

Two days later, the Mid-Columbia Major Crimes Team came together to discuss the case over a video conference call.

Detective Crowler started the conversation. "I don't think we are getting the full story from Kim Marseilles and Scott Larson. And Laurence Visser. I don't buy his charming Dutch guy thing."

"Right," said Sam Mann, Klickitat County prosecuting attorney, "but I just don't think we have enough to make any kind of charge for a homicide here."

"But what about Merz?" Crowler asked. "We've got confirmation that he came into the country again a week before all this went down. Cameras in The Dalles show what we think was his vehicle heading west after the shootout."

"He's a ghost," Mann said. "We don't know where he is or even if that's his real name."

Don Childs of the Portland Immigration and Customs Enforcement office spoke up. Podowski's identification of Merz, a foreigner in the United States on a visa, had prompted ICE to get involved.

"We've looked into Merz and have some theories about him. We have an analyst in D.C. who thinks he might be a hired gun. An actual international assassin, someone with another identity. We've also been looking into Revazov and the parent company that connects them to some other wineries. They have six or seven different wineries, all hugely successful.

"But the closer I look at their stories, the tax and business records we have access to, well they don't pass the sniff test. They all start out small and then just take off and become enormously successful. It's not the typical financial trajectory of an artisan winery. The theory that there is foreign cash coming into them is an interesting one."

Childs continued, "We'll take this from here: My office and the Alcohol and Tobacco Tax and Trade Bureau. We're going to give Darden Wine Holdings a serious looking over. I mean we're really going to get up their ass. We'll figure out the connection with this Merz character."

The German-engineered windshield wipers on Laurence Visser's Mercedes cleared the view so effectively that one barely noticed the pelting rain on the windshield. It was early October, and the soggy Pacific Northwest weather had returned to Portland. Visser drove south down Highway 43 to the upscale suburb of Lake Oswego.

Laurence pulled into the Lake Oswego downtown

parking garage. His Mercedes fit right in among the Range Rovers, BMWs and Lexus SUVs.

Despite the blustery weather, Charlie Albrechts was seated at an outdoor table on the patio outside St. Honoré Bakery. The pounding rain had let up for a moment. Albrects' disheveled bleached-blond hair was matted down and wet. He wore a blue Patagonia raincoat and had a large coffee in a to-go cup on the table. As Laurence approached, Charlie gave him an eye roll for a greeting.

"Charlie, good to see you," Laurence said.

Albrechts shook his head, stood up with his coffee in hand and said, "Let's walk. You can get a coffee after if you want."

They strode together out onto the wet paved plaza adjacent to the shopping center. The sky was filled with dark gray marine clouds and a cool breeze whipped up occasionally.

"I realize that this is not where we want be right now," Laurence said.

"You know how much I do for your wineries, don't you Laurence? I put you guys in front of everybody. And now this, fucking ICE? My accountant is sweating bullets right now. I'm afraid he's going to blow his brains out. They are subpoenaing all of our accounts. And I'm worried they are going to go after my personal records."

They stood at the edge of the plaza, overlooking the lake, Charlie Albrechts glanced around nervously to make sure no one was in earshot.

"The beauty of the crypto we passed to you is that it can't be traced. It's untouchable," Laurence said. "And I know the transactions on the books might look odd but they will hold water based on the way we set things up," Laurence said. "We will take care of the legal costs."

"This investigation needs to stop. We need to make it go away completely if you want to continue doing business."

"We'll take care of it," Laurence said.

"You'd better," Charlie Albrechts replied as he turned

and walked away.

Scott stuck his head into Nate's room and checked to make sure he was engaged with the online class happening on the laptop on his desk. It was his fifth week of COVID-induced online school.

"I'm going to take Bob for a walk."

"Okay."

Rachel was standing outside the duplex, leaning on her Subaru Outback, arms crossed. She was on lunch break from her position as a speech pathologist and clad in some business casual wear: half-height boots, tights, a knee-length skirt and a western-themed shirt.

Bob got excited as soon as he saw her and she bent down to greet him, her distraught expression disappearing for a few seconds.

They didn't need to say anything to each other about where they were going. They'd walked together with Bob through the neighborhood on Scott's standard dog walking route many times.

"So Scott, I need you to tell me what's going on."

"I'm stressed, Rachel. About the investigation, this new job, parenting in COVID. It's just a lot."

"I get that. But you're not letting me in, you're closed off. I mean it seems like since you took this job I never see you and when I do you're just in another world. You are just not here."

"I'm sorry. I'll do better."

"You've said that before, Scott," Rachel said, her tone getting more upset. "We don't ... connect like we used to. I have to wonder, were you and Kim really having an affair? Are you? What the fuck is going on Scott?"

Scott sighed. It was pretty rare for calm, rational Rachel to swear. "Rachel, no, we talked about this. I told you Kim and I are tied up in this but we're not, you know, together."

"You are talking to her all the time these days. I know it, I've seen your phone, I've heard you."

"We have to, Rachel. With these inquiries, the whole Darden Wine team needs to be on the same page. There's a lot I just can't discuss. Non-disclosure agreements and things."

"I want to be there for you Scott but you just have to let me in."

"It'll get better, I promise," Scott said, reaching to hold her hand.

They stopped and watched Bob sniff a particularly interesting piece of shrubbery in front of someone's house.

Rachel sighed. "Okay, now that the smoke is gone, maybe we can finally take that trail running weekend we've been talking about?"

"Sounds great," Scott said. "Let's plan on it."

22

By late October, the investigation into Darden Wine Holdings that now included ICE and the Alcohol and Tobacco Tax and Trade Bureau had hit the media. Even though Kim was a subject of the investigation, Laurence gave her full control of public relations for the firm. Inquiries came at the Darden enterprise at a rapid-fire pace. Everyone from wine bloggers to local newspaper and TV stations wanted to know about the illegal business doings, the alleged affair between Scott and Kim and Camden Ross' death.

Kim hit back hard with a carefully crafted narrative: Darden Wine Holdings was a successful business that supported innovative risk takers in the burgeoning natural wine industry. They had many success stories with wineries in the Western United States. Their investors were private and preferred anonymity.

Yes, Kim had dated Scott at one time but she had been happily married to Camden at the time of his death. Scott was a friend. A friend to her and to Camden. Camden's death was a terrible tragedy.

She shared pictures with the media of Scott skiing and biking with Camden, of Camden and Kim at Revazov events, of Camden, Kim, Scott and Rachel having dinner together that night in spring 2020.

Kim knew the stakes were high in this situation. This growing, successful business could crash and burn if this went the wrong way. Camden, the man she had spent a decade of her life with, was part of the narrative she was spinning. Thinking of his death could bring waves of intense emotions. Sometimes after a stressful day, she'd find herself sobbing after a single glass of wine.

But mostly, the stress and the drama excited, even exhilarated her.

She couldn't see Scott much but when she did, it was hot. The public scrutiny somehow made their affair that much more forbidden and exciting. She was jealous that he was still with Rachel but would take care of that as soon as this blew over.

Right around Halloween, Portland television station KJEP invited Kim for a Zoom interview on the Good Morning Oregon show. Kim dressed up — but not too much. She wanted to come across as the mom next door, attractive and put-together but not overly high maintenance. Relatable. A blouse, some earrings, her hair pulled back.

Kim had an instant rapport with Sherri and Melissa, the co-hosts. They'd interviewed Kim in the past a couple of times ahead of wine festival weekends.

The interview started out on a non-confrontational note with some basic questions about Kim's business and family connections. Then they came to the accusations being made as the result of Podowski's investigation.

"I understand the concern from my husband's family," Kim said. "They were looking for answers about Camden's death. But we need to remind ourselves who Mr. Podowski is and what kinds of things he's done in the past. He is a convicted felon. And much of the evidence he has gathered is quite questionable."

The two hosts grimaced.

Then the interview turned toward losing Camden. Kim worked herself into an emotional state as she talked about their partnership, the struggles and joys of making a business and blended family work and the highs and lows of the relationship.

By the end of the interview, both hosts were practically in tears and they parted by wishing Kim the best of luck.

In November 2020, gyms were open with social distancing. ICE Agent Don Childs was *so* glad to get back to his regular workout routine at Club Sport in Tigard, Oregon. He wasn't a guy to boast about himself but he considered himself "cut." Mondays were chest and biceps. Wednesdays back and shoulders. Fridays legs and abs. The other days he threw in some cardio.

He felt a firm touch on his arm as he was doing bicep curls. He slipped out an ear bud. "Ever tried negatives? They could add even more definition to these already well-developed arms," the tall, shapely young woman said as she ran the back of her hands down his upper arm. She was wearing a mask but her beautiful brown eyes were almost hypnotic.

"Really?" Don said with a smile, taken aback by the unsolicited advice. She was a stunning young woman. Amazing body.

"Here, let me show you how to really make them work for you." She grabbed a lower weight dumbbell and demonstrated. Her slightly sweaty, tanned and toned body was so close that he picked up a musky feminine scent, probably her body lotion or perfume.

"I'm a personal trainer on the side," Lacey said.

"Well, maybe we could talk about you taking on a new client," Childs said.

In a half-hour, they were laughing over smoothies at Club Sport's cafe.

A week later, they skipped the workout altogether and had Bloody Marys in bed at her condo. Childs was on such a high as he climbed down the stairway in her bathrobe to the kitchen to get another refill, it took a couple seconds for the shock to kick in when he saw the man in the blue blazer with slicked-back, shoulder-length gray hair at her kitchen table.

"I'm Laurence," the man said, greeting Childs with a wave.

"I was wondering if we could have a sort of abstract conversation? Care for a little more?" Laurence asked, motioning with the pitcher that came off the blender.

Childs remained silent and took a seat. The veins in his forehead pulsed with tension.

"We have mutual interests, Mr. Childs. You clearly don't want your wife and kids finding out about our friend here. And I want to make sure that the investigation of my firm, Darden Wine Holdings, is done fairly. Very fairly. Do we understand each other?"

Lacey had dressed and come down the stairs and was nonchalantly straightening up the kitchen as Laurence spoke. Childs nodded silently, stood up from his chair and then walked up to the bedroom to put on his clothes.

Kim texted Scott a link to the Oregonian article.

Dec. 5, 2020

The Mid-Columbia Major Crimes Team has completed their investigation into the case of Camden Ross' death in connection with a Sept. 8 shootout on Highway 97. No charges have been filed.

The article quoted Samuel Mann, Klickitat County prosecuting attorney.

> "At this point we have no charges to file in connection with Camden Ross' death. If anyone has further information connected to this case, we encourage them to contact us.
>
> "The killing on Highway 97 appears to have been a case of mistaken identity. Jake Clark picked the wrong guy to shake down for some drug money."

It also presented the Darden Wine perspective.

> When asked about whether Revazov had a connection to Ross' death, Laurence Visser, president of Darden Wine Holdings, said, "Camden Ross was an amazing winemaker. He was a valued member of the wine community in the Gorge. We are so sorry about his passing this summer. We are not connected to Dr. Merz in any way."

23

January 2021. Camden Ross Senior poured himself another Canadian Club as he sat in his home office with Ralph Podowski. The low late afternoon January sun reflected off the snowfall that the Milwaukee area had recently received.

"No thanks, Cam, I'm fine," Ralph said as Ross offered more whiskey.

"If you ask me," Ralph said, "I think they've got the whole system sown up. You remember how it was here back in the eighties with Schumacher Freight. Every time we reported their dirty tricks, they had a way out of it. I think that Darden Wine outfit knows how to buy any outcome they need."

Ross broke in after having a deep draw from his whiskey glass. "We're talking about my son here, goddammit!"

"I know. I know."

Ralph took a moment to think.

"How about a journalist who could investigate Revazov, perhaps even the whole syndicate?" Ralph suggested.

"Remember, we tried contacting a few newspapers about it, in Oregon and here. No interest."

"Well, you could try hiring someone, a freelancer."

Ross Senior paused a minute to think.

"You know, I can think of someone. My old friend Wayne, he's got a granddaughter who studied journalism at Madison. She actually wrote a promotional piece for Cam's winery. I don't know if she'd be up for something serious like this but it might be worth a try."

Mr. Chen showed up on the Zoom call from some tropical locale Scott didn't recognize. In the other Zoom window, Laurence looked relaxed, evidently back at his place in Northern California.

"Scott, wonderful to see you. Tell us about the Dougherty winery," Mr. Chen said.

Scott was overseeing the renovations taking place at Dougherty Vineyards over the winter of 2020-21. In the fall, they had bulldozed the old tasting room and now contractors were building out what would be a stunning new facility.

"It's progressing nicely, but the cost estimates seem to go up on a weekly basis with all these supply chain issues. The Dougherty's want us to scale back. They're afraid of being in even deeper debt than they already are to us. I honestly think we could phase the project in by putting in the tasting room and waiting on the production facility."

Laurence jumped in: "The way the real estate investment trust contract is written, they've committed to the full renovation. A nice side effect of the high construction costs is that the higher they go, the greater the stake we have in the Dougherty property. If the costs go high enough, we'll have a controlling interest."

In the other window, Mr. Chen nodded his head with a satisfied look on his face.

"Hold firm on the tasting room plan and the new production facility, Scott," Mr. Chen said. "If anything, I want to go bigger."

"They are not going to be happy about this, especially Steve Dougherty's younger sister, Susan, who's been attending the meetings recently. She's much less agreeable than Steve."

"I know we can count on your diplomacy in the matter, Scott," Mr. Chen said. "Oh, and give my best to Kim," he added before giving a superficial wave and terminating the meeting.

THE ECLIPSE

Kim's trips to Hawaii with Camden had always been a sore point for Scott. Thanks to new, loosened travel restrictions, Kim was able to arrange a late January trip to the Islands, this time with Scott as her companion.

It was striking how quickly things had changed. Less than a year before Camden Ross was still alive and Scott and Kim were engaged in a clandestine affair. Now they were slowly transitioning into a bonafide couple. After the investigation around Camden's death blew over, Scott broke it off with Rachel. Kim and Scott continued to keep separate homes in Portland and the Gorge but in the Gorge, Kim was starting to spend more and more time at his place.

Kim had, through an arrangement facilitated by Mr. Chen, managed to secure a loan to buy out Camden's daughter's stake in Ross Wines. Camden Ross Senior wasn't pleased with the arrangement but there wasn't much he could do. Had the forms Kim signed before Camden's death not been destroyed, the buyout would not have been easily possible.

Kim was now managing Ross Wines herself and had full responsibility for marketing at four other wineries in the Darden Wine portfolio. Her life was a constant rush.

The press about the alleged murder of Camden and the affair with Scott had few if any negative effects on Ross Wines or Revazov after the case was dropped by authorities. If anything, the additional publicity bolstered both businesses.

Scott had often imagined having some calm time with Kim to savor their connection. Even though he, theoretically, had her to himself now, that hadn't happened.

As they lay on the beach loungers outside their Kihei condo, Scott soaked in the sun for 20 minutes or so and then was ready for another swim. He waded into the water, dove underneath a wave and swam out past the break. As he bobbed up and down, he could see Kim in her sunglasses and hat on the beach. At 51, she was still as glamorous as ever. He did the backstroke a bit, savoring the tropical water and looking up at the puffy clouds floating past. He pondered this new reality. This was what he had wanted for so long.

Or was it?

Scott thought about the last meeting with the Dougherty family on the estate that had been in their family for three generations. Even the cancer-stricken senior Doughtery had shown up.

Scott had explained that due to the additional debt required to finance the renovations, the real estate investment trust that he established now had a controlling stake and did not require the family's assent to make decisions about the property.

"We trusted you Scott," Steve said.

"I think this is the best course of action for the winery you've invested so much in. With the support of Darden Wine Holdings, your business is in the position to thrive. We will still consult with you on renovation decisions," Scott replied.

The Dougherty family stared at him, dumbfounded. It would almost have been easier if they'd protested loudly but they just looked dejected.

Scott swam in and laid down next to Kim on the beach lounger. Soon they made their way from the beach to the twin heated outdoor showers outside their condo. Then they dried off and went inside, opened a bottle of rosé and made their way to the bedroom.

An hour later, they were still in bed. In the otherwise dark room, the daytime tropical sun filtered through venetian blinds making slats of light across their naked bodies.

"That was nice," said Kim.

"I wish we could spend weeks like this, not just days," Scott said.

"Can you get me another glass of wine, love?"

"I mean, isn't that the purpose of all the risk we've taken

so that we can relax, do what we want?"

Scott went into the kitchen and refilled her glass.

"We're there, babe," Kim said as she sat up and took the full glass of wine from him.

24

June 2021. In the dull early morning light, Scott loaded his hydration pack with energy gels and put on his trail running shoes. He was parked among the towering Douglas firs at the Herman Creek trailhead near Cascade Locks, ready to head out on a 20-mile loop up the Pacific Crest Trail to Chinidere peak and then back down the Herman Creek Trail.

As he ground up the first section of switchbacks on the PCT, his legs loosened and he started to work up a sweat. He was somewhat surprised to see a female figure moving on the trail a couple switchbacks above him.

When Scott caught her eye, she stopped, looked down at him and gave him a wave.

"Good morning," she said with a smile.

"Hi there!" Scott said.

Soon he caught up to her and they started chatting. Something seemed familiar about the woman.

"Do I know you?" Scott asked.

"I'm Samantha. I did an interview with your friend Kim a couple of weeks ago. I'm a writer."

"Oh right, I remember you coming by the house now."

"I'm out on a tour of Pacific Northwest wineries."

"Sounds delightful," Scott said.

They ran a bit together, chatting about different folks in the wine industry whom they both knew. She was slim and athletic with a thick mane of brown hair and dark features. They stopped at an overlook and took in some morning rays of sunshine and a spectacular view of the Gorge.

"Scott, you knew Camden Ross, right?"

"Well, yes in a way. A tragic situation."

"His dad is old friends with my grandpa and he got in touch with me about Revazov. I was curious about you because, well, you were with him when that accident happened. And, as far as I can tell, you weren't even in this business a few years ago. You were a history teacher, right?"

"Yes, I am sort of new to this."

"I know it probably isn't the right time. But I'd love to talk to you more about this. I'm really interested in the story behind Camden's death and what he might have known or who he might have upset before he died."

"Well," Scott said, "I think the media has been over this, don't you?"

"I think there are some missing pieces. I'd love to talk to you about your perspective."

Scott paused the conversation for a second.

"Right. Could we talk off the record if we spoke?" Scott asked.

"I think we could. Let's meet on another one of these runs in a week."

"Okay, can we set a time and place now? This may sound paranoid but I think we should keep this interaction offline," Scott said.

"Agreed," Samantha said.

At that point, Samantha turned around and Scott continued on the PCT as it made its way up to the Benson Plateau.

The next time Scott saw Samantha was along the Dog River Trail just off Highway 35.

In the time since their last meeting, Scott had established that Samantha was a graduate of the University of Wisconsin like him and had recently been living in Madison.

Scott kicked off their conversation by bringing up their Madison connection. They figured out that they were both fond of a recently deceased professor at the Journalism

School, Jim Baughman, and that they had a mutual friend in Madison, Rick Leyden.

Soon, Samantha began to fill Scott in on her investigation of Camden Ross' death.

"Thanks to the Ross family, I was able to travel to the Republic of Georgia last month to write a travelogue piece on wineries there."

"How was it?" Scott asked.

"Amazing. There is such a cool wine scene there. I visited so many little wineries. And lots of people make wine in their homes. It's just part of the culture there. And it's pretty much all natural wine.

"In the interest of learning more about Revazov and Darden Wine Holdings, I found out where Dimitri and Sasha are from in Georgia and visited a few wineries there. It's in the Adjara region on the Black Sea.

"Have you ever heard of the Belt and Road Initiative?" Samantha asked Scott.

"Yes, I have a vague notion of what it is from reading The Economist."

"We're talking massive foreign investments in Africa, the Caucasus, Central and South Asia. Highways, oil pipelines, factories. Huge government loans from the Chinese to relatively impoverished countries.

"I met a couple, the Isakadzes. They run a winery outside of Batumi. The winemaker there, Anton, told me that he knew Dimitri, Sashas's dad. Dimitri used to live in that area and worked for a Chinese developer, Zhang Shaozhu, who did a number of big projects in Georgia in the early 2010s. Apartment complexes, shopping malls and some road construction projects. Zhang's company worked throughout the Caucasus region and in Africa as well. Dimitri was one of his top executives in Georgia and worked with the local officials to get things approved. Incidentally, Dimitri was active in a windsurfing club on the Black Sea.

"Zhang loved the wine scene in Georgia and he even

bought two wineries there: one near Batumi and one in the Kakheti region. Sasha lived in the Kakheti area for a couple of years as an apprentice winemaker. In 2014, however, Zhang fell out with the Chinese authorities. Apparently, they found out that he was siphoning money off his construction projects into offshore bank accounts. Now he's wanted internationally for embezzlement and money laundering.

"He's a man without a country. He and his wealth have literally vanished. My theory is that Mr. Chen is Zhang Shaozhu.

"I realize that you're working for this guy. That you're part owner of his enterprise. But you must have a sense of the risks here. This is a house of cards. If his real identity comes out, everything could collapse.

"Camden's father is convinced that his son had information on Darden Wine Holdings and that's what got him killed. Since you are close to Kim, I'm wondering if you can look around Camden's old things, see if you might be able to find what Camden had on Darden when he died?"

"Okay," Scott said. "I will try."

Scott racked his brain about where any evidence that Camden had collected about Darden Wine Holdings might be. Kim might know but there was no way he could bring her into this. She would be totally against what he was doing with Samantha.

If Kim had come across compromising information Camden had on Darden, she'd probably have destroyed it or given it to Laurence. On the other hand, she might save it as a kind of insurance policy, something that could be leveraged against Darden if anything ever went sideways with them.

Scott didn't know the password to Kim's MacBook but he jumped on it one night when she abandoned it for a long phone call with one of her girlfriends. He turned off the lock screen on it while she wasn't looking. A couple hours later, after she was asleep, he hopped on it.

He couldn't find much on the local computer in her photos and documents.

After Camden died, Kim had told Scott that she contacted an IT firm and gotten some help accessing Camden's online accounts so that she could monitor any activity in them. She'd shared what information she thought was "appropriate" from those accounts with Ralph Podowski.

When Scott opened the Google login screen and typed in the first part of Camden's Gmail account, the browser autofilled the rest.

There were all of Camden's old emails. Scott scanned the emails from spring 2020 and browsed through Google Docs and Photos for any evidence of Camden's inquiries into Revazov. Nothing.

He wondered if Camden could have had a separate account for his inquiries. It was possible. Would there be any traces of that account anywhere? Scott searched in Camden's email for a few phrases that he thought might land him some reference to a second account.

The phrase "recovery email" landed a message that stated, "You received this message because this is listed as the recovery email for negociant_plonk12@gmail.com."

Scott opened an incognito window in Chrome, went to the Google login page and entered in the negociant_plonk12 username and then proceeded to follow directions for recovering a lost password using Camden's other Gmail account that was still open. Soon he was in the other Google account.

In Google Photos, he found pictures of invoices from Albrechts Wine & Spirits for various shipments of Revazov wine as well as pictures of a warehouse facility with recycling bins loaded with empty wine bottles and a sink that looked like it was used to dispose of wine.

Scott passed the files on a thumb drive to Samantha at a meeting time they had pre-arranged on the Hood River

THE ECLIPSE

waterfront. They also set up their next meeting.

A day later, Samantha found Scott tucked away at a corner table at Starbucks in The Dalles sipping on a mocha.

"So what do you make of this? Invoices from Albrechts? Pics of empty wine bottles?" Samantha asked.

"From what I can gather, this must have been some scheme to artificially raise production figures and bring revenue in."

"But who paid the bills for the fake wine?" Samantha asked.

"I assume the money came from Zhang. He must have been transferring it to Albrechts through Darden or a shell company or some other way," Scott replied.

"This kind of manipulation violates all sorts of regulations around alcohol sales and taxation, not to mention the money laundering angle," Samantha said.

"Darden is using the business strength of Revazov and their other wineries to borrow more and expand further." Scott said. "In fact, that's what my job with Darden is all about."

"Fake it 'til you make it," Samantha said.

"Right. There's something else," Scott said, pausing. He hadn't planned to tell her about this but suddenly he knew he had to if he was going to go down this path.

"You know the guy Podowski identified as Dr. Ingo Merz? On that bike ride, I saw him with Camden next to the cliff right before he went over the edge. I didn't see him push Camden off. But on Laurence Visser's instructions, I never told the cops about his presence when I was questioned. I told myself it was best not to complicate things, especially given what was going on with Kim and me."

Samantha looked at him and didn't say anything for a minute.

"What should we do?" Scott asked.

"We're going to Wisconsin," Samantha said.

Scott made arrangements to visit his dad in Madison over the Fourth of July weekend and brought along Nate. Kim wouldn't have to know about the other motive for the trip.

Samantha texted Scott while he was sitting with his dad and Nate on the lakeside terrace of the iconic Memorial Union of the University of Wisconsin-Madison. It was a perfect June day to enjoy a Wisconsin lager on the shore of sparkling Lake Mendota.

Scott took a couple extra gulps of his beer before he confirmed that he would meet Samantha at Camden Ross Senior's home in nearby Delafield.

The next morning, Scott told his dad that he was visiting an old college friend in Milwaukee and left him and Nate to themselves. His gut was in a knot as he drove the rental Hyundai east on Interstate 94. He let Google Maps take him to the address. At the end of a long driveway, the home appeared, a giant Tudor-style brick edifice with a four-car garage.

A well-kept woman in her seventies greeted him at the door.

"Sharon Ross," she said, extending her hand.

She led Scott to Camden Ross Senior's study.

Ross was seated behind a large desk in his home office suite chatting with Samantha. He was a white-haired, more diminutive version of his son with almost the same facial features but with eyes an icier shade of blue. Scott had met him in Oregon after Camden's death and they had spoken briefly about his son's fatal bike ride.

Camden Senior gripped Scott's hand hard and shook it slowly.

"What can I do for you, Mr. Larson?"

"Mr. Ross, as you probably remember, we spoke in Oregon. I was on that bike ride with Camden."

"So why are you here?"

"I'd like to talk to you alone for a minute about your

THE ECLIPSE

son's death," Scott said.

Samantha excused herself and left Scott with Ross in his study.

Ross motioned for Scott to sit.

"What's on your mind?" he asked Scott.

"I've been talking with Samantha. And thinking about the people I'm in business with. And what happened to Camden."

Scott paused for a second and gathered himself. He could feel his face going flush.

"My suspicions are that Camden was killed."

"What do you know that you haven't told the authorities?" the senior Ross asked, his face twisting into a grimace.

Scott told Ross about what he had seen on the bike ride, confirming the version of events that Ralph had put together. He explained how he had neglected to mention the man at the scene of Camden's fall when law enforcement questioned him.

Ross looked stunned.

Then, shaking his head, he spoke. "You know what you did, Larson. You covered up murder. And you were fucking my daughter-in-law at the same time. You should be in jail for this."

Ross walked around his desk and over to Scott, who was still sitting.

"Get the fuck up," Ross said.

Scott began to stand and as he did, Camden Senior grabbed him by the shirt collar with both hands and pulled Scott's face to within inches of his. He was surprisingly strong for a man in his seventies.

"My son was murdered! And you were part of it!" he screamed at Scott, looking him straight in the eyes.

He shook Scott by the collar and then released him with a shove.

"Get out of my sight," Camden Senior said.

Scott walked out of the office and out onto a large patio

behind the house.

Twenty minutes later, Samantha emerged from the house and explained that Ross had called a meeting with two attorneys, Ralph Podowski and her to discuss next steps in the investigation she was leading into Camden's death. She asked Scott to continue waiting outside while the meeting got started.

A half-hour later Samantha came out to retrieve Scott.

"It took a while for him to calm down." She led him back into Camden Senior's office.

In the overstuffed leather club chairs surrounding Camden Senior's desk sat Samantha and Ralph and two figures who Samantha introduced to Scott: Cal Winslow, Camden Senior's personal attorney, and Jim Carter, a former federal prosecutor in the U.S. Attorney's Office Western District of Wisconsin.

Scott and Samantha went back and forth, explaining what they had discovered about Camden's inquiry into Ross Wines.

"He *was* onto something. They are laundering money with these fucking wineries," Ross declared.

Jim Carter stretched his large body out in the leather chair. He wore a beige summer suit with a blue tie. "Essentially, this bolsters the case that Ralph put together." He spoke in a deep voice with a Wisconsin lilt. "Darden Wine Holdings was trying to amp up their wine sales figures and maybe bring in some revenue from some illicit sources as well. These invoices are good evidence but I don't think they are a smoking gun. My guess is their accountants and attorneys would find their way out of this by paying some inconsequential fines. I'd be cautious about going to the authorities with this, before we have more."

"So why would they kill my son for this?" Ross Senior asked.

"Most likely, his inquiries were getting in the way of some big plans they had. In fact maybe they could have brought their whole house of cards down," Winslow said.

"What about the murder. Can't we go after them for that?"

"I'm willing to talk to the authorities about what I withheld earlier," said Scott.

The former federal prosecutor responded. "Scott's encounter with Merz on the bike trail and the call from Laurence that day strengthen the likelihood that it wasn't an accident. The problem is that Merz is a ghost. It's a false identity, it's not an adversary that's easy to chase or to connect to the Darden enterprise. The feds dropped this case and they are not going to reopen it easily."

"So what do you suggest?" Ross Senior asked, growing visibly frustrated.

Carter responded. "The real story here is Chen's true identity, which Samantha seems to have sussed out. That explains where the cash is coming from and the motive to move assets into this country. If you could tie Zhang Shaozhu to Darden Wine Holdings, you'd have a huge story. I would go after that first before trying to reopen the murder case."

"I want to take this man down," Camden Ross Senior said. "Whatever it takes."

There was a pause in the conversation.

"I'd be careful," Carter said. "Zhang is used to operating globally and in places where things aren't done quite as civilly as they are in this country."

"We'll expose him," Samantha said. "When we uncover who he is and what he has done, he'll be finished. At least in this country."

Camden Ross Senior gave an exasperated sigh. "Okay, Samantha, I'm counting on you to break this story wide open."

Back in Oregon, two weeks later, Scott made his way on bike to his next meeting with Samantha at the Aubrey R. Watzek Library at Lewis & Clark College, a modernist structure with expansive windows overlooking the forested campus in southwest Portland.

They took a seat at one of the tables adjacent to the atrium. Samantha laid out a diagram on an oversized sheet of paper that outlined the Darden Wine Holdings enterprise. Laurence Visser was at the top and the winemakers at the various wineries listed below. Property owners and real estate partnership agreements were also delineated. Albrechts Wine & Spirits was also graphed into the diagram.

"This represents the wine enterprise that Zhang is building out in the United States. To bring this story together, I need a way of explicitly connecting him to these entities."

"He shields himself well," Scott said.

Scott studied the chart for a few minutes.

"I don't see Wine Jamie here," Scott said.

"Who is she?" asked Samantha.

"Well, in a way, she got me into all this. I met her at a party and she told me about the possibility of owning property for Mr. Chen. I always thought of her as sort of a social figure though, not really part of the business operations. She is well connected in the wine world. And she talked to me like she knew Mr. Chen personally."

They looked over Wine Jamie's web site, blog and Instagram feed. Wine Jamie traveled a lot. She seemed to spend half her time on wine adventures abroad, whether it be in Argentina, Chile, France, or Italy.

"No, it couldn't be that simple."

Samantha studied Wine Jamie's Instagram account.

"Look at this picture." It was a sunset shot taken at a vineyard in Chile. A figure with his back turned stood looking out on the vista.

"I'm telling you, that is Zhang. Look," she said, pulling up some other photos of him that she'd collected on her laptop.

Scott nodded, recalling his brief encounter with the man he knew as Mr. Chen in Frankfurt.

"And look at these pictures from Montenegro. They all seem to be taken from this one house. He's not in any of the shots but I think that's his hand in that one. This must be one of his properties. If we want to find Zhang, Wine Jamie could be the key."

"I might be able to meet up with her socially," Scott said.

"Do it," Samantha said, "And soon."

25

In summer 2021, Kim's life was expanding. The pandemic was on the wane. Business at Ross Wines was excellent and her Darden work was on fire. Things were also getting real with Scott. They had met with architects about Scott's Gorge property and now had a plan.

The old farmhouse would soon be demolished to make way for an abode that truly suited the estate. With five bedrooms and four full baths including a master suite, a high-end kitchen and a spacious living and dining area that spilled out onto a massive deck overlooking the vineyard and mountain, it would be perfect for entertaining. The price tag: $1.75 million.

She was also pleased that the Revazov production facility was moving partially off site to an industrial area in Bingen and that they were opening a tasting room in downtown Hood River. There'd be less traffic near their home but they'd still have occasional wine events just down the pathway.

Kim's son Aiden was starting at Claremont McKenna College in the fall. Thankfully with her Darden work and the income from the winery, she had the funds to easily split the expenses with her ex.

She and Scott had started to spend time together with all their kids at Scott's Gorge home. After the kids excused themselves, she sat alone with Scott at the dining table.

"I'm going to miss the old farmhouse after the renovations," Scott said.

"Oh nonsense," said Kim, refilling their glasses with the

chilled pinot grigio. "Our new place will be fabulous."

"Hey, remember how this all started with Wine Jamie? I hear she's going to be coming through town next week. Maybe we should have her over for dinner," Scott suggested.

"Lovely idea," Kim said. They moved over to the sofa and Kim sat on Scott's lap. She started talking about the latest gossip from Revazov. Scott seemed a bit distant but he listened, asking the occasional question as Kim held forth.

Wine Jamie was just how Scott remembered her. A burst of vibrant energy clad in a flamboyant dress.

Kim and Scott hosted her at Scott's place in the Gorge, as she was visiting some new Gorge wineries that week. She said she appreciated the relative quiet of a home-cooked meal among old friends. Scott picked up some grassfed Oregon country rib eyes and cooked them up on the grill along with some asparagus and baked potatoes. The blustery May weather broke in the afternoon so they enjoyed the meal alfresco with Mount Hood as their dinner companion.

Over the dinner, they popped a "spicy tannat" that Jamie brought from her latest adventure — a tour of some high-altitude vineyards in Bolivia. Kim and Jamie caught up on all that had happened in the last year in the Gorge wine scene. Scott did his best to steer the conversation toward Jamie's travels over the past spring and winter.

After dinner, with a chill in the air, they retired to the hearth inside. Scott got out a bottle of Double Circle bourbon and some tumblers and poured Jamie and himself glasses while Kim stuck with wine. Jamie wasn't shy about asking for refills.

"So Jamie, with all your travel to these fabulous, romantic places, can I ask if you have a special adventure partner in your life?" Kim gave Scott a kick for asking such a forward question but Scott knew she'd be dying to hear the answer.

"Oh, I have liaisons everywhere," Jamie said with a mischievous smile.

"There is one that's special. He's very international. And he loves wine like me. I usually just see him on my travels as he's not able to visit the United States now. I was lucky to quarantine with him at his place in Montenegro last year."

"Sounds perfect for you," Kim said. "We need to get him out here to the Gorge."

"Oh, he knows the Gorge well," Jamie assured them.

Scott excused himself to take his dog Bob out for his evening walk, which he had neglected to do earlier in the day. When he returned, Kim and Jamie were still at the fireplace tucking into yet another bottle of wine. Scott bid them goodnight.

At six or so the next morning, Scott heard Wine Jamie get into her SUV and leave. He got up and went for a run. Once he got back, he made some coffee and Kim soon emerged.

"I learned a lot about Jamie last night," Kim said. "Once she started on her boyfriend, she wouldn't stop. Apparently, he's looking at buying vineyards in Portugal and he already owns them in France and Georgia and here. She more or less admitted that he is Mr. Chen."

"Is that right?" Scott said.

"Apparently, they have this wild connection in bed. This might be TMI but I learned that he's one of those powerful CEO types who gets off on assuming the opposite role in the bedroom. And she's *more* than happy to oblige.

"She said that she wasn't supposed to reveal this but that he's coming for a visit to the U.S. in a few weeks."

"Oh, he's coming here, to the Gorge?"

"Yep, sounds like they're going to be here the first week of August."

Scott met Samantha that afternoon during a break from a windsurfing session at Doug's Beach.

THE ECLIPSE

"This could be it. If we can get a picture of him in the United States on one of his properties, that would provide a real link to Darden for our story," said Samantha.

"It could be hard to photograph him when he's here. I'm sure he's used to keeping a low profile whenever he ventures to the States," Scott said.

They both said the solution to the problem at the same time: "Rick Leyden."

Rick was an excellent commercial photographer. But his drone piloting skills and devious exploits made him extra qualified for this job.

Scott had known Rick since high school and could still picture him scaling a telephone pole using a pair of tree climbing spikes that he'd swiped from a cable TV installer's van. In his junior year in high school, Rick looked about 12 years old but he could get you free HBO or Showtime.

Samantha remembered a more recent story. Rick, who'd matured into a good-looking dude and something of a player with the ladies, had broken up with his erstwhile girlfriend to pursue someone new. The problem was that he had left an expensive set of camera lenses in the furious ex's house.

After a couple hours at The Paradise Lounge, a dive bar on Madison, Wisconsin's Capitol Square, Rick had devised a solution. He drove over to his ex's place, scaled a tree and entered the second story of her house through a window to retrieve the equipment. Sure enough, he got the lenses. But not without witnessing his ex in carnal union with a new lover.

Unfortunately, his shock combined with his drunken state had caused him to knock over a glass of water, making the two lovebirds aware of his presence. In his hasty escape out the second-story window, Rick fell from the tree and broke his ankle. The drive to the emergency room with his ex and her new lover had been a bit humiliating. But he was drunk enough at the time that he didn't care and besides, it made for a good story.

"Leyden has what it takes to get this guy on film," Scott said, "though he's a bit of a loose cannon."

"Agreed," said Samantha.

When Scott got in touch with Rick, he didn't hesitate to say yes.

"Samantha's great. What a hottie. I keep asking her out but no success there."

"Dude, she's like 20 years your junior."

"I know, I know."

Leyden arrived in Portland at 10 p.m. the last Thursday of July. Scott took him out to his neighborhood bar, Dots, for a burger, fries and a couple of beers.

"I brought all the gear you asked for, dude. Drone … check. Multiple cameras … check. Tracking devices … check. I even brought a couple other toys along."

"Excellent," Scott said. Rick was already on Tinder, swiping between sips of beer.

"Dude, are the dispensaries still open?" Rick asked.

"Sure, I think they are," Scott said, a bit irritated. "Listen, Mr. Leyden, you need to concentrate on this job.

The next morning at 10 they met with Samantha at Broder on SE Clinton Street, a hip Swedish restaurant famous for its breakfasts. Samantha had some exciting news when she arrived. Wine Jamie had just posted on Instagram from a winery in the Walla Walla area. She and Rick would head out there immediately.

"So how are we going to find them in Walla Walla," Rick asked.

"I looked at some of her most recent write-ups of the area and it seemed like she stayed at the Marcus Whitman, so I would try that spot," said Scott.

"Okay, let's book rooms there," Samantha said.

"I'm totally cool with sharing a room. For saving money," Rick said.

Samantha ignored the remark.

"Jamie lives in a very modern sort of condo, so if she's

not at the Marcus, you might keep her preferences in mind," Scott said.

It took a while for Sam and Rick to get organized and on the road to Walla Walla. They checked into the Marcus Whitman at about 8. By then all the wineries were closed so they retreated to the "Vineyard Lounge," the hotel's ornately appointed bar. Samantha asked the bartender if she'd seen any signs of Wine Jamie around but she hadn't.

While Rick settled into a couple of draft IPAs, Sam nursed an old fashioned.

"If they're trying to lie relatively low, they're not going to be staying at a public sort of place," Samantha said.

"So that means vacation rentals, Vrbos and Airbnbs."

"Right."

They huddled over Rick's laptop and did some searches for vacation rental homes in the area, zeroing in on the more expensive, over $700-a-night ones.

"This one looks like her style. God, it's amazing." They clicked through the photos of the spacious, modernist home with floor-to-ceiling glass, custom woodwork and high-end furniture, with all the main rooms oriented around breathtaking views of the rolling vineyards.

"It's out among the vineyards. Touts extreme privacy. And it's currently booked. This is probably a likely candidate," Samantha said.

Rick finished his third pint and then went up to his room to pack his gear. By now, it was past 10 o'clock. They took off for the vacation rental home in question, with other possibilities as backup. It was only a 10-minute drive from downtown Walla Walla and out in a pretty rural agricultural area.

They followed Google's instructions and soon saw the turnoff to a private drive emerge in their headlights. Rick continued a bit down the road.

Samantha asked, "Now what?"

Leyden made a U-turn and drove back past the private driveway, then tucked their rental SUV into what was something of a turnout next to the roadway.

"Time for the drone," Rick said. He got out and unpacked his large drone from its carrying case. "These new ones practically fly themselves."

Standing along the road with the vehicle shut off, they were both struck by how quiet it was. They paused for just a second and took in the starry night sky, the dark outline of trellises in the vineyards and the earthy scent of the surrounding farmland.

Rick set the drone back and leaned against the hood of the car next to Samantha. With the large drone controller in his lap, he fired it up and with an audible buzz, the teapot-sized device lifted straight up into the night sky. This was a high-end model Rick used for real estate photography and the live view from the drone's camera was excellent.

The screen showed an image of the mostly dark estate from hundreds of feet in their air. A few lights from the driveway and the house were visible but not much else. The drone descended for a direct view into the windows.

"Holy shit, that's her!" Samantha said as Wine Jamie's big blond hair and voluptuous figure came into view. Wearing a slinky kimono, she was sprawled out on a long sofa with a glass of wine. Another figure with their back turned was in the kitchen area.

Rick put the drone into hovering mode and they watched the two figures. Sure enough, the other occupant appeared to be Zhang.

Samantha was practically hyperventilating with excitement and anxiety.

"I guess I'll go in and put the tracking device on now," Rick said.

"You're going to do what? Fuck, I'm scared Rick."

"It'll be fine. We should get out of here soon anyway, right?"

Rick called the drone back, then left the vehicle and headed into the vineyard. He was gone for what seemed like forever to Samantha but then just as she thought he'd never return, the car door suddenly popped open and there he was.

"I got a bit disoriented out there but I found their car. It's a rental Lexus SUV. I put that little fucker way up inside one of the fenders. Before I put the drone away, let's take another gander."

"I think we should just go," Samantha said but Rick had the device in the air before she could object.

As the drone closed in on the house, they could see the occupants had moved to the bedroom. Zhang's slim body was splayed across the bed, hands tied with rope and eyes blindfolded. Wine Jamie appeared to be playing the dominatrix. Rick flipped the drone into hover mode and handed the screen over to Samantha.

"I think we get the idea," she said, shaking her head.

Rick took the drone display back and continued watching.

"Oh my God, I can't believe what she's doing to him. I didn't even know that was a thing," Samantha said, unable to keep herself from looking over at the screen.

"You're young," Rick said.

"Let's go back to the Marcus Whitman," Samantha said. "Job well done."

Rick recalled the drone and they were off.

The next morning Rick sauntered into the hotel restaurant at about 9 to find Samantha productively pecking away at her laptop. He charged a Denver omelette, a quad-shot mocha and a Bloody Mary to the room.

"Okay, so now the fun begins. We get to chase them around, right?" Rick asked.

"We'll keep an eye on their whereabouts but we don't want to make ourselves known," Samantha said. "It would be useful to get some shots of Zhang in the United States if he gets out in public. We really need to get a picture of him on site at one of his own properties with his business team here."

Rick agreed to monitor the tracking device and set about exploring charming downtown Walla Walla. After returning to the hotel room for a nap, Rick's phone alerted him that Zhang and Jamie's SUV was on the move. Samantha came over to Rick's room and they watched the little dot on the tracking app make its way to one of the Walla Walla area's many wineries.

"Okay, we're on," said Samantha. "I'm going to let you go in, Rick, especially on the off chance that Wine Jamie recognizes me as another wine writer."

"Wine at noon? I must answer the call of duty," Rick said.

The first winery was an uptight sort of place with highly manicured landscaping and an imposing tasting room building with large, stately wooden doors. A BMW 7-series sat next to Zhang's Lexus.

Rick opened one of the heavy doors and entered the small but ornately done tasting room. Jamie and Zhang were nowhere to be seen. Rick did a four-wine flight rather quickly and then bought a bottle and headed outside. As soon as he walked out onto the outdoor picnic area behind the winery, he saw them. They were seated at an out-of-the-way table under a tree, sampling from an open bottle. It was a beautiful 80-degree summer afternoon. But the bright sunlight and shadows made it poor conditions for getting a recognizable photograph of Zhang's face at a distance.

Rick took his bottle and occupied a table a couple tables removed from the two. Eventually, Samantha joined him with a bottle of chardonnay.

Zhang looked comfortable. He wore a polo shirt, jeans and some sneakers with a baseball hat. He laughed easily as he conversed with Wine Jamie and sipped vino. Rick was able to get a few surreptitious shots of him from a distance.

The couple moved on to another tasting room. Rick and Samantha followed but didn't enter this one for fear of being recognized. They did catch up with them at a third winery and this time Rick entered at the same time they did. This winery had a rugged western theme to it.

Rick sidled up to the bar.

Just one seat removed from Jamie and Zhang, he could hear the couple going back and forth about the grenache blanc they were drinking.

"The floral notes on the backside of this one are so lovely," said Zhang.

"No, no," said Jamie. "I'm overwhelmed by the fruitiness of it," she said, swirling her glass.

"I'm getting just a hint of cinnamon," Zhang said, looking thoughtful.

"Really?" Jaime said, putting her nose in the glass and then taking a sip.

"Excuse me," Rick said to Zhang, interrupting. "What would you recommend?"

"Are you drinking white or red?"

"Whatever you are."

"Try the flight of whites. They are most worthy of consideration."

The attendant poured Rick a flight of white wines. He started on the sauvignon blanc, swirling it in his glass and then sticking his nose in it for a long, exaggerated sniff.

"My god, it's so complex …," Rick looked around, then glanced at the tasting list. "I'm getting oaky notes and … a light minerality on the finish."

Zhang gave him a questioning look.

"Are you guys just visiting?" Rick asked, hoping to avoid any more wine talk.

"He is," said Wine Jamie, "but I'm local to the Pacific Northwest."

They conversed for a bit. Rick asked Zhang to take his picture and when he handed him the phone it was on selfie mode taking three shots a second.

Rick and Samantha followed the couple to another winery but laid low this time.

The summer bash at Revazov was the day after

tomorrow. They anticipated that Jamie and Zhang would be heading back to the Gorge for that, so they decided to call it a day and planned to head back to the Gorge first thing in the morning.

In its first years of operation, Revazov established a tradition of having a big summer bash in early August but had skipped the tradition in 2020 due to the pandemic. It was an invitation-only event and had acquired a certain mystique in its first two years. This year the event returned with proof of vaccination required. Scott got Samantha and Rick invites.

It being summer 2021, people were ready to let loose following over a year of pandemic restrictions. Samantha instructed Rick to hang out for the full length of the party and if Zhang made an appearance, get a photograph.

The party kicked off around eight. Gradually, the visitors began to occupy the large lawn outside the Revazov tasting room. The crowd was heavy on twenty- and thirty-somethings connected to Sasha and the wine industry. There was also an eclectic mix of older Gorge personalities including winemakers, restaurateurs and wind sport business owners.

Rick was first in line at the bar and struck up a conversation with Katie, the Revazov tasting room manager. She looked forty-ish and told Rick that she had been in the wine industry for over a decade.

"So why don't you have some of your minions take over here and enjoy yourself for a bit?" Rick suggested.

"That's the idea. Delilah and a couple others should be arriving soon."

Rick nodded and said, "Excellent. Have a drink with me when you get off?"

"Sure."

Armed with a full glass of Estate Pinot, Rick mingled for a while, chatting with a natural winemaker who seemed a bit spacey and then a guy who designed and sold something called "foil boards." Eventually, he drifted over to Kim. She had a flute of sparkling wine that seemed to call for frequent refills.

Rick had to admit Scott was onto something with Kim. She was a real MILF in that sexy white summer dress that highlighted her ample bust line and showed off her shapely tan legs.

It was strange to think about how he'd first heard about her four years ago on that visit to Portland when Scott had just started dating her. Apparently, Kim and Scott's relationship still had some intrigue. Scott had told Rick that Kim could not know about the mission that they were on to get photos of Zhang. They had made up a story about Samantha writing a wine travel piece and Rick accompanying her to take photos.

It was hard to keep the fake story straight as he chatted with Kim and the wine kicked in. Soon a DJ started up some dance tunes. When Kim heard the Dua Lipa song "Levitating" she got excited and told Rick that this was one that she and her daughter loved to dance to during the pandemic. Soon Kim kicked off her wedges and joined a few youngsters shaking it on the grassy dance area to the catchy beats. Rick eventually joined the fun, too.

As the sun went down the crowd grew exponentially. At 11 the classic country band that Scott had convinced Sasha to invite, The Oregon Trailers, came on. They belted out some Waylon Jennings tunes to start. When they fired up an old Eric Clapton song, "Promises," Scott couldn't help but grab Kim and bring her out on the dance floor. A wave of nostalgia came over them both as they two-stepped to this old favorite.

> I tried to love you for years upon years
> You refuse to take me for real
> It's time you saw what I want you to see
> And I'd still love you if you'd just love me

After the song, Kim disappeared into the crowd while Scott took in a few more tunes.

After a half-hour or so, Samantha approached him and pulled him aside.

"Zhang is here. I just saw him. Where the hell is Rick?"

Scott began searching for Leyden. He walked around the party and checked the tasting room. No sign of him. He went into the Revazov production building and looked through the dark offices on the second floor. Finally, Scott trekked up to his house where he found Rick in the hot tub enjoying some time with the tasting room manager.

"I need you back at the party, Rick," Scott said.

"Listen man I'm working on some intel here," Rick said as they walked back to the party.

"What intel is that?"

"I think she might know about when and where some of Zhang's meetings with his team will be."

When they returned the band had stopped playing and the crowd had gathered round to hear Sasha say a few words about the year's successes. Scott and Rick scanned the onlookers. Sure enough, there was Zhang, standing on the patio of the tasting room, looking on proudly at his enterprise. He was smoking a cigar.

Rick took out his professional camera and began taking shots of Sasha's speech with full flash. Knowing Zhang's position, he whirled around and took a shot directly of Zhang before he slipped out of view. Rick continued taking shots of the crowd.

After Sasha's remarks, Rick and Samantha stood off to the side and reviewed the photos. They weren't great but there was one with a reasonably clear image of Zhang at the party.

"Rick, come on, let's go!" Samantha said as she pounded on Rick's door at the Lyle Hotel.

Soon, a bleary-eyed Rick opened the door in his boxer briefs and asked what time it was.

Samantha let him know that it was 9 a.m., shoved a cup of coffee into his hand and commanded, "Get dressed." Samantha could see the woman from the night before make a hasty retreat to the bathroom.

Rick got dressed and then got in the SUV with Samantha.

Samantha said, "The tracking device still shows Zhang and Jamie at their rental place in White Salmon, but they are bound to get moving soon. We need to stay on these guys."

"Actually, Katie said that they are taking Mr. Chen to the new production facility in Bingen this morning. And I think the wine distributor guy might be there. Charlie something."

"Charlie Albrechts?" Samantha said.

"Yes, that's it."

"Oh wow. If we could capture that threesome at that location it would be such a coup."

Samantha pulled out onto Highway 14, quickly picking up speed as they headed out of Lyle and onto the winding route west toward Bingen.

Soon they were driving down the main drag of Bingen, the town down the hill from White Salmon. They cruised past a motley assortment of businesses before getting to the west end of town where the new Revazov production facility was located.

Just as they approached the turn off, they saw Laurence's Mercedes CLS pulling into the road to the facility. Samantha kept going and turned onto the next road headed toward the river.

Just as she put on her turn signal, she saw Scott approaching from the rear in his Saab.

They both pulled into the private driveway of another industrial business situated on the south side of Highway 14. It being Sunday morning, the large parking lot next to the warehouse-like building was deserted. The three of them got out of their vehicles.

Scott consulted the satellite view on Google maps to get an orientation regarding where they were relative to the Darden facility. He figured that they could make a stealth approach to the place on foot.

The three of them made their way through trees and bramble until they came to a vantage point where they could see Laurence's Mercedes parked in a gravel driveway next to the Darden building, a large sheet metal structure. There was a white Tesla Model S parked alongside Laurence's car.

A large garage door to the building was open and a group of three men — Laurence, Zhang and a man Scott identified as Charlie Albrechts — were standing just inside, talking.

Rick got his telephoto lens out and went forward to a spot at the edge of the trees where he barely had any cover and snapped a few photos.

The group moved deeper into the building and Rick returned to Samantha and Scott.

"I couldn't get much because of the lighting. I think we need to get into that building somehow," Rick said.

Rick led the way as the three of them circled the building. On the far side there was an exterior stairway that led to a platform with a doorway.

"I bet that goes to a loft office area," Rick said. "That would be ideal for a shot of them."

"You hang back and be ready to drive, Samantha," Scott said. "Rick and I will see if we can go in and get some pics."

Rick and Scott ascended the exterior stairway.

Scott felt the knob on the door at the top of the stairs. The door was locked, but had a window.

They stood there, not sure what to do, whispering to each other. "If a train goes by, maybe we can smash the window and get in," Scott said.

They waited.

After a couple minutes, Scott said, "I'm going to go see if I can walk through the front. You wait up here."

Scott descended the stairway and carefully walked around the edge of the building, then peered into the building through the garage entryway. The lights were on and the three men were looking over some machinery on the opposite end of the 5,000-square-foot space.

What the hell, he'd need to take a chance.

Scott quickly and quietly walked to the internal stairway to the office loft. He ascended the stairs and opened the door to the office which thankfully made little noise. Then he crawled on the carpeted floor to the external doorway and quietly let Rick in.

The dark office had windows looking out over the warehouse area below so they stayed hunched down on their knees.

Scott popped his head up to get a view of the goings on in the warehouse. It was lit up and Zhang, Laurence and Charlie Albrechts were walking around the space, likely discussing the build out.

"Okay, this is the perfect opportunity for the shot we're looking for," Scott said.

Rick got his camera out, knelt at a window and started snapping photos. They had what they needed after a couple of minutes.

As soon as they opened the exterior doorway, they saw Laurence waiting at the bottom of the stairs.

"Scott, I saw your friend taking photos. This is a problem," he said.

Scott said, "I want out, Laurence. I can't work for Darden anymore."

"I need the camera, Scott. Otherwise, I will call the police on you two for trespassing."

"Like I said, I want out. And I don't think you're going to call the police about anything," Scott said as he moved past Laurence assertively.

"This isn't going to work, Scott," Laurence said in an elevated voice as Rick and Scott walked away from the warehouse. The Tesla and the other two men were already gone.

When Scott and Rick reached Samantha, Rick initiated a

round of high-fives. They had the photos that they needed for Samantha's story. Mission accomplished.

26

Kim heard from Laurence when she was out at the Harvest Market in White Salmon. She was aghast when he told her that Scott had quit the business and seemed intent on defaming the Darden enterprise.

When she got back to the house, Scott was in the kitchen making himself lunch. He seemed oddly calm.

"Did you get some salsa, love?" he asked. "I'm working on a monster burrito here."

"I just got off the phone with Laurence. He said you're out? That you and Samantha are going to the press with all sorts of false accusations about Darden, about these business ventures we are a part of."

"Kim, it's been hidden under layers of paper, but we are working for a criminal enterprise. I'm going to come clean about what I saw that day up on Syncline. When this article comes out, it's going to be over for them. They will be forced out of the country."

"Don't do this, Scott. We've worked hard for all this."

Scott walked up to Kim and put his hand on both of her shoulders.

"It's going to be okay, Kim."

"Fuck that." She started to tear up. "Fuck that. What about our dream, this property?"

"We'll make it happen another way, Kim."

"Scott, they will win. They always do. We need to stay on the right side of this for us, for our families."

"This is the right side, Kim."

"You don't know what you're doing Scott. Darden Wine

Holdings is what's made it possible for me to take over Ross Wines, it's what made it possible for you to own this property. And what about our kids' future? Laurence said something about reminding you of your family."

"Oh no."

Scott's seemingly calm, confident mood disappeared. He began frantically looking for his phone.

"Shit, shit, shit."

He called Nate's mom. No answer. Nate was back in Portland with her this week.

"I gotta go to Portland to check on Nate."

"Scott, you should talk to Laurence," Kim said.

Scott left the house, initially heading for the Tundra but then heading to the garage to get the Saab.

After backing it out, he accelerated so hard that the front wheels threw up gravel five feet into the air as he started out on the driveway that led out of the estate.

He raced down winding Cook Underwood Road, overtaking two vehicles on the narrow two-lane and made the Hood River Bridge in record time.

As he entered I-84 from the on-ramp adjacent to the bridge, he floored it, burying the Saab's turbo boost gauge in the red zone and entering the flow of traffic well above the speed of the vehicles around him.

He weaved between cars, semis and SUVs as he barreled west toward Portland at 90 miles per hour plus. The old Saab was surprisingly nimble at such speeds. Every so often, he hit the call button on his mobile phone mounted on the windshield to ring Nate and Nate's mom but neither answered.

It was a typically beautiful Pacific Northwest summer day in Portland with clear skies and temps inching into the 70s by late morning. Gerhard and Lacey both sat sullenly in the Amazon-branded Sprinter van outside a residence in southeast Portland. Earlier in the day, they had followed

Nate from his mom's house to a friend's place in the leafy, upscale Colonial Heights neighborhood. Now they waited for some sign of movement.

Gerhard wasn't pleased with this assignment. He'd done kidnapping jobs in Latin America and the former Soviet Republics. That kind of extortion was routine there. But it generally was not a good idea in the United States. This is what Mr. Chen wanted, though, and he had to clear his record after that clusterfuck with the private eye.

Finally, after two hours, it happened. The 12-year-old, dressed in Vans, Dickies and a baggy T-shirt, emerged from the driveway on his mountain bike and moved confidently along SE 33rd Avenue over to Lincoln Street, then south on 32nd Avenue. He playfully weaved a bit as he rode, grabbing air whenever a driveway's tapered curb provided a good ramp.

As Nate crossed the intersection at SE 32nd and Division, Gerhard and Lacey got caught behind a couple cars. They knew Nate was likely headed back to his mom's house and if he went inside, they'd be stuck again. Lacey cursed as she maneuvered the Sprinter through the foot and vehicle traffic in this congested area of Division Street, which had loads of popular shops and restaurants. Nate appeared at first to have disappeared but then, there he was adjusting something on his bike in a gap between parked cars. This was their chance.

Lacey slowly brought the van to a stop next to Nate. But when Gerhard pulled on the lever to open the sliding door, it was locked.

Nate sensed something weird was going on when the van pulled up and sort of blocked him in between the parked cars. He heard the van door opening. Something told him to get moving so he hustled his bike over to the sidewalk and started rolling. When he took a quick look back, he saw a man emerging from the van and moving quickly toward him.

Nate started pumping his pedals hard and turned right on SE Clinton, a street designated as a low-traffic bikeway that always had a steady stream of bikers on nice days. He picked up the pace, taking advantage of the downhill slope. Gerhard ran after him with Lacey following behind in the Sprinter.

As he ran amongst the cyclists, Gerhard found himself alongside a skinny and heavily tattooed guy on a fixed-gear bike. The guy seemed bemused at this middle-aged fellow in a tracksuit running after a kid on a mountain bike.

"Dude, is that your kid?"

"I need your bike," Gerhard said.

"What?" the guy asked, confused.

Gerhard checked the hipster cyclist, sending him and the bike flying across the middle of the roadway in front of two other bikers headed the opposite direction.

"You fucking crazy fuck!" the hipster uttered, sprawled out in the middle of the roadway.

Gerhard mounted the fixie and started pedaling to catch Nate.

Nate wove between cyclists in his highest gear, blasting through the no-car, streetside restaurant zone at 26th and the four-way stop at 21st and continuing as Clinton flattened out. He turned around occasionally to see the man in the tracksuit, now on a bicycle, a few blocks behind.

As Nate approached the terminus of Clinton at 12th Avenue, he could see the movement of railway cars. He turned left when he hit the one way on 12th and approached a slow-moving freight train. He'd hopped one of these trains when it was at a stop. This one was moving, but slowly.

He rode past the cyclists waiting for the train to pass then dismounted his bike a few feet from the moving train. With one hand Nate grabbed a ladder on the back of a railcar and pulled himself up, his bike dangling from his other hand. It was precarious but he managed to get in between rail cars and tuck back so hopefully he wouldn't be spotted.

As the train slowly moved down the tracks, Nate saw the man arrive at the intersection and look around. Nate pulled out his phone, only to see about 20 missed calls from his dad. He called him back.

"Dad, Dad, I need you to come get me. I'm being chased by a crazy guy on a bike."

"Where are you?"

"I'm on the train, Dad."

"What train?"

"It's the train at the end of Clinton."

"You mean the Max?"

"No, the real train."

"Holy shit. Okay. Are you going toward downtown?"

"I think so."

Scott had been looking for Nate in the Richmond neighborhood where they lived. Now he headed west to intercept the train. His idea about where freight trains traveled in the city's network of streets was fuzzy. From SE Division, he got on Grand Avenue going north, then turned left on Stark and parked right before the train tracks.

He ran up to the tracks and looked to the right to see the rear of a freight train heading north. Then he turned to the left and saw a struggle between two people alongside the tracks about a block away. He sprinted alongside the railway and as he drew near, he made eye contact with Nate.

In seconds a Sprinter van pulled up, blocking his view.

As Scott reached the van, it pulled away, heading up Washington Street.

Scott's well-trained runner's legs pumped hard as he followed the van. It was headed toward the main thoroughfare of Martin Luther King Jr. Boulevard. He knew it would be lost if it turned onto MLK, but a line of three vehicles waiting to take a right turn brought the van to a halt.

In a split second he spotted the object he needed: a metal folding chair lying among homeless camp debris on the side of the road.

Scott approached the Sprinter, still stuck in the line of cars and smashed the passenger-side window with the chair. He reached in, unlocked the door, opened it and got in. A dressed-down Lacey, who he knew from the episode with the real estate agent way back when, was in the driver's seat.

In the back of the van, the man Scott recognized as Ingo Merz had his arms around Nate and a roll of duct tape in his hand. Nate was squirming around as the man tried to work the tape around Nate's hand.

"Dad!" Nate screamed, terror in his voice.

"Drive," Merz commanded from the back of the van.

The van started moving and then turned right onto busy, four-lane MLK Boulevard and quickly began to pick up speed.

Scott lunged from the passenger seat and grabbed the steering wheel, pulling it to the right. The van bucked up on the curb and went hurtling through a parking lot, smashing into the glass facade of a retail flooring showroom and coming to a stop.

Lacey disappeared out the driver's door while the German exited through the back. Scott was left with Nate.

It took an hour or so for the Portland Police to finish with them. Scott decided that their best bet for a safe house would be to head down to the Silverton, Oregon area where his friend Ray Johnston lived on a family farm with his brother Jerry. Rick and Samantha arrived at Scott's car and Scott gave them the address of Ray's place.

They all agreed to turn off their cell phones for the drive down in case they'd been hacked and were acting like tracking devices. They scoured their cars as well.

At the Johnston compound, Ray welcomed Scott and Nate at the entry gate. Perched on a hill, the compound had two separate homes and a lodge-like structure connected to one of them that encompassed a guest suite, office and garage.

Rick and Samantha soon arrived and Ray set them up in the office, which was outfitted with two high-end computer workstations. The brothers had a custom low-voltage electrical business that did network wiring, audiovisual setups and security.

Ray got Scott a Coors Light and Ray's girlfriend Sherry took Nate aside to dress some scratches.

"Scott, it's good to see you. Sorry it's under these strange circumstances," Ray said.

"It's been a fucking day, dude."

"What the hell is going on?"

Scott didn't know where to begin but did his best to fill Ray in on the circumstances that brought them there.

"Man, I told you to stay away from that Chinese businessman," Ray said, shaking his head. "I'm a little worried that they are going to find you guys here. How sure are you that they don't have a means of tracking you?" Ray's line of work made him digitally savvy and that was on top of a pretty good paranoid streak.

Scott went over how they'd kept their phones off and checked for tracking devices.

"Nonetheless, we'd better be ready for visitors."

"What does that mean?" Scott asked.

"Follow me," Ray said.

He led Scott and Nate to an enormous garage that felt more like an airplane hangar. It had three garage doors, one large enough to fit a full-sized recreational vehicle. Along one side of the space there was an automotive workshop complete with an engine hoist and car lift. A faded late-sixties Pontiac GTO was partially disassembled.

Ray led them to a white metal box about the size of a wardrobe that was mounted to the wall. He punched in a code on the digital display and the door clicked open. Racked neatly within were at least 20 firearms, ranging from handguns to deer rifles, to shotguns.

He handed Scott a tactical, short-barrel shotgun. "Have you ever used one of these?"

"Not since shooting skeet at a Boy Scout campout," Scott said.

"Here's how you take the safety off. You pump it like this." He squeezed the pump action and it made a satisfying mechanical noise. "If you fire it, be ready for a huge kickback," Ray said.

Ray retrieved a Mauser deer rifle for himself and some kind of assault rifle for his brother. Nate asked if he could have a gun, too. Ray said that they could do some target practice tomorrow, but not now.

"Jerry and I will go outside and keep a look out."

Kim got a call from Laurence shortly after she heard from Scott that he had found Nate.

"Scott was worried that you did something with Nate," Kim said to Laurence.

"Oh, that's nonsense," Laurence said. "We were looking for Nate so that we could find Scott. We're worried that he's going to do something harmful. Something that's not good for anyone."

"Yes, me too," Kim said.

"Do you have any idea where he might be?" Laurence asked.

"He said that he was going to stay with a friend, out of the Portland area. That might mean Ray who lives down toward Silverton."

"What's Ray's last name?"

"Johnson or Johnston, I think," Kim said.

Zhang downed the flute of pre-flight Champagne in one gulp and motioned to the flight attendant for a refill. He was seated in the first-class section of a Lufthansa 747-8i at

THE ECLIPSE

Portland International Airport. The flight was set to take off for Frankfurt in 17 minutes. There he would catch a connecting flight to Montenegro, which conveniently, had no extradition treaties with the United States or China.

He was certain that this problem could be resolved, but he wanted to get out of the United States as soon as possible.

He spoke with Laurence about the failed kidnapping.

"Drive down there and talk to Scott," Zhang said. "Let's make him an offer he can't refuse."

"I'm on it," Laurence said.

Laurence made his way south from Portland to the Silverton area. When he pulled into the driveway to the Johnston farm, he faced a locked gate at the front of the driveway. He pressed the buzzer and in a minute a man holding a rifle opened the side gate, greeted him and asked him what he sought.

Ray Johnston advised him to call Scott so Laurence headed back to his car.

Scott's phone buzzed and he saw that it was Laurence.

"Scott, Laurence here. I'm sorry about what happened with Nate. We just wanted to talk to you and we knew we could find you if we found Nate.

"Let's work this out in a way that's beneficial for all. You can come clean from your investments with us. We'll give you a stellar reference and you can walk away with a handsome profit from the equity in the property."

Laurence was always hard to argue with. For a millisecond, Scott considered the offer.

"It's over, Laurence. The whole thing," Scott replied.

"Scott, if I could just come in and chat with —"

"Man, you just tried to kidnap my kid. I'm not going to negotiate."

Scott could hear Laurence pleading, but he took the phone from his ear, held it in his hand and pressed the end call button.

Gerhard parked off an access road and began making his way through a wooded buffer that ran along one side of the farmed acreage owned by the Johnstons. He had a 9 mm semiautomatic pistol shoulder holstered under a windbreaker.

The wooded buffer went past a barn and some outbuildings connected to the farmed acreage. Gerhard stayed on the pathway that ran inside the buffer and worked his way up to the houses and lodge.

The residential area of the Johnston compound sat atop a hill with an excellent view of the surrounding farmland. Lights mounted on the structures illuminated part of the lawn and the central patio and walkway that connected the two homes and lodge.

Gerhard stayed low in the wooded area and surveyed the scene. He could see two men, conspicuously armed, pacing around the well-lit buildings.

He went back down to the area near the barn. There was a nineties-era Ford pickup truck parked partially in the shadows. He looked around the edge of the barn and found a water spigot and hose. Using his combat knife, he cut a four-foot section of hose then took it to the pickup and inserted it into the gas tank.

"Oh fuck me!" Jerry exclaimed when he saw the flames coming from the truck by the barn.

Then he ran over to Ray and said, "I've got to get down there and put that out."

"It's obviously a diversionary tactic," Ray said.

"How about you cover me? We can't just watch the farm go up in flames," Jerry said.

"Okay," Ray said. "Let's make it quick. Scott has the lodge."

Scott was hanging out with Nate in the great room area

of the lodge. Nate was watching a "Cobra Kai" episode on the enormous TV while sipping a Coke and snacking on some microwave popcorn.

Scott occasionally checked in with Rick and Samantha. They were working through the photographs Rick had assembled, getting ready to put together the story to send to the editor at the Los Angeles Times.

The package they were sending him included photographic evidence of Zhang's business interest in the Revazov winery operation as well as photos Samantha had picked up from the internet that documented some of his history as a developer and then as a globe-trotting fugitive. In the text of her article, she made the case that Zhang was the owner and gray eminence behind Darden Wine Holdings and had very likely ordered the murder of Camden Ross.

As Scott moved between the office and Nate, he held the pump action shotgun over his shoulder as Ray had instructed him. It had a loaded magazine but an empty chamber.

Suddenly, Scott heard a loud crash in the entryway of the lodge as the door gave way. He pumped the shotgun, loading a round into the chamber.

Then Laurence walked into the great room.

Scott aimed the shotgun at Laurence. He'd never pointed a gun at anyone really and his whole body was shaking and so was the barrel of the gun.

Laurence put his hands in the air and Scott caught sight of a holstered handgun he had tucked into his waist.

"Scott, Scott, we need to talk. If you publish a story about the firm without consultation it could open you and your colleague Samantha up to some serious legal and financial consequences."

"Laurence, you need to leave," Scott retorted.

Laurence began slowly walking toward Scott.

"Nate, get down on the floor," Scott shouted without taking his sights off Laurence.

"I need you to turn around and leave," he said to Laurence.

"Okay," Laurence said and stopped, his hands still in the air. He was now just a couple feet away from Scott.

"Turn around," Scott said.

Suddenly, Laurence lunged and grabbed the barrel of the shotgun, but as he grabbed onto it, Scott yanked the gun back and fired.

The blast hit Laurence's chest at point blank range and Laurence's whole body flew backward and collapsed on the floor.

The recoil destabilized Scott, almost knocking him on his ass. Just barely, he managed to stay on his feet.

As he regained his footing, Scott stared at Laurence's body. Dazed, he couldn't believe what he had just done. As he heard Nate hesitantly say "Dad?," he lowered the gun and looked over toward the TV.

And then he caught movement out of the corner of his eye and there was a deafening shot, this one knocking him to the floor.

Scott lay on the floor looking up at the ceiling. He couldn't stand up or even sit. The German was on the edge of his field of vision. He gasped for breath and when he touched his chest with his hand it was wet.

There was another loud blast and the German fell away and Ray appeared and was yelling, though the sound seemed muffled.

Things went blank and then there was Nate looking over him as he was being carried out of the lodge.

"Dad, dad, are you going to be okay?"

"I'll be fine buddy, I'll be fine."

Scott could feel Nate squeeze his hand.

Rick rode in the ambulance with Scott toward Salem Hospital.

Scott didn't make it.

THE ECLIPSE

The story appeared the next day in the major West Coast dailies including the Los Angeles Times, The Oregonian and The Seattle Times. Using evidence pieced together by Samantha, the story convincingly tied Zhang Shaozhu to Darden Wine Holdings and made inferences that connected Darden to Camden Ross' death. The recent photographs of Zhang captured by Rick Leyden were particularly compelling as Zhang had not been publicly photographed in several years.

A couple of days later, one of the TV news stations in Portland did a piece where they interviewed a number of the winemakers about the scandal. Everyone claimed to be shocked by the revelations.

Scott's remains were flown back to the Midwest and his memorial service was held a couple weeks later in Madison, Wisconsin.

In a matter of weeks, Darden Wine Holdings disbanded and liquidated its assets. Dimitri and Sasha vanished and Revazov ceased operations completely. Various clauses in the agreements that Scott had signed when he purchased the estate that became Revazov were called into effect and Wegner Bank took possession of the property.

Despite Samantha's piece on Zhang Shaozhu, as well as considerable follow-up coverage by various news organizations, his whereabouts remained a mystery.

In September, Rick flew out to Oregon to help Scott's dad and brother wrap up the details of his estate.

Rick and Scott's family had just a few days to move Scott's possessions off the Revazov estate. Scott's family gave Rick Scott's old Saab.

Rick decided to drive it back to Wisconsin with Scott's 12-year-old dog Bob along for the ride. He promised to return Bob to Nate as soon as things settled down a bit.

Just before he was about to head back to Wisconsin, Rick drove the Saab to Kim's place in the Portland West Hills. When he knocked on the door, he got her daughter and then eventually Kim emerged.

They went to the backyard.

"I'm sorry I haven't been in touch. I've been processing a lot," Kim said.

"I'm sure you have. Look, Kim, I have a few things of yours in the car. I also just wanted to say, well, that you meant a lot to Scott. God, he really fell for you."

Kim nodded and looked down. She was tearing up.

"I know. I can't believe we lost him."

Rick gave Kim a hug.

"So where to from here?" Rick asked.

"Camden Ross Senior's legal team is coming after me for the Ross winery. And I think they'll get it.

"That's okay," she said, sighing. "I have a new opportunity in the wine industry, in South America. Bolivia, actually."

"Sounds just about right for you," Rick said. "Best of luck."

EPILOGUE

June 2027. Tucker Park, Hood River, Oregon.

Nate woke up in the tent as his one-year-old pup, Brady, licked his face. He could see his girlfriend Olivia's hair buried in her sleeping bag. At 7:30, she was still fast asleep.

He pulled his jeans on and unzipped the tent. Brady wiggled out first and went on a sniffing fest around the campsite while Nate put on his puffy. It was cold enough that he could see his breath. Nate leashed Brady up and they took a stroll around the campground.

When they returned to their campsite, Nate opened up the back of the Tundra. It was a total mess of windsurfing, wingfoiling and camping gear. He got out the French press and put some water on his grandpa's old Coleman camp stove.

As the stove's burner made a low roar, Nate put the coffee in the French press and waited for the water to boil. He looked around the campground and he thought about his dad and how they used to camp here when he was little. Then he thought about the place where they used to live in the Gorge. His dad's house, the one way up in the hills. Boy, that place was sweet with the hot tub and view and all.

He poured the boiling water into the French press. He got out the cooler, retrieved eggs, butter, buttermilk and blueberries and made the pancake mix.

Olivia emerged from the tent when she smelled the pancakes and bacon. The three of them enjoyed breakfast in the strong early morning sunlight.

As they drove into town from Hood River Heights, they could see that the river was covered in whitecaps. It was going to be a big day.

Brimming with excitement, they headed for the Hood River Bridge and then the Hatchery. They couldn't wait to get on the water.

ABOUT THE AUTHOR

Mark Dahl lives in Portland, Oregon with his son Rowan. He is director of the Aubrey R. Watzek Library at Lewis & Clark College. He enjoys many outdoor activities in the Pacific Northwest including trail running, backcountry skiing, windsurfing, bicycling and backpacking.

Made in United States
Troutdale, OR
08/19/2024